I
AM HERE
TO KILL
YOU

Chris Westlake

Cover design by Elizabeth Ponting, LP Designs & Art
Editorial services provided by Jeff Jones,
www.jeffajones.blogspot.co.uk

www.chriswestlakeauthor.co.uk

For Mum and Dad, my wonderful parents

Saturday 17th August 2019

Grant

In the pit of my churning stomach I always knew that, after tonight, *nothing* would ever be the same between us.

Sucking in the final dregs of warm white wine, I eye Rachel's empty plastic cup, smeared with red lipstick. Oh, the shame of playing catch up to my wife! Whatever would my mates think?

Did we really only put the kids to bed a few hours ago? It felt like a different day, a different world. Although it was only seven on the dot (we'd told Mia and Sophie it was eight), the August sunlight gleaming through the blinds gave the bedrooms a mid-afternoon feel. First came the bedtime story, then a hug, swiftly followed by a kiss and (recently added) a high-five. Mia desperately delayed the inevitable, firing out dialogue on any topic that sprung to mind. Tonight it was the *Dumbo* film we'd watched in the front-row of the cinema back in spring. *He hated those big ears, Daddy, but they were his greatest gift.* Seven-year-old Sophie raised disbelieving eyebrows. *Just what was her little sister like?*

Fresh from the shower, my short-sleeved shirt sticking to my body, I'd tip-toed down the wooden stairs, heart in my mouth, for even the slightest suggestion of noise gave my princesses a reason - an excuse - to call me back, to shout my name. *Daddy.* Rachel waited for me at the bottom, in the landing. Her nod was a signal, a secret code. Mission accomplished. We'd already briefed the babysitter. We could go.

Outside, holding Rachel's clammy hand, we walked in silence. Finally, we were alone. Big sigh. But it still felt like there were three of us. That nagging voice perched on my shoulder, asking questions. *It's all fine and dandy you going out and having a great time, but how are your two darling cherubs going to sleep in this heat?* Had a point. The air remained uncomfortably hot. When I'd held my darlings close - kissed them goodnight - their bodies prickled from a day in the sun, a day at the fete.

That was then, of course. This is now.

With the wine swishing around my belly, the alcohol seeping through my pores, I'm a tiger released from the cage, free to roam, eager to make up for lost time. I – *we* – deserve this. Mummy and Daddy have been replaced by the much more exciting Grant and Rachel. Date night. Okay, so maybe our night had been gate-crashed by a good chunk of the 2,000 residents of the town, huddled together like sheep inside this barn, but - right now - who gives a shit?

God only knows what I'd be without you.

Whenever the song comes on, I imagine The Beach Boys riding a wave on a Los Angeles beach; for her it's different. She's always been soppy. Romantic. Call it what you like. Pulling at my hand, her cheeks glow with mischief. My forehead creases in resignation. I can't deny her a dance any longer. This is *her* song, the opening song at our wedding, in *this* barn, seven years ago. Her wide, watery eyes tell me she is nostalgic. Standing up, my feet are laden with lead. My black shoes sweep up strands of straw lying on the bumpy concrete floor. This barn must be fifty feet long and twenty feet high, yet it feels like it is shrinking in every direction to the point I duck my chin into my chest to avoid bumping my head. Plenty of these merry, frolicking dancers were at our wedding; they surrounded us in a perfect rectangle as the newly wedded couple took centre stage. I'm being paranoid. I'm exaggerating my self-importance. Glancing around at the shiny, perspiring faces, apart from a few peeking middle-aged ladies, nobody is focused on us.

My hands graze the smooth of my wife's back. Slanting my forehead, I savour her favourite Acqua di Parma perfume, saved for rare special occasions (so much rarer these days). The tip of her nose massages my cheek.

"God only knows what I'd be without *you*, Mr Grant Edwards," she whispers.

Squeezing Rachel's hand, I rest my chin on her newly bronzed, freckled shoulder.

"God only know what I'd be without *you*, Mrs Rachel Edwards," I say.

Our feet stop moving. We'd uttered the same, glorious words in (roughly) the same spot at our wedding. Our hips sway from side to side, a ship riding choppy waters. I hold her tight, enjoying the warmth and glorious radiance of her body.

And then, I look over her shoulder.

At *her*.

Standing in the shadow of the entrance to the barn with her hands on her hips, a thigh gloriously exposed by the cut in her red dress, she scans the room. Whilst my chin rests on Rachel's shoulder and my hands cup her waist, my eyes remain glued to another woman.

She is wearing *that* dress.

The woman's succulent red lips curl at the corners. Her eyes stop scanning. Instead they fixate on me, fixate on the romantic vision of me embracing my wife. She makes a subtle, barely noticeable movement of her head.

Rachel's eyes widen as I pull away from our embrace. I know that look. I know everything about her. It is a look of concern. "Sorry, darling," I say, conscious of my burning, flushed cheeks. "Nature calls. Won't be long. Promise..."

Momentarily, the brightness in her eyes, fades; she reaches out her hand and says something I wish she didn't, something I wish I could erase.

"Remember what I said, sweetheart. God only knows what I'd be without you, Grant Edwards."

My eyes focus on the array of polished shoes and heels as I move closer towards the glimmer of light outside. My nostrils fill with the tangled scent of cologne, perspiration and Carling. A few curious eyes follow me - I *think* - but it is like I am in a tunnel and they peer in from outside. I have sucked in air, but I have not yet blown it out again. This is my most vivid, my most disjointed, dream.

I exit the barn.

The light has begun to fade, and the cool breeze is a splash of cold water against my flushed cheeks. Nothing, I muse, burns hotter than guilt. The deafening noise of innocent pleasure begins to quieten behind me. Finally, there truly is only two of us; only, my wife is not one of them. Out of sight, out of mind, that's what they say. My hand is pulled seductively by another woman now. I need to forget my wife - for now - and focus on the moment. God only knows I don't love *this* woman. I barely know her. She is older than me, maybe by fifteen years, but that merely adds to the appeal. Was it weeks or months ago she came into my life? Why did I even enter that shop with my wife and kids? And what enticed her about me? Did she recognise that I was craving excitement, a release from my everyday burdens and routines? And to think, even though she invades my mind, is a taunting, seductive obsession, she has only ever uttered seven words to me.

I'll see you at the barn dance.

Skipping along like a couple of giddy school kids, I glance at the seductive crease of her cleavage, at the pale, soft flesh; my eyes move downwards, focus on the inch or two of purple, silk bra. The voice is there again. *Look away, you bastard.* I do so, but straight into the eyes of a farm cat, stretched out in a yoga pose on all fours in the fading grass. The narrowed piercing green eyes seem to know everything.

Our steps quicken in silence, away from the parked cars and onto grass, spotted with dried cowpat; the flies hover like helicopters. Pausing at a chest-high metal gate, the woman turns to me. Her voice is lighter, less husky, than I remembered. I didn't expect these words.

"You really are a bad boy, aren't you, Grant?" she says, shaking her head, dimples forming in her cheeks. Her twisting, twirling tongue is coated with saliva. How would that metal stud feel in my mouth, on my lap? Seemingly reading my mind, she lowers her hand, widens her smile. "Getting excited, are we?"

The path, sheltered on both sides by hedges, narrows. Stopping, she turns to me and wraps her arms around my neck; her tongue pokes inside my mouth, slithers like a snake. She pulls away, puts a single, upturned finger to my mouth, tells me to be quiet. Oh God. That's what I do when I give the kids a sweet. *Don't tell Mummy.* We are all conspiring, then and now. Mummy must not know the truth.

"Please don't tell my wife," I say.

She laughs. She laughs *at* me. "Don't worry," she says. "I have a husband too, you know. I don't plan on telling anyone what I'm about to do to you..."

My face must soften, the lines must fade, for she kisses the centre of my forehead. This, I muse, is a sensual gesture between lovers. Who seduced who? The lines are blurred. "Come with me," she says, her eyes sparkling. She does not need to ask twice. I scurry behind her, chasing her coat tails.

She pulls open the wooden door and then pushes me inside. It is pitch black. Faint yellow lines seep through the cracks in the roof. The door shuts behind me. She is here with me, somewhere; I can hear her subtle, rhythmic breathing. I just have no idea where. A match strikes and a face lights up - pale, exquisite and alluring in the darkness of the barn.

What the *fuck* is going on?

She lights a candle, and then another. I look around, and then up. There is a larger gap in the roof, maybe thick enough to push an arm through. The barn is tiny, possibly a perfect square, no more than fifteen feet by fifteen feet, and I could touch the ceiling with outstretched arms. Bales of hay stack high around the edges.

"Oh we really *have* chosen a bad boy, haven't we? This one's eyes are always wandering..."

I jerk my head, startled. Oh my God. There are two of them. I turn around, looking for answers. I'm reassured by the row of white teeth, by the sparkle in the eyes. Her fingers massage my chest between the gaps in my shirt buttons. "Thought you'd be man enough for two of us..."

I *did* like it, of course. This was a wonderful fantasy. Part of me wanted to gloat to my friends. If only *I* could. And this one was a bit different, wasn't she? The final words, though, felt like a challenge, like a threat...

"Just lie back, and imagine what Heaven might look like..."

The floor is hard and bumpy against my back. My outstretched hand massages the hay. It feels oddly damp and clammy considering the blazing sun beating down all day, considering the smouldering heat in this tiny barn.

"Close your eyes. There's a good boy..."

Stretching my arms behind my head, the two women work quickly and methodically - *expertly* - first on my wrists, then on my ankles. I long to open my eyes, to see for myself, but I know what they're doing; the harshness of the rope grazes my skin.

"My friend is kind of kinky," the voice soothingly says.

I wait for them to pull at my trousers, tug down my pants, to feel the curve of their bodies against mine, to savour the close intimacy. And yet they seem to be moving away, becoming detached. My heightened senses can't feel them; I'm no longer sure I can hear them, either.

I sniff. What is that? My eyes shoot open. They *are* close. Four eyes stare down at me, just inches from my face. My body rattles against the concrete floor. The smiles are wide and full of teeth, and yet they are manic.

Crazed. A middle finger wags. Just like I do when I put one of the girls on the naughty step. My body clenches as I try to pull my hands apart. Nothing happens.

"You're a dirty little bastard, Grant Edwards. You *all* are."

"Who are...?"

"*Men are...*"

I pull my head from the floor, manage to fix my eyes on the corner. At the bales of hay. An orange flame haunts and spreads. The whole barn is on fire.

"Untie the rope!" I shout. "Let me free! I promise I'll change..."

The giggles are mocking. The door pushes open a few feet. There are voices. One. Two. Three...?

"Forget imagining what Heaven might look like, Grant. Welcome to Hell..."

I know that they have left, that they've left me to burn to death on my own, because the wooden door to the barn shuts, and the glimmer of light from outside fades away to nothing...

One year earlier
Saturday 25th August 2018

Katherine

God, was this *really* a school? The sloping slate roof and the row of chimneys reminds me more of a derelict mental hospital than a long-forgotten school. I picture bruised and battered residents walking the corridors in grubby blue overalls, their minds frazzled, not so much from illness but from the drugs, from the electric shock treatment.

I know it was a school, though, because my dear, dead brother, Ben, was a short-lived pupil here.

The image invades my mind as I reach the crumbling, chest-high wall, sheltered by majestic oak trees. It isn't a memory (even though I was there) because I was too young to make sense of my surroundings. 1972. His first day of school. My older brother by four years strode across the lawn in his grey shorts, his socks pulled up to his knees. Mum trailed a few feet behind, her forehead layered with a film of cold, uncomfortable sweat, struggling to push the pram up the torrid slope.

Luckily, I remained the infant in the pram. I never had a first day at the school; they moved the children to a new wooden building with a flat roof the term I enrolled.

I inhale the damp, musty scent as I smile and say hello and shimmy past the rows of chairs. The drab grey curtains are always open and yet, even with the stifling August sun yellowing the grass outside, it remains relatively dark inside the small, square room. My legs feel weak as I take my seat at the back. I glance at my wrist. 11am. Just on time. We always (optimistically) allow a minute for any unexpected late arrivals. I begin my ritual of counting the heads. Twelve. Not bad. Not good, of course - but still. Two less. Hardly an avalanche, is it? Peering between two of the heads, I catch Rose at the front of the room, facing the troops. She is more of an under-twelve's football coach appealing to his team to keep their heads up when they're 5-0 down at half-time than Jesus addressing his disciples.

"We're a few down from last week, ladies." Rose's voice suggests bronchitis. Her middle finger, bitten to the bone, rubs at her dark, shadowed eyes. Coughing, her eyes flip open. "Which is good when you think about it. Hopefully a few less people in this world need our help."

Or, maybe, a few more people got bored and couldn't face another dull meeting? I glance at Apinya. Does she read my mind? She turns her slip of a figure around, raises her perfectly sculpted rainbow eyebrows. Apinya, with her long limbs and flat chest, is Laurel to my Hardy. *Same words as last week.* Apinya opened her heart (and her mouth) at her very first meeting. Within minutes, the group knew more about her than they ever have about me. Her father from Pattaya (about sixty miles south of Bangkok, apparently) had wanted her to settle down with a local man and look after the home, but Apinya rebelled. She wanted more from her life.

She only went and fell in love, didn't she? She escaped the depravity of - what *she* called - the slums. And this is where she landed. Here. Pontbach. She said she simply couldn't believe how lucky she was to find such a beautiful town inhabited by such wonderful people.

The women cooed; the women fell in love.

Apinya is one of the few people of any shade of colour in Pontbach. You don't get many ethnics in Wales, let alone in a sleepy rural town fifty miles from the closest city. We all say we're frightfully liberal, of course, but most of the residents eye her with fascination, like a bird not seen before in the garden. She is like Dafydd - the only gay in the village. Even the bigots say (behind gritted teeth) she is a fantastic advertisement for outsiders joining the town. Naturally, of course, she remains an outsider. If only, I think, other outsiders *were* actually interested in joining our gorgeous little town.

"That said," Rose continues, deep, straight slits carved in her cheeks, "we welcome anybody – not just women, of course – to join us here at Crossways School. I have no doubt we'd all be very welcoming."

I glance around the room again, at the five straight rows of (mainly) abandoned wooden chairs, searching for anybody who is not a woman. Traditionally, this species is called men. This is just for amusement. Of *course* there are no men. There never has been, not in the twelve years Rose has run the meetings. It would take a very brave man - like Thor with his hammer - or a very dumb one, to attend this group. I haven't seen any Thor's in the town recently, and so I'd opt for the dumb option.

Rose moved to Pontbach about twelve years ago. We

met at the summer fete, an annual event held on the rugby pitch. We held this year's extravaganza last week. I never made it to the evening barn dance that year, and I don't normally break routine. I hadn't been out of the house for weeks. Conscious of my chalky, lifeless complexion, I painted a smile on my face but diverted my eyes. Standing in the queue for candy floss, I shuddered when a dry, calloused hand grazed my arm.

"Its Katherine, isn't it?"

I nodded my head, ensured my smile was the right way up. At the time, I didn't want to engage with people I knew, let alone strangers.

"I don't think I've seen you around here before?" I asked. We hadn't met, but it *did* feel I knew her.

"I've not long moved to Pontbach," she said. Her smile was warm enough to thaw an iceberg. "I suspect we have a few things in common, Katherine."

Her pained face explained that she, too, was mourning - her husband had recently passed.

"Did he drown like both my parents did?"

Holding up her hands, Rose took a step back. Firing the words at me, she apologised for my tragic loss, said that she'd found solace in the church, asked if I cared to join her. The shake of my head may have been too quick, too rigorous.

"My parents were both very religious," I said. "I lost faith when my brother died, and then I *completely* lost faith when Mum and Dad joined him."

Back home, when the rest of the town partied at the barn, I told my husband about our exchange. His face dropped. *Did he drown like both my parents did?* What sort of a horrid thing was that to say to a woman who'd just joined the town, whose husband had just passed away? He was right, of course. It *was* wrong. Unforgivable.

But my husband didn't persist. He *did* forgive. My downbeat, negative behaviour often gets forgiven, not just by him, but by the other residents in Pontbach. After all, how many of them can say their brother was murdered, that both their parents drowned?

Rose wasn't deterred, either. We always bumped into each other as I ventured out more and more over the next few months. She always greeted me with a hug; I disappeared within her soft, cushioned body. She never gave any indication she was offended by my initial rudeness. A few months later, when she asked if I'd like to join a group she was setting up to help people just like us, I agreed. Saturday at 11am, she said. People like us? Mourners? Turns out it wasn't just for people like us, but anyone who needed some extra support, anybody who wanted to share their difficulties.

Rose addressed the seventeen women who attended the first meeting by rubbing the dark shadows of her eyes. I'm the only one of those seventeen women in attendance to witness Rose opening the meeting in the same way today.

With my attention wavering - *again* - I imagine Ben, sat cross-legged on the hard, wooden floor, palms pressed together, eyes closed. This room was the assembly hall. I confess, this place holds a morbid fascination for me. I've only ever been in this room, the toilet and the kitchen, with its long laminate worktops, empty of nearly everything (particularly life). Red rope cordons off the stairs (the building was a mansion house before it temporarily became a school). The hallway spirals in many different directions, with long, narrow, dark corridors, leading to closed doors. I tried to open one of the doors once, but - inevitably - it was locked. I jumped when I heard the voice behind me. *Are you lost, Katherine?* It was Rose, of course. Once again, I was a schoolgirl sneaking inside my parents' bedroom, searching for a wardrobe leading to a parallel world, to Pandora's Box, to excitement, to anything but *this*.

Casually, I turn to my left. My heart jumps.

We have a new member.

My mind recites the words. *We have a new member. We have a new member.* Where did she sneak in from? She wasn't there a moment ago. Or was she? Members often leave. Sometimes they rejoin. Rarely do we have a completely *new* recruit. I just *know* this one is different, too. She has a purpose. She is here to stay. My eyes flicker, trying not to be too obvious, to be caught.

"We are all here for a reason," Rose announces to the group.

Exactly. We are all here for a reason. She says this every week. She has asked me, both openly and privately, for my reason.

To overcome the tragic death of my parents and my older brother.

Nobody in the village *ever* talks about Ben, though. I understand why people don't talk about his death, but why don't we celebrate his life? There again, who am I to complain? I rarely bring him up, either. I deliberately try not to draw attention to myself. I deliberately try to melt into the background.

Distracted heads turn. Who is *that?* What is her story? They look for bruises, for cuts. They observe her body language. She gives little away. There are few clues. I bet the women in the group will never guess her true story. A silk scarf covers her bowed head. The baggy top is too hot for the summer; it gives little indication of the body hidden underneath. She is diminutive, though, and - possibly - she is fragile, like a newborn bird. Rose likes them when they're fragile.

I don't look for clues. I don't try to work out who she is.

Steam emits from Rose's china cup. She seems oblivious to the newcomer. How could I have been wary of her? Fine, dark stubble coats her upper lip. The grey cardigan dangles like a tent from her folded shoulders. "Now, would anybody be kind enough to share with the group? No pressure, of course. Just being here together today makes us stronger..."

My hands grip the sides of the chair. I want to put my hand up, to say a few words about this and that, about the things that really plague my mind. On the other hand, I know it is best I remain oblivious. My head rotates, pleading to the room. I glance left. What? Where has she gone? It is like she wasn't here at all.

I graze my silver metal tongue ring (*what* a rebel) against the underside of my front teeth.

"I'll share."

The voice came from someone at the front, I'm sure, but then it doesn't really matter where, because it didn't come from me. Closing my eyes, I unclench my hands.

I'm free for another week.

Bernard

Boys with toys, that's what they say, isn't it? Well, I consider, this is *definitely* the right toy for *this* boy.

Sat three or so feet off the floor with the luscious green lawn stretching out in front of me, a thought comes to me - maybe I should take up golf? Think about it. A golf course has eighteen holes (or so those in the know tell me); that amounts to thousands upon thousands of yards of immaculate, nurtured lawn to savour. After all, they employ greenkeepers to ensure the course remains meticulous. *Absolutely* I could take up golf! Driving around the course on an electric buggy in my favourite Canali trousers, taking photos of the ponds, parking up next to the delightful sand features - what in life could provide greater satisfaction? If only I could escape hitting any of those damn, dimpled white balls. What a dreadful chore *that* would be. Whoever it was who said golf ruined a good walk was likely a genius.

Taking a swig from the champagne flute, I smile. I'm getting carried away, aren't I? I should probably just stick to this marvellous lawn tractor. Hours of fun. With the steering wheel in one hand and the champagne flute in the other, it's a shame really that I can't buy a third hand (a cigar wouldn't go amiss, either). I wipe a layer of salty sweat from my top lip with the back of my arm, then jerk my hand back on the steering wheel as the buggy veers towards a bush.

Inhaling the glorious scent of freshly mowed lawn, grass gathering in mounds, the lawn as spectacular as Old Trafford on match day, I'm struck that I'm alone in over an acre of land. *My land.* I open my mouth wide so I can hear my own singing above the roar of the engine.

Here's a little song I wrote. You might want to sing it note for note. Don't worry, be happy.

The garden is a frequent discussion point at my celebrated dinner parties. Frankly, I make sure it is. When the guests gaze out of the dining room window (tipsy on Dom Perignon Vintage) and they *gasp*, then I know my work here has been done. Suddenly, I'm Hitchcock on the opening night of *Psycho*, savouring the audiences reaction to Janet Leigh's untimely shower death (bless her). The house (correction: the *mansion*). The garden. The indoor swimming pool. Unknowingly, their gasp is their judgement of my life's work, my reward for long, lonely hours in the office when, most likely, the rest of the town idled in The Swan or The Oak, intoxicated on a cocktail of booze, gossip and unrealized dreams.

I bring the tractor to a halt. Motionless, a sitting target, the sun is like a laser beating down against my neck. I take a quick sniff of my armpit - I definitely need a shower before dinner. Perhaps I should cool down with a swim in the pool first, though? Or - maybe - I could work up a real sweat in the gym first *before* cooling down with a swim?

Decisions, decisions, decisions...

******

That workout was a terrific idea; it really got the happy endorphins flowing and made the relaxation that followed so much more satisfying.

Clad in my jeans and white tee-shirt in the main living room, I stretch my legs out across the sofa. The world is a peaceful place with the TV turned off, the phone put away. I truly understand why people pay a fortune just to stay in a tent in the middle of nowhere practicing Buddhist poses and yoga and drinking jasmine tea.

Blinking open my eyes, my wife, Diane, stares back at me. Her smile is wide and set, with a tiny gap between her two front teeth. Her hazel eyes fix on me, face alight with contentment. My two boys, eight and ten, have their blond hair brushed forward in a straight fringe. They are freshly scrubbed, straight out of the bath; both look awkward in their freshly ironed shirts. I'm there too, slender and handsome in my favourite grey suit; the proud family man.

That was then. This is now.

The family portrait hanging on the living room wall was taken on my 35th birthday, twenty-two years ago. Part of me wishes I could pause time. I'd happily live this day over and over, like Bill Murray in *Groundhog Day*. The slender and handsome man is now portly and tired with straw arms and legs, despite the gym, despite the swimming. Our two boys fled the nest as soon as it was feasibly possible to do so. They hardly speak to me. They *never* come to visit. Diane is no longer my wife.

What was I supposed to do? Live the rest of my days alone? I was forty-nine years old; either I shrunk and withered, or I started again.

I look away, to distract myself with something - *anything* - in the room, but - *again* - I'm drawn back to the portrait. Sometimes I think it is a curse, on par with Dorian Gray's portrait, hidden away in the upper room of his house. How could I think this about my wife and

my children? Occasionally I'm tempted to hide the
portrait away in the loft, with the draught and the
spreading cobwebs - out of sight and out of mind. I
never would. Even though it brings tears to my eyes, I
cling to the happy memories. And besides, how could I
dump Diane in the cold, heartless loft, away from
human life?

"I caught you, Mister. Sat on your own. Billy No
Mates, you are. Daydreaming again, weren't you?"

The silence, and the solitude, is broken.

I lower my head, hoping my red-rimmed eyes aren't
visible. I hadn't noticed her enter the room, but then
she is so delicate, so light on her feet. Her buttocks sink
into the sofa next to me; the legs fold underneath her
like a toddler. Strands of lustrous dark hair brush
against my arm, sensual like a feather. Her caressing
hand tingles my cheek.

I smile. "Sorry, Apinya. You're right. You caught me.
Just having a quiet moment to myself."

My eyes drop to the row of bright, straight teeth, to
the delicate mole just above her lip. I often find myself
staring at my second wife in wonder, like she is a work
of art. How can a person be so perfect, so
unblemished? Mesmerised, I take in the angular
contours of her face, the flawless olive skin. How did
this beautiful, divine creature ever become part of my
life?

I push away the taunting voices. Plenty of people in
the town have an explanation or three. The chaps from
the pub - Dave and Geraint, for example - have said as
much to my face. I don't begrudge them - they're the
honest, brave ones. They don't mean any harm. Not
really. I'm reminded of Debbie McGee on the sofa with

Mrs Merton. *But what first, Debbie, attracted you to the millionaire Paul Daniels?*

Apinya's thumb circles the indent in my chin. "Don't be a silly sausage. I want my husband to be happy. That is my job, Mister, to make you happy."

I don't say anything. Does my smile translate as a grimace? My ears feel like they've reddened. Her lips edge closer to my cheek. "And besides, if I don't make you happy then you may ask for an exchange, send me back to Thailand..."

I pull my head back. Has she been reading my thoughts? "Oh no, I'd never do that. Why would you think that...?"

She cackles loudly. My eyes cloud over as she playfully slaps my wrist. "I'm playing with you, silly. Besides, you've been a busy boy today haven't you, whilst I've been at my group? You were on that tractor thing of yours for hours, mowing the lawn or whatever it is you do. And that garden is so big, so much lawn! You deserve some peace and quiet, bless you. You must be tired. Don't mind me."

Her bony knee digs into my chest. All her joints are sharp - her knees, her elbows, her ankles. They contrast with mine, which are cushioned with fat. Usually, I ask how the group went. Often I'll enquire about Rose and Katherine. Particularly Rose. Today I'm not convinced my interest is genuine. I try not to be disingenuous. Looking up at Apinya, I'm aware my face is probably pleading, like a puppy wanting a treat. "I am a bit tired to be honest, Apinya. An early night wouldn't go amiss. After all, we have tomorrows for a reason..."

Apinya's nose rubs against my cheek before she kisses my lips. Her legs effortlessly expand. Which way will this go? What is wrong with me? My wife's young, beautiful, lithe thighs wrap around my rotund, aging belly, and yet here I am craving my bed (to sleep).

"I was thinking the same thing, darling. An early night is just what the doctor ordered!"

I follow the confident swagger of her pert buttocks as they move further away. She turns around just as she reaches the living room door. Her eyes straighten. Her smile widens.

"Bedtime, Big Boy."

Hearing the flutter of her feet tiptoe up the wooden staircase, I close my eyes. So many men my age would kill to have a sexy young wife with an insatiable sex drive. Me - I'm worried she might kill me off. If Diane were still here, then I'm sure she'd be content with naked cuddles and tender kisses in the morning. What would she think of this? She'd probably bounce back and forth with laughter. No. Don't compare her to Diane. That's unfair and heartless on Apinya.

The shout from upstairs is loud and caressing. "I'm *waiting...*"

Pushing the bedroom door open, my jaw drops. Apinya lies on her back on the bed, her knees slightly raised, hands pressed flat. She has changed for bed. Only, she has not put on striped, cotton pyjamas. Four-inch black high heels dig into the cotton bed sheet. A red bodice makes her midriff impossibly slender and it squeezes her breasts up and out. The tiny black leather skirt flutters over naked buttocks. Parting her legs, my eyes follow the trail all the way up her thighs.

"Has this woken my tired, darling husband?"

The frog in my throat hops. We've been married for two years and yet she still manages to turn my fifty-seven-year-old self into a giddy teenager discovering top-shelf magazines for the first time.

"I think I am fully awake now, yes."

"Relaxation is good for your heart..."

"I'm not sure this will do my blood pressure any good though, Nurse..."

Her laugh is loud and thunderous.

I perch on the edge of the bed like a hospital visitor delivering grapes. Immediately, Apinya gets to her knees, tugging at my jeans. I try not to look at my pasty, bumpy legs, at the red dots, at the blemishes. I'm tempted to tug back when she unrolls my pants. She asked me to shave, said it was hygienic *and* sexy; I feel like a pre-pubescent teenager.

"You certainly *have* woken up," she says, looking me in the eye, holding me in her hand.

That has never been a problem. There have never been any humiliating behind-the-counter purchases of Viagra for me. Quite the opposite. Thrusting my pelvis forward, my eyes move to the ceiling. My open hand presses down against the top of her head. Desperately, I try to think of horrendous things. People with piles. Brexit. Margaret Thatcher naked.

It is too late. None of this is anywhere near potent enough.

Apinya jerks away, coughing and spluttering. I don't dare to look at her, at the white goo flowing from her mouth. This was supposed to be the warm up. The referee hasn't blown his whistle yet. I've blown mine. My wife wanted me inside her, to give her a good time. I know, and she knows, this isn't going to happen now.

The sting to my cheek thrusts my eyes open. My darling wife sits over me, one knee either side of my belly. Her open hand is ready and willing to slap me again. I put my arms up, not to push her away, but to protect my face.

"You fucking loser!"

"I'm sorry-"

"You're sorry? *I'm* sorry I married you..."

"Don't say that..."

"Am I asking too much for my husband to actually fuck me once in a while?"

"Of course not."

"I could have any man I want-"

"I know. You are beautiful-"

"I chose you, and this is how you repay me?"

"You excite me so much, Apinya. I couldn't help it. I'm sorry..."

She pushes her hand to my chest. Uses my body as a springboard. Bounces off the bed. The bedroom door slams shut. Apinya is no longer light on her feet as she thunders back downstairs. A herd of elephants rampages through our house. The room is suddenly dark; I am suddenly alone. I huddle up under the duvet, my body naked and sticky and trembling.

A thought intrudes my mind, mocking me. I imagine Apinya sat in the living room, arms folded across her chest, vehemently staring up at the family portrait on the wall. I'm reminded of my earlier thoughts.

Given a chance, I'd *definitely* turn back the hand of time to the day that photo was taken.

Ray

Saturday night, I feel the air is getting hot. Like you baby.

I nod to Geraint and Dave when I rock up in The Swan but then, when I return from the bar with a pint of Fosters, I walk straight past them. The Chuckle Brothers appear forlorn, like they're the last two kids left in the line to be picked for football, because they're *shit*. Leaning against the pillar in the corner of the pub, I deliberately wait a few moments before throwing them a second nod.

"You're not contagious are you, Ray? Not caught crabs again have we?" Geraint smirks. "Don't worry, Dave gave it to your missus in the first place."

Dave runs his hand through his mop of wavy, silver hair. Mullets weren't fashionable even in the eighties. As he is the only one of us with any significant hair, we like to find fault with the style. We don't need to try very hard. Somehow, at the age of fifty-three, he manages to pull off a metal hoop in his left ear. His black leather jacket always makes me think he has a motorbike parked outside. Wagging his middle finger, he tells Geraint he is a bad, bad man. Geraint is far from offended. His gaunt, lined face broadens. He accepts this as a compliment.

"Don't worry, gentlemen," I say. "I'm not contagious. Heard the filth are out tonight, running random checks. Thought I'd keep my distance from you two muppets in case they arrest me for crimes against banter."

I can almost sense steam emitting from their heads as they struggle for a decent retort. I grab the opportunity to take in the other (dozen or so) residents of The Swan, mainly shiny, upturned faces silently staring at the flashing screen up on the wall. I shake my head. This is Saturday night and it is hardly heaving, is it? No wonder. The government is intent on taxing anything that is remotely fun. What is the point in keeping us all alive until we're a hundred if you then have to pay for all the care that goes with it? With these prices, it is much cheaper to get a crate of lager from Aldi and vegetate in front of the TV. No wonder we have an obesity problem - nobody bothers to walk to the pub anymore.

You could pop an apple in the gormless, open mouths and release an arrow before anybody noticed. It's only rugby league highlights, for fuck's sake. This is the summer - the season is over. This isn't Wigan. They've got nothing better to do up north than bake pies (and eat them, judging by the locals) and watch rugby league on the tele. Nobody in Wales gives a fuck about rugby league. We only watch when there's no real rugby on, and even then we hope the wife doesn't notice the difference. There again, it doesn't really matter what they put on in this gaff. Golf. Tennis. Darts. *Women*'s fucking football. We've all been transformed into bra burners, and nobody is man enough to argue against it. Put sport on the TV in the pub and - instantly - we're sucked in. The regulars in The Swan become Germans, hypnotised by Hitler's rhetoric. It's fucking boring.

Geraint and Dave are my regular drinking buddies,

and I mean them no harm. They see me as a slacker, as a lightweight, because I'm only in the pub three or four times a week. They made an exception last Saturday - they got drunk at the barn dance instead. Occasionally I don't join them; they don't take offence. It is one of my odd quirks. They eye me open-mouthed when I complete The Sun crossword, like they're in the presence of Stephen Hawking. I'm not deliberately anti-social. Sometimes it's healthy to take a step back, view things from outside the goldfish bowl. It's not like I'm into meditation or mindfulness or any of that fancy crap. Not like Bernard, hidden away in his castle with that Yoko Ono wife of his. No doubt if a spaceship landed in The Swan then the aliens would take one look at us lot and report back that they'd found an undeveloped civilisation.

Tonight I'm just not in the mood for socialising. It's been a hard day on the job. My body feels like it has gone twelve rounds with Tyson Fury. My mind is frazzled, too. I would say my brain feels like I've gone twelve rounds with Stephen Fry, but I don't want to take the piss. I've had the extra burden of showing Rob the ropes.

He's a decent kid but - for *fuck's* sake - sometimes it feels like I'm working with a twelve-year-old, not a bloke who claims to be twenty-two. God, I was married and had a young boy at his age. They say kids grow up so young these days, but sometimes I think they don't grow up at all. What is it with 'children' living with Mum and Dad when they're forty? We set our boy up with his own gaff when he was in his early twenties. Fair play to Rob, though, he is nothing like these Millennials they harp on about in The Mail. Aren't they supposed to be perpetually offended? Rob's jokes would make Bernard Manning belly laugh in his grave. And even I'm sometimes uneasy with his obsession with the female form.

Fair play, overall, I could have done a lot worse.

I catch the eye of a guy heading towards me. Don't recognise him, which is unusual around here. Sure, a couple of thousand people live in the town, but you tend to know the regulars. I angle my body to give him more room; I'm not sure if he is heading for the toilet, or maybe the door. Red-rimmed eyes, prominent underneath a bony, protruding skull, zone in on me. My fist knots into a ball. Maybe he knows me from the old days, has a score to settle? It's happened before. He pulls back his hand. My eyes remain fixed on his. He offers his hand. I shake it, hoping he doesn't notice me blowing air from my cheeks.

"I'm Tony," he says. "Fancy a game?"

"Sure." I'm too slow to think of a reason why I *don't* fancy a game. "Ray."

We're no longer strangers as Tony slots a silver coin into the side of the pool table. As he racks up the balls, I busy myself by swishing the amber nectar around, making the taste last. Realise I'm a tad peckish. The wife is forever on a diet, keen to lose some lard from the hips and the tummy, even though I tell her I love her that way (she has this slightly plumper Nigella Lawson thing going on); regardless, that jacket potato she served up for tea barely touched the sides. I glance at the bar, even though I know it's pointless. They don't offer up nuts in glass bowls any more, do they? Something or other about it being less hygienic than licking a toilet. I read about it in one of those magazines laying around the house. Clearly, the Cosmopolitan writers hadn't visited the toilet in The Swan.

"Not seen you round here before," I say.

"That's because I've not been round here before," he says, smiling. "I'm from out of town. Part of the team doing the building work at the leisure centre."

Glancing down at the ripped table, I'm thankful that at least this guy knows which order to put the balls in. Sometimes the guys with the swagger and the bravado are the worst players. Tony breaks; the crack of balls is familiar and comforting. Instantly, he becomes reds. He pots a few more balls, pausing after each to allow time for me to congratulate him. I remain silent. He's not a bad player; he doesn't need me to massage his ego, or his balls. Inevitably, a red ball rattles around the pocket but fails to disappear, remains on the faded green felt. *Close*, I think, *but no cigar.* I tell him it was bad luck. I don't tell him he wouldn't have needed luck if he'd hit the fucking ball properly.

"Looks like I've got my work cut out here."

"Just do what you can," Tony says.

I take a quick glance at my wrist. Look over at Geraint and Dave who, of course, are looking over. They don't have anything else to do. I lean over the table, the cue grazing my light stubble. I stifle a laugh. Time to get to work, I think.

Five minutes and forty-three seconds later, I sink the black ball. There are a few snorts from my usual table. I shake Tony's hand for the second time since meeting him. This was better than staying in and watching *Who Wants to be a Millionaire?* I muse.

"Good game, mate," I say.

I try not to sound condescending, but I suspect the harder I try, the worse it is. Tony prances around on tiptoes with colour to his cheeks. He jerks his head to the side, checking whether anybody noted the game. Geraint and Dave bow their heads, stare into the abyss of their pints (something they're experts at). Maybe I misjudged him? Maybe I've punctured his ego?

Tony juts out his chin. "Fucking hustler."

I hold up my hands, keep him at arm's length. Instinct kicks in. Thirty years or so ago this was my usual Saturday night. His smirk shows me he's taken it as he should. Just a game. His plastic masculinity is still intact. "Like playing against Paul Newman..."

"Hey," I say, "I never pretended to be anything other than a great pool player."

I seize this lull in activity - in conversation - as an opportunity. Need to be quick, before he starts again, badgering me for a second game, a rematch. I drain the glass until all that remains is froth and bubbles. The last thing I want to do is draw attention to myself, to impress this guy; I just want to get out of here. I can tell by his wide eyes that he sees this as a challenge. I may as well have flopped my cock out on the table and asked him to show me what he's got.

I can see the pinkness of his lips through the glass. I dig at some dirt in my nails, killing time like I'm in the queue at the supermarket and don't want to appear impatient. Glance up, then glance back down again. Wish this guy would hurry up with his whole Tarzan thing; it's beginning to get embarrassing. I resist the urge to look at my watch again, to stifle a yawn. Looking over, Dave raises his eyebrows. Eventually, a jubilant Tony slams his empty glass down on the table.

"Can certainly tell you're a drinker," I say, trying not to smile. I tell him I'm off, that its past my bedtime.

"I'll come with you," Tony says. "I fucking *hate* rugby

league anyway."

I wave to Geraint and Dave as I pass their table.

"I won't tell the wife you've pulled," Geraint says.

I hold my middle finger behind my back as the door shuts.

It is an hour or so from closing time, and there are only a few drunken shadows stumbling around on the dimly lit high street. We call it the high street, but really it's the only street in the town with any shops on it. I love it like this. I love it when the streets are completely deserted. Occasionally a fox scurries halfway across the pavement, jerks its head to the side to look at me, before continuing to the other side. It feels like we share a moment. I've noted it a few times in my diary.

"Heading towards the bridge?"

"Nah. The other way."

Course he is. He's sticking with me. My hands ball inside my pockets. I nod to the guy in the pizza shop, do the same to the one in the chip shop. Momentarily, I'm tempted to stop off and pick something up – *anything,* so long as it is greasy and smothered in salt – but this isn't really an option. It won't be a meal for one. Of course, just because I've got a takeaway, it doesn't mean she's required to eat any of it. Some things aren't designed for sharing. I know the score, though. She'd silently stare at the food, whilst pretending she isn't. The guilt will eat away (ironic, really) at me until I'm just not enjoying the food anymore, until I feel compelled to offer her some. *You sure? I wasn't going to ask.* She'll shovel the food into her mouth like she's worried it will vanish if she doesn't. Once the high has faded and the guilt hits, she'll blame me for encouraging her to eat rubbish when she didn't want to. Is it really worth the drama just for a greasy

Doner Kebab?

Turning the corner, heading away from the high street, I flinch, stop dead in my tracks. Tony does the same.

"You alright, love?"

I stay at about six feet, like I'm in the queue for the cash machine. There are two of us - two *men* - and I'm aware that, even on my own, with my shaven head and bulky build, I'm the last person a single girl wants to meet down a dark alley. There is just one of her. She may not want our attention. She may think we're predators. Sat cross-legged on the edge of the pavement in a pair of baggy pink shorts, the girl looks up. Running a hand through her straggly, dirty blonde hair, she shakes her head.

"Just embarrassed," she says, with a trace of a smile.

My knees click as I crouch down to her level. I try not to dwell on the puddle of sick, a perfect circle, casting a spotlight on the girl. "Don't worry," I say. "We've all been here. Me more than most..."

The girl sucks in some air. Her eyes flicker, maybe afraid to take in the size of me. "I'm twenty-one next month. When will I ever learn...?"

I study her face, searching for a flicker of humour. *Only fucking with you.* There is none. She's deadly serious. She's *certainly* grown-up. God, it's nearly thirty years since I was twenty-one. Should I tell her my age? I'm old enough to be her dad, and then some. No. It would be a pointless exchange that might freak her out. Besides, there are more pressing issues at hand. I don't want attention to be on *me*.

The girl takes the silence as an opportunity to keep talking. "Thing is, I hardly ever go out anymore, not since I had my little girl. I feel terrible for thinking it, but it feels like I've been let out of prison for the day. Wanted to live it to the max, you know? The drink has gone to my head, I guess. I'm a proper lightweight now, aren't I? Was downing shots in The Oak. Me. Cass. Amy. Becky. We all were. I only popped out for some air, to clear my head. Not sure what happened..."

I glance at the puddle, just for a second. There must have been blackcurrant in those shots. I look over my shoulder. The street lights suddenly seem very bright, making my world a blur. This girl, with her shorts barely covering her bum, coiled over in a pool of her own vomit, conjures up the sort of image the media love to latch on to. *Sad state of today's youth.* And yet...and yet, she is sweet, just a young girl ashamed that she has drunk too much. I want to cover her up, hide her from any prying eyes. She doesn't deserve to be seen like this, looking so *unladylike.* I was right when I said I'd been there. Only, when I was her age, I was doing so much worse. She is only causing damage to herself, not to others.

"Can I take you somewhere? Away from her...?"

Blood flows to my cheeks, I can feel it under my skin. I know how it might sound, but I can't think of any better way of saying it - I'm not great with putting words in the right order. The girl smiles, lips layered with moisture. What does that smile mean?

"No, I'm good. Just...You don't have a tissue by any chance?"

I spring up, suddenly twenty again. Dig into my pockets. Feels so tight, like there isn't enough room for my hands. As a young dad, I was always asked for tissues, for wipes. It was a dirty business. Now my boy is grown up and I've probably got a few years until they're asking Granddad for tissues.

"Not got any, Ray?"

I'd forgotten he was there. I shudder at Tony's voice, coming from nowhere. He'd been so quiet. What's he been doing all this time? Tony bounces, feeling the cold, like he is on the touchline at the football. He crumples his face and shrugs his shoulders.

I know one solution, but I'm wracked with doubt. Is this too much? Is it a bit odd to suggest? But I've come this far, and I really want to do *something* to help. I'm floundering, and the feeling doesn't sit well.

"I only live down the road. Give me two minutes, okay?"

Turning to Tony, this guy I've only known an hour or so, beaten him in pool and nothing more, I say, "You wait here, yeah? Make sure she's alright..."

Jogging down the hill with my phone to my ear, I call a taxi, barely able to get the words out. Pushing the key into the front door, the house is warm and organised, a stark contrast to the mayhem out on the street. I should have stayed home after all. I clutch at a handful of tissues from the kitchen table; there is *always* a plentiful supply. I turn to leave.

She stands in the hallway. Blocking my path. My beautiful wife of twenty-six years. Katherine.

"What's the matter? What's going on, Ray?"

I stand in the kitchen with a handful of tissues. It is hardly a scene from CSI. You can't get anything past Kat, though. She always smells a rat. I don't know whether it has something to do with my youth, when there were plenty of rats to smell. But then, she was something of a wild child, too, by all accounts. These days she is content to keep the home, draped in her thick jumpers that hide her delightful curves. She is a housewife, a homebody, with a son who has long flown the nest.

Of course, I wouldn't change her for the world.

"You've left the front door wide open. It's freezing out there. Anybody could have got in. Burglars. Rapists. Murderers. You can't be heading out again, surely? You've only just got in. Ray, what *is* going on?"

The questions rattle around my skull, bruising my brain. I'm on the back foot. Now she's mentioned it, this *does* look odd. She needs an explanation. I don't have a decent one.

"Somebody has been sick on the pavement, love. Drunk. Just off the high street. Not far. Bit of a mess. Said I'd pop back and get some tissues. Feel a bit bad. We both know I've been in that position myself a few times..."

"Somebody?"

I look away. Of everything I said, that's what she picked up on. My darling wife should be a detective, not pottering around this house most of the day. I'd hoped she wouldn't pick up on it. Of *course* she did. "A girl. A woman. She's only a kid, really. Twenty, going on twenty-one. She just needs some help, Kat..."

The words linger. It sounds like I'm pleading, like I'm seeking her approval. Dave and Geraint mock me for being under the thumb, for Kat wearing the trousers. I've hit a nerve, though. The power of manipulation. I've never been to her Saturday group - of course - but I know what they talk about. Girl Power. I'm telling Kat that another member of the female species needs our help. On another day it could be Apinya, or even Rose. I'm testing her.

Her face breaks and softens and the scorn vanishes;

suddenly, my wife is beautiful again. "The world needs more men like you, Ray Roberts," she says. "Knight in shining armour, that's what you are."

With a quick kiss on the lips and a brief goodbye, I'm out of the door. My calves strain as I climb the hill. I reach the top and look around.

She isn't here.

I'm not panicked. I'm disappointed. She must have sorted herself out, found her friends. Which is good. *Fantastic.* But I missed my opportunity to be a hero, to make Kat proud. Knight in shining armour, that's what she said. I turn on my heels, my job done. And then, something grabs my attention.

What's that on the other side of the road?

It's Tony, the guy from the pub. He has his back to me. My fists tighten into balls. Blood flows to my burning face. My feet quicken into a jog. All of me - sixteen stone of brawn and anger - transfers to my right shoulder, as I barge him. Perfect connection. Tony's upturned arms flail into the air. He stumbles and staggers like a punch-drunk boxer, bending at the knees to stay on his feet. I don't look at his face - I don't *want* to - but I know it has crumpled into one of confusion and anger.

"Here you go, love," I say, aware of my crackling voice. I don't stay six feet this time. I deliberately invade her space, parting my legs and widening my body to offer a protective shield. Black mascara smears her puffy, blotchy cheeks. Her eyes dart to the road, to the pavement, reminding me of a puppy that isn't sure if I'm going to stroke or slap her. Right now, I suspect that she'd prefer a slap to a stroke.

"Thank you," she whispers, a flickering smile

appearing and then disappearing. She holds my eyes. I nod. Unspoken words. *I understand.*

"It's my fault. I shouldn't let myself get into this mess..."

I begin to speak, begin to tell her that no, it is *not* her fucking fault, that she should never blame herself; just as I open my mouth, just as I'm about to spit out a barrage of words, the girl puts her hands to her eyes, shielding them from the taxi's blinding lights. Taking both of her hands, I pull her up. The girl is unsteady on her feet, but I resist slipping my hand around her waist to balance her.

The driver peers out of the window, eyes widening as he spots the stains on her top. My heart sinks. What must he think? A paralytic girl with a guy old enough to be her dad. He isn't going to take her, is he? I can't blame him. This is his business, his livelihood. He's self-employed, just like me. He has to fill in tax returns, too. He thinks she is going to make a mess in the back of his cab, create a massive valet bill.

"Where does she need to go?"

I want to kiss him. Maybe he has a daughter of his own? Maybe he has a heart of gold? Right now, I don't care. The girl manages to give the driver her address. He nods his head. Knows where it is. Slipping him a note, I tell him to keep the change. Feels like a drugs deal. The driver says he'll make sure she gets home safely. The car reverses - turns around - and I watch as the engine fades, the light disappears.

He is still here. Tony. I can almost smell him. I can sense him next to me on the pavement edge, just a dark shape. Thought he might have taken the opportunity when the taxi turned up to slip away. Think he *should* have taken the opportunity. One. Two. Three. Four.

Five. The digits pass in and out of my mind. I want to stand in silence, in the biting cold, for a handful of seconds, just me and him. I turn around.

"What the fuck were you doing?"

Tony looks straight ahead, hands bunched in his pockets. "Don't know what you mean, Ray. You asked me to stay here and look after her whilst you did your whole Superman thing, and that's what I did."

"You *know* what I fucking mean."

His eyes drop to the floor. He straightens his back. Sucks in his belly. "Thought you'd be thanking me. What's the problem? She was a pretty girl. She was cold. I kept her warm..."

"She was drunk. She was sitting in a puddle of her own sick. You had your hands on her. I saw you. What is *wrong* with you?"

"Didn't hear her complaining..."

I don't even think about it. Pure instinct. I bend my knees. Rotate my body. Transfer my weight. My left hook slams into the side of his jaw. Knuckle against bone. Tony drops to the floor like a felled tree. I stand over him, feet apart, fists still rolled into balls whilst Tony, kneeling on all fours, hands and knees digging into the tarmac, shakes his head. No way is this chump going to stand up and fight back. Nobody is around - he can tell his mates in the pub he fell down the stairs. No shame. This is hardly ever about physical pain. Clutching a handful of hair, I pull his head down and smack it against my knee. He rolls onto his back. Digging my knee into his chest, I pummel punch after punch into his face, his bloodied cheeks smothered with saliva.

An image invades my mind, one I'm constantly trying

to push away, and somehow - *just* - I manage to stop hitting him.

Standing up, I brush myself down. I walk up and down for seconds, possibly minutes, my cheeks hot despite the cool breeze. Tony purrs like a helicopter ready to take off. He presses his hands down against the floor, gingerly rises to his feet. I turn to him and he flinches, puts his hand up to cover his face.

"If I ever see you around here again, Tony, I *will* fucking kill you. Do you hear?"

The man - a stranger again- nods his head.

Sunday 26th August 2018

Sheena

The duvet rolls in a neat ball to the side of my naked body. My eyes fix to the ceiling. I know I'm smiling.

The sun has got his hat on, hip-hip-hip-hooray. There is no need for an alarm. Regardless that its Sunday, there is no real need to get up. Not anymore. Not here, in Pontbach. I don't have a job, and yet I still have money. I know its morning because light slips through the flimsy bedroom curtain. Another day. But unlike back in London, where I was just another faceless person, herded here, there and everywhere but with no real purpose - no real reason to exist - now I look forward to waking up, to another day full of wonderful possibilities.

Not that anybody in Pontbach has really seen my face, seen who I really am. That will change. Soon. Deliberately, I've been a ghost. Sure, I've allowed a few glimpsed shadows, like Katherine and Rose in yesterday morning's meeting, but they were so fleeting I left them confused and befuddled. But I've seen plenty of faces in the few weeks I've been here, just from afar.

I can't hear anything. I could be deafened by noise in London and yet still be lonely. Now, all alone in my bedroom in Pontbach, my body is covered in goose bumps. No TV. No voices. No passing cars outside.

Not even the ticking of a clock. Possibly just the hint of my breathing as my belly rises and falls. With my head engulfed in the fluffy pillow and my long blonde hair scattered everywhere I think, with a smile, that if rose petals were dropped from the ceiling onto my naked body then it would be like the scene from *American Beauty*.

When it happened, about two months ago now, I was ready to move anywhere just so long as it was away from London. Literally, I was prepared to just close my eyes and stick a pin in a map. Daniel, of course, had other ideas. He knew the day would come. In a way, he prompted it. He'd secretly planned, thought ahead. He never let on. Kept me completely in the dark. This is one of his (many) weapons.

"There is only one place you should go to," he said. "Pontbach."

I raised one eye, waiting for him to expand. He stayed silent. Pontbach? Was that in Wales? Wasn't that country full of mountains and sheep? I shrugged my shoulders. There had to be a reason. There always was.

"Do your research," he said, reading my mind.

Twenty years ago this would have meant a trip to the library. These days, of course, a fountain of knowledge is available at your fingertips. Still, initially there didn't appear to be that much information. About sixty miles inward from Cardiff. Just over two thousand residents. Three pubs. A Thursday market. A small brick bridge crossing the Wye River.

I wondered how I'd stay awake. Where was the drama? Part of me wanted to go back to Daniel, ask for more information, just a starting point, but I feared his disapproval and I dreaded the thought of letting him down. And so I kept clicking the mouse, continued flicking from screen to screen until the headings expanded before me.

There it was. The reason he said it was the only place I should go. My fingers trembled at the enormity of the reason.

Creaking my head to the side in my new home now, I look down at the reflective laminate floor. There is not even a glimmer of fluff on the skirting board, no mess whatsoever. A spider appears from underneath the bed, confident and cocky, almost dancing. Smiling, I press the back of my hand on the floor, inviting the spider into my palm. The spider weighs up whether I'm friend or foe. He has no reason to trust me.

"There you go. I'll do you no harm. I'll look after you. You're safe with me."

The spider pauses – *stops* – almost as if to take in the words, a fish checking whether a hook is attached to the worm. Certain this is no trap, he climbs onto my hand, ascents up my bare arm.

Everyone, and every *thing*, trusts me.

I roll the spider between my two fingers like a ball of chewing gum. Flick it away. The spider is like a newborn calf. It scrambles away, before disappearing down a tiny crack in the skirting board.

This is the stimulus I need to get out of bed, to end the bliss. Pressing my feet down on the cold floor, I pull the curtains wide, open the window. I push my head outside, not caring if the neighbours can see my naked body. The cold air makes my body shiver. The sky is clear and vibrant. What wonderful power God has, I think, to make it a good day or a bad day for billions of people, just by deciding whether to make it rain or shine. I inhale deeply. Crisp. Fresh.

"Beautiful," I say, bending at the waist and pushing my arms forward, a cat that has just woken from a nap. The floorboards creak as I make my way to the mahogany fitted wardrobe, the centrepiece of the bedroom. Twisting my neck to the left and then to the right, I crinkle my nose and bare my teeth, stare unblinkingly at my reflection in the mirror. "Absolutely beautiful."

My fingertip creates a smudge down the mirror. I'm reminded of the soreness in my wrist, of the sharp, glorious incision in my skin. I pull my fingers to my nose; the scent is dull and familiar, like lead from a battery.

I think back to the early hours of the morning. I stood right in this spot. The window was wide open then too, the breeze caressing my naked body. It was cold and black outside then, and my body, tinged blue, shivered and shook. My pink nipples stiffened and darkened, not from the cold air outside entering my room, but from the blood flowing through my body. The whites of my eyes reflected back at me in the mirror, growing wider as the scissors plunged into my wrist. I closed my eyes and, as the pain hit me, the tingling crept up my thighs.

Looking down now, the droplets of blood have dried, darkened to the point they are nearly black. My smile widens. My teeth glisten. My fingers trace the outline of the letters I smeared onto the mirror.

Carnage.

Bernard

The lines appear etched in his cheeks. His freckled forehead slopes backwards. The head shakes from side to side. The expanding eyes fix on me. He says nothing. The look tells me everything I need to know.

I repel him.

Blinking the sweet sweat from my eyes, it takes me a few moments to realise I'm no longer asleep. When will I learn? The dream is recurring, yet it never fails to trick me.

I take a sideways view of the alarm clock. 8:14. Sunday. Wish it was an hour earlier. Whatever time I wake, I always wish it was an hour earlier, just to give me some time before I have to face the day. I stretch out my arm to the other side of the bed. My hand continues grazing the silk bed sheet. I pat my hand down, like I'm building a sandcastle.

Apinya isn't in bed.

Memories of last night's argument flood my mind. Was it even an argument? Apinya just shouted at me. Despite the light in the room and the glowing August sun outside, dark clouds hover and fester in my world this morning.

Showered and dressed, I tiptoe down the stairs. She doesn't notice me enter the kitchen; I observe her for a few moments at the stove, frying eggs and sausages and simmering baked beans. She always strived to be the perfect wife. The oversized apron hangs to her knees. Her hair is tied in a bun. The beautiful scents make my nostrils twitch. This house is already beginning to feel like a home again, like it did when I lived here with my first wife and our two children. I stand motionless in the doorway, a smile forming. I want to hate her. She deserves to be hated. How can I? Apinya does a double-take when she turns around. I extinguish my glimmering smile, like water on a fire. Her reaction is almost comical. For a moment, she wonders if an intruder is in her home. *Our* home. For a moment, I wonder if she's right.

"How long have you been there?"

"Not long. Just admiring the view."

This is intended to sound affectionate, a loving husband complimenting his beautiful wife, and yet heat burns my cheeks. I feel like a Peeping Tom, like I've been caught spying with my trousers by my ankles. Apinya pauses; she isn't sure of the correct way to greet me. She throws down the oven gloves and wraps her arms around my neck, planting a kiss on my lips. "I'm so, so sorry," she says.

"It's okay."

"It's really not okay, Bernard. You mean everything to me. You treat me like a princess. Yet this is how I repay you?"

Breaking our embrace, she sits down on the sofa, tightening her arms around her chest. I'm reminded of my eldest boy; he did this when Mummy told him off. But then, he was about ten at the time. Whilst I sit down next to Apinya, it feels like I'm observing her from afar. "You have your reasons," I say.

"That's not an excuse."

It is almost a question. The auburn eyes are pleading.

She wants me to reassure her that it is an excuse, that her behaviour is justified because of the terrible things that happened to her in Thailand.

"We all do things we regret," I say.

"Sometimes the memories build in my mind until they bubble over. I get so angry, and then I take it out on the one person I truly love."

"I should take it as a compliment in a way..."

"I hate myself for it."

"Don't. Just don't."

"Didn't you see the signs?" she asks. "Didn't you see it building?"

I lose eye contact. "I didn't, Apinya. You were out at your group in the morning and I was still in the garden when you returned. We didn't spend that much time together, did we? Maybe my mind was elsewhere."

She strokes my arm. I flinch. She doesn't notice. "You were distracted yesterday, darling, I could tell. Thinking about your family. That's why I gave you some time. I tried to help."

"I was. And you did give me some time. I appreciate it."

Apinya jumps to her feet. "I've cooked you breakfast, sweetheart. You deserve it..."

I tell her it smells great (which it does) and minutes later I tell her it *tastes* great (which it *absolutely* does). Apinya plays with her food, pushing it around her plate with her fork. Again, I'm reminded of the kids. I have no idea how many mouthfuls she eats (if any) before she scoops her food onto my plate. I'm tinged with frustration. No wonder I have an inflatable dingy around my waist whilst she remains as slim and perfect as the day we met. My endless sessions on the treadmill merely compensate for eating for two. Apinya tops up my cup of tea.

Sitting in silence, I glance occasionally at Apinya. Her watery eyes redden. She looks up at the ceiling and then at the clock on the wall. Today is Sunday. We have no plans. I long to quieten the guilt, gnawing away at my heart.

"I'm sorry," I say. "You're right. I should have paid more attention. I shouldn't have let it build up to the crescendo last night. It was my fault..."

Apinya's creased face softens. Jumping off her stool, she plants a wet kiss on my forehead. "Thank you, Bernard," she says. "It means so much for you to say that."

Wednesday 5th September 2018

Sheena

I step over dandelions as I walk along the bumpy path in my flat shoes. Flowers are beautiful. Flowers are harmless. They don't deserve to die.

Before locating the information Daniel wanted me to find, I discovered that Pontbach is picturesque and delightful, the perfect place to unwind. Fair play, whilst the contributors to the forum probably had too much time and not enough life, their observations were spot on. Of course, the internet didn't suggest actually coming to *live* here (are you *crazy?*), not unless you'd retired and were already counting down the days till you die.

Naturally, I'm not ready to die. I'm happy to push the clock hand forward a notch or two for some of the other villagers, though. Part of the thrill - as I'd already discussed with Daniel - was deciding which ones.

Time is passing. I'm itching to get started. I've made my presence felt with the men in the local pubs, just by not having a dick. Their tongues dropped and they shuffled uncomfortably on the wooden stools. The men may not yet know my name, or where I've come from, but they're talking about me, that's for sure.

Daniel said to bide my time, to watch and learn before I made my first move. Patience, he said, is a virtue. Think of it like a chess game. Who am I to argue with my intellectual superior? And so I am a shark circling my prey, ready to attack.

Call me a callous, shallow cow, but at first I was struck, not by Daniel's intellect, but by his beauty. The sharp contours of his face appeared carved from mahogany. His lips were the colour of rose petals. Slim, strong wrists poked out of cuff-linked, cotton shirts. The last thing I sought was love. I longed to find myself, not to find somebody else. Our first handful of meetings were brief. I did most of the talking. His questions allowed me to open my heart.

What excites you, Sheena?

What frightens you?

What makes your life worth living?

With his fingers laced and his chin perched on his thumb, he barely even nodded his head. His eyes encouraged me to keep talking. When I was in a room with him, the rest of the world ceased to exist. I fell in love the first time we met, even though I knew my affections were inappropriate. The implications were much greater for him. Only much later did he confide that he felt the same way. Who could have imagined that, seven years later, he would be there, and I would be here, living in a town I never knew existed?

The wooden porch provides shelter; the faded light is like a blanket over my head. My arm brushes away a fly. I take a cursory glance at my left wrist. Pushing open the sturdy door, my immediate world turns an even darker shade.

My flat shoes are soundless against the tiled floor. The musty scents bring back childhood memories. Navy blue books, torn at the edges, pile high on a metal trolley. Only a glimmer of early-autumn sunshine filters through the stained glass windows; it does little to lift the gloom. Despite this, I can't help but be drawn to the quiet, to the confined solitude. This is the perfect place to hide away from the chaotic world we live in. My jaw drops. Jesus stares down at me from the cross. What does he see?

Does he view me as a kindred spirit?

I know what to expect. I may have spent the last handful of weeks in relative isolation, but I've been busy. I've studied the routines. There are only two of us in the church. Normally, at this time of day, there is only one. She sits on her own, three rows from the back, a cardigan hanging from her stooped shoulders.

"Rose?"

Untangling her hands, she lifts her bowed head. Up close, her grey, lined face looks like it has been used as a dartboard. She blinks at me like wind has blown dust and debris in her eyes. Of course, I am not significant to her in the way she is to me. Yet. My wide, practiced smile is calming. Her foggy eyes suggest partial recognition. Her lips crease into a smile. She sees me as a friend, and not a foe, just like the spider.

Everybody sees me as a friend. Even my enemies.

"I'm so sorry, Rose," I say. "I didn't mean to startle you. I just saw you here and I thought it would be rude not to say hello. Gosh, it feels like I know you and yet you probably don't even know who I am, do you...?"

She knows that her startled face most likely appeared rude. She has a few false starts before she gets her words out. "I *do* recognise your face, dear. I just can't quite put my finger on it. Oh, I know now. You've come to the group, haven't you? I don't think you introduced yourself? I apologise, I don't yet know your name, and yet you know mine..."

"Sheena Strachan."

"Well, Sheena, welcome to the village. And welcome to the church."

"That's very kind of you, Rose."

We both turn forwards. Rose clasps her hands together but then pulls them apart again. I sense her blowing air from her mouth. She is a lady of routine, and her routine has been interrupted. How can she possibly focus on her prayers with me hovering over her, a moth drawn to the light?

"Do you come here often?" I ask. I'm aware this sounds like a chat-up line.

"Every day. Same time. It is kind of my *thing*."

"I admire your commitment to the Lord."

"Thank you, dear."

I lean back in the pew, stretching out a long, naked leg. "I'm sorry. I shouldn't have disturbed you, should I? Sometimes I just can't help myself. I had no idea this was a special time of day for you."

Rose is apologetic now, realising that maybe she has been overly brusque. After all, this lovely young lady is new to the village; she is probably lonely. I release a subtle smile as Rose holds up her hands, assures me that this is God's home, that everyone is welcome here, she has no more right to be here than I do.

"I'm sorry to hear that your husband passed," I say.

Her tired eyes narrow, and I picture a question mark drawn in the middle of her forehead. "Sorry, I heard about it in the village," I say.

Rose smiles. "Don't worry. It's fine."

"Was it a long time ago?"

She sagely nods her head.

"Before you moved here?"

"That's right. Yes."

Her heavy-hooded eyes seem to lighten. "So how are you settling into the town, Sheena?"

"Oh it's such a lovely place. Everybody is so friendly. Not that I've actually *spoken* to that many people. I can be a bit shy, if I'm totally honest with you."

I can feel her warming to me. She probably thinks this is an ordeal for me, that I'm pushing myself to engage. "So what did you think of the group?"

I gush. "Oh, I thought that *you* were absolutely brilliant."

Rose exposes a row of mustard teeth. "You do flatter me."

"Not at all. The control you had over the group was incredible."

From her strained, rasping laugh, I don't know if she smokes, but she certainly used to. I glimpse her stained fingertips. "Control? I'm not sure that is the right word for it, dear. But thank you."

"The group idolises you. The women would do anything for you. *Anything.*"

She looks at me nonplussed. Am I being serious? The lines on her forehead vanish. Surely this nice young lady wouldn't joke with her in this way? "Most of the women respect me, for sure, which is nice. I'd hate to control them, though. Truth be told, I try to do as little as possible. I merely encourage them. I try to let them do it all for themselves. Work things out. Let them give me the answers they already know. I find that is much more effective."

She's aware I'm looking at her with adulation, like she is the guru of all things wise. Her dead skin shows some life.

"If I'm honest, Rose - and I do try to be honest - I wasn't quite so impressed with all of the group-"

"*Really*? What do you mean? Who?"

I hold up the palms of my hands, tell her that it is nothing really, that maybe I shouldn't have said anything. "Don't get me wrong, they're a lovely bunch. You're very lucky in that way. I just got the impression some of the women are in it for themselves..."

The colour fades from her cheeks. I'm not sure if she's shocked, or aghast. "I hadn't noticed. Maybe I'm blinkered, been too close for too long. They say it sometimes takes an outsider to see what has been there all along..."

"I just don't think some are as committed to the cause as you. Some of the women looked like they're there just to fill some time, for something to do. You've given up a lot of time. You deserve better than that..."

"Maybe you have a point, dear. Attendance is up and down. Women come and go."

"Do any always attend? Are there any you know you can rely on?"

Rose doesn't hesitate to reply. "Well, Katherine is an angel-"

"Katherine?"

"Yes, she sits at the back. Pretty lady. She came to the first meeting twelve years ago, and she's been coming ever since. Never misses a meeting bless her. And there's Apinya - of course - she's been good as gold, ever since she joined the village..."

I laugh. "Oh yes. Apinya did stand out somewhat."

"You could say she is an outsider here, but she's slotted right in with no problems at all."

"An outsider? Oh, I relate to her then," I say.

I stand up. Tell Rose that I've taken up far too much

of her time, that I'll speak to her in the next group meeting. I lean down to lightly embrace my new friend. My mouth lingers close to her ear, brushes against it.

"Don't forget to pray for your daughter too, Rose," I whisper. "We both know who's really to blame for that now, don't we?"

Her body physically flinches. She turns, ready to fire out questions, but she faces my back, and I'm nearly at the door, bracing myself for the brightness outside.

Bernard

Whilst I've always adored my home comforts, I can't deny the sudden urge - the *need* - to get out of the house, to be around other, breathing people. Subconsciously, part of me just wants to show Apinya I have a life she isn't part of. Certainly, she's entirely aware of my past life - she only has to look at the pictures on the walls - but I long to convince her that I have a present, a *future*.

Empty, defeated eyes return my gaze in the full-length bedroom mirror. Who is this stranger? Stretched, zigzagging crows-eyes meet in the middle. Are my teeth a shade darker? How am I going to show Apinya I have a present and a future when the stranger looking back at me in the mirror looks unconvinced?

I sling my usual cuff-linked shirts to one side of the metal rail. This is the attire I'd choose to wear, and so instinctively I know it is inappropriate. Too smart. Too formal. Too stiff. What are the clothes I'd wear when I rough it, when I'm in the garden or when I visit the tip? My hand delves deeper. My nose crinkles, like I don't quite recognise that smell. Yes. These look more promising. The faded blue tee-shirt has a couple of holes beneath the armpits where moths have eaten their breakfast. With my arms stretched upwards, I stumble like a punch-drunk boxer as I struggle to get my head through the hole. I unroll the tee-shirt down over my protruding belly. Perfect. My pristine brown leather shoes remind me of a delightful temptress, luring me to slide them on my feet. I grab hold of a pair of running shoes, long ago disposed to the back of the cupboard because the soles had come away. Ruffling my fingers through my hair, I try to hide that I combed it earlier in the day. I need to fit in.

Downstairs, a barefoot Apinya widens her eyes and pulls her hand to her mouth when she sees me. She is even more beautiful when she does not wear make-up. Rather than covering imperfections, she merely covers her fresh-faced beauty. For the last few weeks or so she has treated me like a king, waiting on me hand on foot. I know I overreacted, that my thoughts at the time were irrational.

"Where are you going, sweetheart? It's the middle of the week."

"To the pub, darling. I just fancy a quick pint."

She is right to raise her eyebrows. I never tell her I'm just popping to the pub for a quick pint.

"Is it a fancy dress party?"

I fight my irritation. She isn't trying to be funny. She genuinely thinks, from looking at what I'm wearing, that there may be a fancy dress party at the pub. Still, I don't answer her. My straight face tells her that no, it isn't fancy dress. I peck her puckered lips and head out of the door before she can ask any more questions.

Entering The Swan, I feel like I'm walking around a holiday resort in my Speedos. I don't linger at the door, and I don't look around, but instantly I can tell there aren't any women in the establishment. I can almost smell the male testosterone. I'm the only person at the bar and yet still I struggle to get served. I try not to look at my reflection in the mirror. I know I won't be able to resist grimacing. Thumbing the pockets of my jeans, I longingly eye the dry white wine.

"Pint of Carling, please."

Leaning against the slippery bar with the pint in my hand, I flinch at the sharp nectar. Do people intentionally drink this? Do they drink it because they enjoy it or do they drink it to get drunk?

"Don't see you in here much, Bernie. Have you come to invite me to one of your much-celebrated dinner parties?"

I smile at the trio huddled around the table. "Alright, Geraint." I nod at Dave and Ray. "Just fancied a quick pint, chaps..."

Dave and Geraint are here every night, as far as I can tell. They are part of the furniture. Apinya is close to Ray's wife, Katherine, yet, as far as I'm aware, she doesn't really know her at all. Ray is a regular, a drinker, but I don't think he comes here as much as the other two.

The three men eye each other. It feels like I'm here for a dare. Geraint leans forward, ready for another bite. "Just come from the garden, Bernard? You been riding around on the mower of yours again?"

My waved hand is dismissive. "Oh these things? Just threw on any old clothes."

The Three Amigos stare at me. I'm an exhibit at the zoo. In my limited experience, men horse around by hurling abuse at each other. *I need to fit in.* "I save my best clobber for when I take your mum to the Bingo, Geraint..."

Maybe this wasn't the right thing to say? Geraint's eyes widen. His fists ball. I glance at the door. Can I get there before he does? I suck in a mouthful of stale air. Ray slams his fist against the table. The table shakes.

Ray starts laughing.

"You didn't expect that, did you, Geraint? They don't call Bernard the Archbishop of Banterbury for nothing, you know. Pull up a pew, Bernard."

Geraint's face softens. My body no longer feels like it needs oiling. Sliding a chair towards the table, I make sure my throat remains far enough away from Geraint's outstretched arm, just in case. I open up my chest, try to look like this is my natural habitat, like I'm a monkey hanging from a tree.

"Still into your trains, Bernard?" Dave asks. "What was that group you said you were a member of again?"

I lower my voice. "The Engine Shed Society. I'm one of only 340 members."

Dave's lips can't hide mischief. "I'm genuinely surprised by that, Bernard. I'd have thought the Engine Shed Society would have had millions of members."

I shake my lowered head as the men break into laughter. I stare at the floor and wait for them to change the subject.

"She was here again last night, Ray, when you were playing Happy Families with that gorgeous wife of yours..."

Dave leans across and stamps his thumb against Ray's forehead. Dave is single. Always has been, as far as I'm aware. I'm not sure if this is a lifestyle choice or because he can't attract a woman. He wears his leather jacket well. The silver ring in his left ear goes with his long salt and pepper hair. There must be a woman in the village who'd take him in. I'm sure Dave wouldn't mind staying in and playing Happy Families with Ray's wife. Most of the men in the village have a soft touch for Katherine. Not many of them would be brave enough to say that to Ray, though, not unless it is in jest.

"Who's that then, Dave?" I ask. "Who was here again last night?"

He turns to me with a wolfish smile. "This newcomer to the town. I overheard her tell Mike at the bar her name was Sheena. You'd love her. She's a cracking piece of skirt."

Sheena? I've not heard that name before. I'm not sure whether to be complimented or offended that, apparently, I'd appreciate 'a cracking piece of skirt'. Presumably, Dave thinks I have a good choice in women, which is something.

"Ordered a gin and tonic, like she's in Hollywood or something..."

"Proper posh," Geraint says.

"Sits over in the corner," Dave says.

"Did she say anything to you? Has she spoken to you yet?" I ask.

"Only with her eyes."

"You should have seen what she was wearing," Geraint says, smiling.

Nobody says anything for a few seconds. I sense another opportunity. "What was she wearing?" I ask.

Geraint slaps me on the shoulder. "I'm glad you asked, Bernie. That was another thing. She was dressed for a night out, not for this dump. She had on this long white dress. She looked stunning, so she did."

The three men stare into space, seemingly absorbing this information.

"I can only think she's here to pick up a guy," Dave says. "Why else would she come to the pub on her own?"

"She's got my interest," Geraint says, wiping his lip.

"But you're married?" I ask.

Geraint glances at his two comrades. "Wasn't looking to get the wife involved, Bernie. Unless you and Apinya are interested in some freaky shit? Now, where's my car keys...?"

The three men laugh. I'm buoyed by the attention. "Seriously," I say. "It must be difficult for women joining the village. We do tend to live in a goldfish bowl in Pontbach, don't we? Maybe she's just looking for friends?"

"Friends with benefits?" Dave asks, tapping the bridge of his pointed nose.

"Or maybe just friends..."

"Did Apinya struggle when she came over from China?"

"Thailand."

"All the same."

"She did find it difficult to acclimatise to the new way of life. But now she's fine."

"She certainly *is* fine," Dave says.

"Anyway, I'm just saying that next time she's here, maybe you should try and talk to her? She might just be lonely. Make her feel welcome. I'm sure she'll appreciate that."

"Have you ever thought of becoming an Agony Aunt, Bernard? Auntie Bernie? Maybe I'll take your advice," Dave says.

I finish my drink. I perceive the men are impressed by my speed. I contemplate getting another, maybe buying a round, but I could see myself coming back late, drunk and abhorrent. I don't fancy another night sleeping in the guest room - I'm on a roll, and that spare bed tends to give me horrific back pains. I decide to make this my last drink.

Rising to my feet, I shake the craggy hands. "I've enjoyed the company, gentlemen. Maybe I'll come back in a few weeks to see how you got on with that young lady, Dave?"

"I'll give you all the gossip," Dave says.

Walking back to the house, I blow out hot air. It feels like I've just finished a Best Man speech I've been dreading. I'm glowing with satisfaction.

That wasn't so bad, I think.

Saturday 22nd September 2018

Katherine

I've lost count of the group social gatherings I've attended. Social beavers? Hardly. I've been a member of the group for twelve long years. Even if we only met up three times a year then that would be thirty-six events. *Ooh, Matron.* It is not even like we *enjoy* these events. Why do we meet at all? Is it because that's what normal, healthy people are expected to do, because we're all just trying to fit in?

I flinch when Ray kisses the nape of my neck. I hadn't even noticed him enter the kitchen. I glance at the cup of tea stewing on the table.

"Fancy a brew, darling?"

His smile has many cracks. He shakes his head. Even though it's not gone ten in the morning, I sense he fancies something stronger. My husband is hardly an open book. Wear his heart on his sleeve? Hardly. You have to crack him like a coconut to reveal any genuine emotions. But recently things have progressed to a whole new level. Now his body is there but his mind is on a completely different planet. Of course, I've asked him if he is okay and - of course - he's reassured me he is. I've tried to pinpoint when things changed, and the closest I can get to is that Saturday night he returned from the pub to pick up tissues for some young, intoxicated girl.

I'm certain he hasn't told me everything about that evening.

"So where's your party today, Kat?"

I smile. He is teasing. This is a flicker of my old husband. We both joke at the formality of our gatherings. "As you know, Raymond, this is hardly a party."

"Will Apinya be going?"

"Guess so..."

"Did I tell you Bernard joined us at the pub the other week? Left his train set at home. Apinya must have let him off the leash-"

"Bernard? That's not like him..."

"Think he was making an effort to fit in. It did seem a bit of an ordeal. Got the impression he wanted to get one of his books out!"

"What a darling."

"Anyway, where you off to? I'm proper jealous. You girls always have so much *fun*."

I slap his arm. Even after all these years of marriage, I'm surprised how firm my husband feels. His arms (and legs) are like tree trunks. You'd need an axe to chop him down. He had a reputation when I first met him, and he still does. He went to the football every week. It is no secret that the football was a sideshow. My husband (boyfriend at the time) went to fight. The rest of the community (quite rightly) said he was a hooligan. I took a more pragmatic view - he only fought other men who wanted to fight him back. It was a release, a form of escapism.

Everyone says he gave it all up to protect me instead. They're partly right, I guess; they just have no idea what happened to make up his mind.

"We're just meeting down the river. A few drinks. Some food. I doubt I'll be long..."

His mouth is a perfect circle. I deliberately fired out the words, uttered them like I'd pressed the fast forward button, hoped that he wouldn't take them in. Who was I kidding?

"Down by the river? Are you joking? Whose smart idea was that?"

I look away. "Rose."

"*Rose?* Why? She knows what happened to your parents. That's why she tried to drag you back to Church when she first arrived in the town. We both know that's why she formed the damn group in the first place, so you could both grieve-"

"I'm sure it was much more complicated than that..."

"I don't like it."

I take my cup to the sink. Move away. Talk to his back. "I can't live in fear all of my life, Ray. I can't keep running from all my bad memories. There are too many. I need to live my life..."

I imagine his face behind me, eyebrows meeting in the middle. He agrees wholeheartedly with these words. For him. Not for his precious, delicate wife. *Feel the fear and do it anyway*, that's what he thinks. He told me as much about his fighting days. But he's a big, grown bear of a man. He'd hate his mates to know he was scared of anything. He'll just be amazed these words have come from my mouth.

"Just take care of yourself, okay? If it gets too much then make your excuses and come home. I'll be waiting for you."

I turn now. Part of me loves my protective husband. I tie my arms around his neck and rest my forehead against his. "I'll be fine," I say, my words trembling.

Bernard

"Remember I'm out later, Bernard..."

I look up at my wife. Judging by her widened eyes, lines must appear on my already creased forehead.

"I did tell you," she says. "It's the social with the group."

"Oh yes. Sorry, I forgot."

"I won't go if you don't want me to."

"I *do* want you to."

"Charming, Mister."

I smile to Apinya's back; she is already loading the dishwasher. She does everything so much quicker than me.

"So where are you going?"

"Picnic down the river..."

"*What?* You do know that's where Katherine's parents died? How is the poor woman going to cope with that...?"

Apinya turns around. Digging her elbows onto the worktop, her hands cup her ears. "Oh my God. What the *fuck*? How did they die?"

My ears prickle. Apinya is not aghast. She is not horrified. She is fascinated. I feel I'm gossiping. What choice do I have? I have to tell her now.

"Nobody knows. Not for sure. They drowned. The detective at the time suspected foul play, but nobody is sure why. They closed the case with no suspicious circumstances. Basically, it was either an accident, or they took their own lives in some sort of suicide pact..."

"*Suicide* pact? But why would they top themselves?"

"Well, I don't know. But you need to consider that their son, Ben, who was Katherine's older brother, was murdered back in the eighties, and naturally that hit them hard-"

"Murdered? *Here?* In this town?"

I put my two hands up to tone down her excitement. "No. He moved away. To Rhondda. Nobody talks about it. We don't want to upset Katherine..."

"How terribly fucking *exciting*," Apinya says.

"Promise me you won't ever mention it...?"

Apinya narrows her eye in mock offence. I stifle a laugh. Returning to the dishwasher, my wife's muffled voice asks what I'll be doing when she's out. I tell her not to worry about me, that I'll sort something out.

"You could catch up with one of the guys you went to the pub with the other week. Who knows? Katherine's husband, Ray, might be at a loose end, too?"

I examine my fingernails. How do I explain that I don't think we have that kind of friendship, that if I keep turning up unannounced then I'll probably outstay my welcome? I've never really been one of the boys, even when I was in school, and I'm not convinced that will change any time soon.

"I don't think they go to the pub in the day," I say. "We don't have a *Wetherspoons.* And besides, I think I fancy doing something different."

Apinya doesn't ask any more questions. Instead, she skips upstairs to make herself look beautiful.

I scan through the numbers on my phone. Reaching the bottom of the list, I start from the top again. I try to think of somebody who'd appreciate me contacting them, who'd actually be excited to do something with me today. What about...? No, it has been so long and besides, she'll be at the social with Apinya. I glance to the ceiling, to the sky above. I'm not religious - don't believe in the afterlife - but even I can't shrug off the feeling Dad is looking down at me, shaking that freckled forehead.

All of this - the house, the money - is because of him. I don't advertise it, but I don't deny it. My dad was the real deal. Scratch under the surface and it doesn't take long to discover I'm just a pretender. Dad founded the accountancy firm in the town and then he set one up in Cardiff and then another in Swansea. He handed the firms to me, and I just kept them going, kept the money coming in. Then, as soon as Dad was six feet under the ground (which was a lot sooner than most people expected), I sold the company. I didn't dare do so when he was still alive, of course. That would have been far too courageous. The kids hated this decision almost as much as they hated my decision to marry a young Thai bride who, they said, was *clearly* after my money. *What sort of a silly old man are you, Dad?* They didn't see it as my money, did they? It was Granddad's money. I frittered away Granddad's money on my own pleasures.

My thoughts are interrupted by Apinya twirling in a violet dress in the middle of the living room. I suddenly feel like an overprotective father letting her daughter go on her first date. Just how much leg does she need to show? I thought they were gathering for a picnic down by the river?

"You look sensational," I say.

Her white-toothed smile tells me that was exactly

what she wanted me to say.

"Sorted something out?"

I nod. "Yes. Should be going hiking a bit later."

I probably will, do, too. I like the idea of being in the mountains, looking down at the tiny town below me, building up a sweat.

I don't see the point in telling her I'll be going alone.

Rose

What *is* that stench? It has been lingering for a while, rank, stale and rancid, an uninvited guest. I've been aware of it for a while - minutes, hours - I think, but I've tried not to give it any attention. My eyes move around the room. My head remains forward; my body remains motionless. I don't *need* to know. It doesn't change anything. I crinkle my nose. I *am* the smell. These are yesterday's clothes. I haven't bathed or brushed my teeth today and, come to think of it, I'm not sure I did yesterday, either.

Who cares? What does it matter?

I normally enjoy sitting by the window in the front room that overlooks the street. I like to people watch. I'm a nosy little Madam. People are natural when they don't realise someone's watching them. It is like taking a photograph when they're not looking. I don't want to see the outside world today, though. I don't want to see smiling faces or hear laughter and chatter. The curtains are drawn. I can tell it is a blue, cheerful day outside, but in my world, everything remains grey and cloudy.

Morbid thoughts often invade my mind. Usually I push them away, but today I can't be bothered. I want to face reality. How long could I sit here on my own, in this little terraced house, before anybody noticed I was dead? Would Mrs Thomas next door knock on the door or call the police before she smelt my decaying body? Or would one of the group wonder where I was? Maybe Katherine?

We have history, of course; we have a connection. More so than even she realises. Yes, I hope Katherine would miss me.

The clock on the mantelpiece tells me it is five past eleven. For some reason, the time reminds me of the day. Saturday. There is no morning group today. They are meeting socially instead. I shake my head. *She'll* be there. I hope they have fun.

I should go for Katherine. I suggested the river so she faced her torrid memories. Time has passed. I hoped it would help both of us. The venue seems ridiculous now. Cruel. What would Ray think? He can be so frighteningly overbearing, so watchful.

Still, I just can't face going.

My head rotates, moving from wall to wall. The white paint is flawless. I enjoyed putting on the overalls, getting my hands dirty. The walls are bare, just an expanse of white. Didn't anybody think it was odd that there were no photographs in this room?

I turn to the chest of drawers in the corner of the room. This is an antique. The delivery men questioned whether I really wanted to take it with me to the new house. I gave them a look, and they quickly struggled to load it onto the lorry. Strange, but now it is here I never touch it. Whilst the house smells of polish (or it did, until I started stinking it out), this chest of drawers gathers dust.

I don't even think before I do it.

My knees dig into the carpet. Pulling open the drawer, my hand drags it out. I am out of breath when I sit back down. I sweep the front of the blue photo album. The palm of my hand is black. Opening the album, she stares straight at me. Her eyes sparkle, her smile is alight.

I haven't seen her in years.

How did Sheena know about her? Why-oh-why did she talk about her?

Lowering my lips, I kiss her sweet, adorable face. Then, I slam the book shut.

Looking to the curtains, shut tight, I think it is about time I let some light into this room. After all, I've got things to do, people to see...

Katherine

Today is the kind of day that believers look to the heavens and gasp in admiration. My mum carried a pocket Bible with her everywhere, hidden away in her handbag. My dad, on the other hand, didn't need to carry his - he knew the teachings word-for-word. Today is the kind of day my parents, were they still alive, would have looked up to the unblemished blue sky and praised the Lord.

I'm no longer religious, of course. How could I be? Deep down I know my older brother would still be alive today were it not for religion.

Sometimes I wonder how it happened, when it began. I was so proud to be Ben's little sister. My friends giggled and played with their hair when they talked about him. When they came to the house, they checked for his muddy trainers at the front door. *Is Ben here?* Whatever the situation, he was the coolest kid in the room. He must have noticed their smiles, must have noticed their exaggerated laughs to his unfunny jokes, but he always remained relaxed, he always took it in his stride. The boys in my year literally fought over some of my friends, but my handsome older brother didn't need to; he had them wrapped around his little finger.

If *only* it was that straightforward.

My thermal socks remain dry as my trainers sink into the soft, dewy grass. I've unzipped my cardigan. Occasionally, I've shielded my eyes from the plucky late-September sun. I glance to the River Wye flowing to my side, then look away, managing to blank it out. People-in-the-know will expect me to be nervous returning to the river. They don't know I sometimes walk down here in the mornings, that I've trained myself to calm the memories. They don't know *anything*.

"Well, *this* is nice," I say, actually meaning it.

I feel like I'm on stilts hovering over Apinya's tiny dancer's frame. She is as delicate as a newborn chick. Does she sleep with that smile on her face? No wonder Bernard is so happy these days. He's won the lottery with this one. Mind you, she hasn't done too bad out of it, has she? I can't imagine she had a life of luxury in Thailand (she told the group as much), and now she is Lady of the Manor, living in that beautiful mansion on the outskirts of town, reminding me of Josephine Baker in her castle. I'd probably live in a permanent state of euphoria, too.

My flimsy cardboard plate is piled high with cheese and ham sandwiches, curled crisps and sausage rolls. Apinya seems oblivious to the long table filled with food (in my mind there is a big finger pointing at it saying 'eat me'). Seemingly, it offers no temptation, no lure. Biting into a sausage roll, I tell myself I'll starve myself tomorrow, that maybe - quite possibly - I'll never eat again.

Apinya darts away with surprisingly long strides, ignores what I said. She returns with an opened bottle of white wine and two plastic cups. "*Nice?* This is my idea of *Heaven*. I'm out in the beautiful Welsh countryside, surrounded by my favourite girls. What is there not to love?"

I should pop whatever happy pill she's taken. Do they

prescribe this stuff on the NHS? How does she do it? The women from the group aren't 'my girls'. I've been a member of the group since the beginning, and she's only been part of the town for a couple of years. But then, even *in* the group, we're like chalk and cheese. Apinya embraced everything about the group. She is a kid at Disneyland racing from ride to ride. I need to be prodded with a stick. Even then, I've never opened up about the memories that taunt me, about my real regrets. How could I? Rose enthusiastically thanks me for my contributions; she is an expert at hiding her disappointment. I know what she wants to talk about. *She* knows it isn't going to happen.

Swivelling my neck, I note that attendance is good. Maybe twenty women. Funny that the numbers go up when drinks are involved. No men, of course. Plenty of smiling faces. Rose *will* be happy. Resentment claws at my throat. Where were these smiling faces when the heating broke that bleak overcast afternoon in December? The only three you can rely on - through rain and (literally) snow, are myself, Apinya and, of course, Rose.

"Where's Rose?" I'm suddenly aware she isn't here. Rose usually arrives at these gatherings first, setting up, making sure she welcomes everybody.

"I was going to ask the same thing..."

We both turn around. I take a second look. It's *her*. Sometimes I can waste a day figuring out where I've seen somebody before, only for it to hit me they served me at Sainsbury's or Asda. I know *this* woman. But then, who could forget her? Platinum blonde hair falls to her chest. The blue, faded jeans appear sprayed to her long legs. My eyes taper at her narrow hips and tiny slip of a waist. I stifle memories of myself as a young woman - as a different person - thirty years or so ago.

"I'm Sheena. Between you and me, I'm a bit of an intruder here. This is quite a big thing for me, you know? I've come to a couple of meetings, but slipped away early. Not had the balls to actually say anything yet..."

She even has a gap between the top of her legs. I can't see it, of course, but she'll possesses the kind of pert, upturned arse that causes heads to turn. Wonder if she's been in any of the local pubs Ray goes to yet? I push away the image of a plump eight-year-old girl with ruddy cheeks and dull, lifeless hair - I was *supposed* to be the ugly duckling that turned into a beautiful swan. Well, I did - for a while. I despise myself for scanning this woman's body, searching for imperfections - what has she ever done to me? It's not *her* fault. Washboard tummy. Glowing skin. Smiling, I shake her outstretched hand. Her smooth skin is soft like velvet. I introduce myself, my upper lip quivering. Apinya embraces the woman like she is a long-lost friend from the shitty streets of Bangkok.

"Isn't Rose *amazing?*" Sheena coos. Her sky-blue eyes widen. "Don't know how she does it. Sets a really calm, welcoming vibe, doesn't she? Was going to pluck up the courage to actually speak to her today. But like you said, I can't find her anywhere..."

A tinge of guilt hits me. Why have I never thought of Rose through these rose-tinted eyes? Because I'm reassured that she is older, larger, less attractive than I am? Of course Rose takes on responsibility for the whole group. She rarely gets the support - or the credit - she deserves. Still, I'm taken aback by Sheena's unabashed admiration; it's like she's meeting the pop star whose poster has been on her bedroom wall since childhood.

Apinya shrugs her shoulders. "I know she's missed the last couple of meetings because she wasn't too well. Thought she was better, though. I just assumed she was coming."

I did, too. Took it for granted. I never really worry about Rose; she is always alright, even though - blatantly - she is never *quite* right. Unzipping my handbag, I make sure they're both aware I'm sending Rose a concerned text.

Aprinya breaks the silence. Reaches for a third cup. "Look on the bright side, though. With one less head, it just means more wine for us ladies!"

I'm sure Sheena will make her excuses. She'll say she's a disciple of the Gwyneth Paltrow *Goop!* lifestyle, something like that. I turn away, ready to avoid any embarrassment, but when I turn back, Sheena is holding out her hand, like the poor thing hasn't drunk *anything* for a week. I put my phone back in my handbag.

"So you're from out of town then, Sheena?" Apinya says, winking. "Like me."

"Yes, I'm from London, a proper cockney. Left that life behind me, though. Moved here a couple of-"

"Why *here*?"

Sheena stifles a smile at my question. "Fancied a complete change, somewhere nobody knows me. This fitted the bill perfectly. So picturesque. So idyllic. Nobody is a stranger..."

"But what will you do for work? For money?" I ask, heat rising to my cheeks.

"I'm sure something will pop up," she says, like she's talking about a bus.

I turn to Apinya, smiling. "Bet she has a rich husband hidden away somewhere, paying for everything..."

"Yes, I hid him under the floorboards."

I join in with the laughter. Secretly, I'm impressed by the quick reply. I glance at Apinya. Doesn't she think it was a strange decision to move from London to Pontbach? It's different for me. I've lived here all my life. Why would you want to jump from the big sea, with endless possibilities, into a goldfish bowl, where the same things happen day after day? Why would anybody willingly make that choice?

"I think it's amazing," Apinya says. "So brave."

Sheena smiles warmly.

"You really think the meetings were good?" I ask. "It is just – you know – you didn't stay for long..."

It's been a long, long time since I thought the meetings were good, since I believed in their purpose. Regardless, Sheena appeared and disappeared like a phantom. How can she think they were good? She gazes down at the grass, riddled with nettles and rabbit holes, then looks up at me, holds my eyes, like she's reading my thoughts. She won't like what she reads. "I know, you're right. I feel bad about that. It was disrespectful of me..."

My hand brushes her arm. Did Apinya *really* just give me a disapproving look? "I'm sorry. I didn't mean it like that..."

"It's just tough, isn't it? Being the newbie. I'm not the most confident at the best of times. There were so many women there who'd probably spoken plenty of times. I guess I was kind of overwhelmed. I told myself beforehand that it was best to just jump right in, but *that* didn't happen. Did feel like a dirty voyeur though, just quietly sat in the corner watching all of the action..."

"Pervert."

Apinya doubles at the waist with laughter. Sheena continues talking. "Guess all of us ladies are there for a reason, aren't we?" she holds my look. "We all need help, though it may come in different shapes and sizes. For me, it was enough just to be in the same room as the other women. Strength in numbers, yeah? Doesn't really matter that the group has no real, defined objective, as such..."

Apinya raises her glass. *Strength in numbers*, she says. Three plastic cups push together. Imaginary clink. We both reassure Sheena, say the right things, tell her that - yes - just going to the group is the first step to recovery, what she is doing is fantastic.

People know why I go to the group, or at least they *think* they do. Some of the women's trauma is etched on their faces. Others have physical bruises. They must wonder about Sheena, though. She must appear like the fairy godmother, here to show us how wrong we are, here to show us the right way. My busy eyes flick over her body, searching for an imperfection, for something to justify hating her less. God only knows I have plenty of reason to hate her. My lips curl at the corners. *Finally*. There is a blemish on Sheena's left wrist - barely noticeable - a couple of sore, red scabs. She is human. She bleeds. Probably fell over. Unless - just *maybe* - somebody did it to her. I don't think it would be that rich boyfriend hidden away in London. I loosen my imaginary grip of her neck.

"You've barely been to a few meetings and already you've picked up that we don't have any real objective," I say, smiling. Am I stirring the pot? I *do* feel mischievous. This dreadful wine is going down *very* easily. Apinya tops up my glass every time I take a sip. Feels like a gust of wind could knock me over. Need to be careful. Don't want to end up like my parents.

"Oh, don't get me wrong," Sheena says. "I didn't mean that as a bad thing..."

"But you're right, though. We *don't* have an objective. Why not? I've been going to the group for twelve years now. Sometimes I forget the reason I went in the first place."

Sheena places her hand on my arm. Her face is twisted with concern. "You've probably chosen to forget, Katherine. Deep down, none of us truly forget..."

Apinya chips in. There are two of them now, and one of me. "The group wouldn't be the same without you, Kat."

"Exactly," Sheena says, turning to Apinya, her face wide with glee. I know my face reddens. It has been a while since people paid me compliments. "You've been going twelve years? That's an achievement in itself, don't you think? This group is part of the community. As soon as I moved in, people started telling me about it. No way do all of the women live in the town. Some of those must travel from nearby villages..."

"That's true," I say. "They do."

"Just think how many women you've helped in that time."

My feet wobble on the uneven surface. Wine trickles down my hand. "Impossible to tell. Women come and go. They just disappear. We don't have a tracking system. We don't phone them to check they're alright. And if they did get better, was this because of us, or despite us? Maybe if we *were* more organised, if we did have a clearly defined purpose, then we could help more women...?"

I look around, suddenly aware I've raised my voice. Women have deserted their plates and their cups and turned to me. Could it be that somebody has actually said something slightly controversial? I should feel uneasy. I don't. I *do* exist outside my own little home, regardless of what Ray thinks.

Apinya whispers, "Think we all get mad sometimes, Kat. Not sure this is the time or the place, you know-?"

"I just mean-"

"Like Sheena said, it can't be all that bad now, can it, or you wouldn't have been going all these years, would you?"

"I didn't say it was *bad-*"

"I'm sure you have *plenty* of other things you could be doing instead. And remember, Rose doesn't get paid for the work she does-"

"I know that-"

"She is a volunteer. She gives up her own time. Sometimes I'm sure she'd prefer not to listen to a bunch of middle-aged *white* women droning on about their first world problems-"

"Oh, just call me *Karen-*"

"If anybody thinks they can do a better job, then they should go right ahead and put their names forward, darling..."

"I'm sure there isn't."

I glance away until I'm free of prying eyes. Did Apinya sense my ego inflate and decide to pop it with a needle? Bang. Like a balloon. Apinya is suggesting I put *my* name forward. Rose isn't getting any younger. Her health isn't great. One day she'll need to stand down.

Sure, people will be sad. They'll be a party with sausage rolls and crisps, just like today. And then she'll soon be forgotten, just like my brother. I'm the obvious replacement because I attended the first meeting. Should I be punished for this? We're both painfully aware, despite my sudden bravado and my criticism of Rose, that *clearly* I couldn't do a better job. I'm a backbencher shouting criticism at the person who has dared to stand up and do something. They know I should have kept my mouth shut.

"Maybe Kat has a point, Apinya."

We both turn to Sheena.

"I mean, you're *both* right. The group *is* disorganised, but I wouldn't have come if it was militant. *Far* too scary. And, frankly, I want to *be* Rose. She *does* do an amazing job, and nobody could have done any better. So selfless. Such a trooper. A real inspiration..."

Apinya has one eyebrow raised. We both know it is her turn to have her bubble burst. Sheena has built her up, put her on a pedestal, ready to push her off. Sheena turns to me now. Jesus, she is no longer an ostrich with her head buried in the ground. She is not quite flying in the sky, but she's rising.

"But just listen to Kat's passion. Clearly she's fanatical about this group-"

"Not as much as Rose," I say. Do I look like I'm crawling out from beneath the bus I've just thrown myself under?

"Rose has been running this group for twelve years. That isn't easy. The devotion was bound to wane at some point. She is only human, after all. I mean, she hasn't made it today and she hasn't told anybody, either. Maybe I'm just an outsider looking in, but Kat's words sure hit home. Maybe the group *could* do with some new stimulus. Last thing I'd ever want to do is to step on Rose's toes, but I think maybe you ladies could help her a bit. You've both got great ideas. Truth be told, I think she'd be *grateful*..."

Apinya eyes me. We've *both* been cornered. We wait for the other to say something. I'm an expert at this, waiting for somebody else to speak so I don't have to. Apinya breaks first. "I can help a bit more if it takes some pressure off Rose."

Two pairs of eyes zone in on me now. "Me too, of course. If you think it will help."

Sheena holds out her arms and the three of us hug. Maybe the wine is talking, or maybe it's because I'm wanted, but I feel kind of exhilarated.

We pull apart. The lines from Sheena's face disappear. "I have the feeling this could be the start of something *amazing*," she says.

Thursday 27th September 2018

Bernard

I can't deny it; part of me got a perverse kick out of Apinya looking like the sad dog for a change.

This life wasn't intended. In my daydreams, during my more and more frequent idling moments, I pictured bumping into my English Rose in the library or at the coffee shop. The more I lingered at these establishments, however, my certainty that this would never happen grew. Whoever would have thought that women these days don't fall over themselves for tired, middle-aged, paunchy men? My bodywork was none too great and it wasn't clear how many miles I had left on the clock, either. The younger models looked much more appealing.

And so I turned to online dating. My inbox bubbled over with messages from beautiful women. I couldn't believe my good fortune. This was all too good to be true. And it was. Who would have thought that robots were so advanced? Who would have imagined so many damsels in distress needed a SIM card to phone their dying mother? Admittedly, not all of the women were fake. Some were genuinely horrendous, taking the opportunity to belittle the way I looked, my age, the fact I was born a man.

And so, my mouse stirred, and I flicked to different,

alternative websites.

Looking back, the website seduced me. Suddenly, the clock turned back a century. Thai women, apparently, prided themselves on keeping an immaculate home, on looking after their husbands, on staying beautiful. This wasn't right, I thought, typing in my details. This was degrading, I considered, handing over my credit card details. This wasn't real, I contemplated, as I said hello to a lithe, delightful young lady. And yet, I mused, this distorted reality appealed infinitely more than anything else on offer.

The villagers think I'm naive, that I'm a victim; I knew exactly what I was doing.

I've never been *that* husband. I don't ask Apinya to keep an immaculate home. I don't ask her to look after me. I don't ask her to do *anything*. And I don't love her because of her undeniable beauty. I love her because she stops me from being alone.

And so, whilst I don't set a curfew - I don't *own* my wife, for God's sake - I just assumed she'd be home on Saturday evening before dinner, definitely before six or seven o'clock. After all, the ladies were only meeting for an afternoon drink down the river. She said it was a picnic. I returned from my hike, with my thighs crying out for forgiveness, hours earlier. How many afternoon drinks could they possibly consume? Admittedly, it took me a while to notice she wasn't home. By about eight I started to fret. Maybe she'd fallen in the river? Perhaps she lay in a ditch somewhere? I left it until about nine; I didn't want to be an overbearing husband. It passed my mind - was Kat home? What was Ray doing? I messaged Apinya, asked if she was okay, if she was safe. No reply. I messaged her every hour until just gone eleven. My ears twitched when the key scraped down the front door. She missed steps as she scrambled up the stairs. The wooden banister creaked as, presumably, she clung onto it for dear life. No hello to me, sat in the living room? Whilst that irked, I presumed she was intoxicated and, ultimately, I was just relieved she was home, that she was safe.

Next morning I cooked a fry-up. Was this sadistic? I don't know. Honestly? I couldn't stop myself. Wandering into the kitchen in her dressing gown, eyes half-shut, I swear to God she turned a shade of green when she smelt what I was cooking.

"Good night?"

"Ummm."

Four days have passed; we're strangers living in the same house. I'm perplexed why. I never mentioned the night out and, frankly, I don't disapprove. Am I jealous she's out having fun? For sure. I only managed an hour or so down the pub the other week and even then, I was a zebra mingling with the horses. My wife, however, needs friends. She needs a life away from me. We both do. Something has changed, though. Who was she out with? Has somebody said something about me? My dear wife is going through the motions with me, saying what is expected; her heart and mind, however, is elsewhere. I've always wondered, underneath the superficial layers, if she hates me. That feeling has only intensified.

I don't even know where she is now. She wasn't lying in bed next to me when I woke. Maybe she went for a run? It's still only mid-morning. What is the accepted protocol with these things? When is a loving husband expected to get concerned?

Sat in the dining room, looking out at the garden, the

doorbell makes me jump. I glance at the mahogany clock. 11:20. The postman has already been (no mail). Maybe it is a delivery company? Maybe it is a sales call? Loneliness has torn my heart from my chest, but still, the thought of any human contact right now makes me nervous.

Opening the front door, I'm conscious that I take a second glance. How rude must that look?

"Rose," I say. "What - I mean, how are you? Do come in..."

Frankly, she looks no better than I probably do, which calms my nerves somewhat. Apinya's youth and looks have always unsettled me, made me feel inferior. Inside the house, she perches on the edge of the sofa, eyes rotating around the room like a four-year-old girl on her first day of school. She's lost weight. Considering that she's always been what I'd politely call rotund, I'd expect this to be a positive development. However, the skin hanging from her chin makes her look like a Basset hound. The darkness under her eyes is as pronounced as birthmarks. She truly doesn't look well at all.

"You *do* look well, Rose," I say.

She growls like a revving motorbike. She always did have a way of telling me I was talking nonsense. I smile.

"Cup of coffee? Still milk and two sugars?"

She nods. "Some things never change, Bernard."

Her eyes fix on the family portrait on the wall. Returning with two cups of steaming coffee, I'm aware that Rose has barely uttered a word. I don't *mind,* it just befuddles me. Surely it is standard convention to explain why - after all this time - you've turned up out of the blue? Sitting down next to my guest, I cross one leg over the other in the way Apinya tells me is *not* very

masculine (but then Apinya is not here, is she?).
Luckily, Rose doesn't give two hoots how I look.

"I haven't been attending the group, Bernard."

"*What?* Since when?"

"Hasn't she told you?"

I shake my head. She doesn't look surprised.

"But you *made* that group. You *are* that group. You
talked about it all the time. Quite incessantly, to be
honest, over and over-"

"I get the point-"

"But what happened?"

"Who knows? I'm not sure myself. They're probably
already trying to dethrone me, like witches around a
cauldron, not realising I don't even *want* to come
back..."

We sit in silence. I don't want to pressurise her.
Thoughts well in my head, though, and I'm desperate to
turn them into words. Who are these witches? Is
Apinya one of them? And, more significantly, just how
must Rose feel now the most important aspect of her
life has been removed?

"You still make the best cup of coffee ever, Bernard,"
Rose says.

This is a deflection technique. Like I said, I'm not
naive. Still, I fall for it hook, line and sinker. My ego
inflates. Often it was just the two of us in the office,
and I took pride in making her coffee. It was my way of
showing I appreciated her. Officially, she only worked
in an admin role, but she put her heart and soul into
that job. My biggest consideration when deciding
whether to sell the business was the effect it would have
on Rose. I'll never shake off my guilt. It was the right
decision for me but - undoubtedly - the wrong decision

for her.

"So tell me what's happened. I don't understand."

Rose puts her cup down on the side table. Seconds pass. She isn't going to answer me, is she? She is going to finish her coffee and then leave me like she never came here at all.

"Have you noticed a change in Apinya, Bernard?"

"Apinya? No, I don't think so. She is still as delightful as ever. Still the life of the party..."

"Bernard..."

She knows me better than anyone, even though we haven't spoken for months and months.

"She's been a bit distant recently. Something is on her mind but she isn't telling me. And she went out on Saturday and didn't come back until late. And she was *really* drunk. But that is kind of charming in a way..."

Rose shakes her head. *She* doesn't think it is charming. "The group social. Of course. I bet *she* had something to do with that..."

"*She...?*"

"Bernard, have you heard of a woman called Sheena?"

Sheena? Oh, of course.

"I've never met her, but I confess she intrigues me. I popped to the pub the other week for a pint - like us guys do - and the chaps talked about her. Sounds like she's made quite an impression."

"Chaps?"

"Yes. You know. *Men...*"

"I know what *chaps* are. Which ones?"

"The usual suspects. Geraint and Dave. Oh, and Ray."

Rose's dull eyes light. "Katherine's husband. Interesting."

"What is this all about?"

Rose holds my gaze. "I think it is all to do with her, Bernard. The change in Apinya? Because of Sheena. The reason I'm not going to the group? Because of Sheena. And God knows what she's doing with the men in the pub..."

Rose flinches at my laugh. I didn't mean it to be cruel. But this is madness. "Are you sure this isn't paranoia, Rose? We spoke about this before..."

"*You* decided I was being paranoid..."

"Yes. Quite. But the men in the pub had never even spoken to her. She caught their attention because she is - apparently - an attractive young lady. She was just in the pub for a drink. I'm not even sure Apinya *has* changed, or if she has, that it's not a positive change."

Rose's forehead crinkles. She knows I have a point. Sometimes she believes what she wants to believe, like a conspiracy theorist adamant the world is flat, despite all the evidence to the contrary.

"Can you just keep a cautious eye on Apinya, Bernard?"

"She is my wife. It is my duty to do that regardless."

Rose finishes her coffee. "Are you *alright*, Bernard?"

Oh wow. Things have got *really* bad. She turns up unannounced at my beautiful house looking like a corpse, talking nonsensically, and she is worried about *me*. I'm surrounded by the latest gadgets, living a life of luxury, and yet she sees straight through all of this.

"We should have kept in contact more, shouldn't we?" I ask.

"Yes. We should have."

"We make a right pair, don't we?"

Her smile turns into a laugh. "Yes, we do."

"So what are you going to do about this Sheena

woman?"

I'm taken aback by the coldness of her hand, by the tightness of her grip. "She knows things I haven't told anybody. Only *you*..."

She takes in my shocked expression. I nod. "So I'll ask again. What are you going to do about this Sheena?"

"I need to be braver than I've ever been, Bernard. The first thing I'm going to do is to go back. I want to speak to him. See what he knows."

I keep my face straight. Try to hide my horror. "Okay," I say. "Promise me a few things?"

"Yes."

"You'll come round for coffee more regularly? You'll keep me informed? And you'll ask me for help if you need it?"

Rose rises to her feet. "I promise, Bernard," she says.

Sheena

Opening the door, she is just as I expected her.

Her unlined face suggests that she is probably in her early thirties and yet, oh dear, that beehive hairstyle and drab, lifeless navy cardigan belongs on a lady ten years older. I could quite easily imagine her in a black and white photograph on the mantelpiece. Thick lenses magnify the hazel, unblinking eyes. Papers threaten to drop from the folder balanced precariously in her left arm. Holding up her faded identification badge (oh, she *has* put on some weight) in her right hand, the flushed cheeks and the glistening sweat on her forehead tell me she is frazzled and overworked. Absolutely perfect, darling.

"My name is Melanie Taylor. I hope you were expecting me today, Sheena?"

My smile is warm enough to thaw her worst expectations. The poor woman must come into contact with all sorts of horrific people in her line of work. It comes with the territory, so it's difficult to feel sorry for her. God knows what she expected of me. I'm sure my pencilled name has stared at her from her diary for weeks. She has read about me, discussed me with senior colleagues. Of course, they told her to tread with caution. Isn't the world today so frightfully cautious? Maybe she thought I'd open the door with an axe in my hand, or a detached head under my arm?

My open hand invites her into my home. "Of course," I say. "I've had your visit in my calendar since the letter arrived. Been quite nervous about it, if truth be told."

She pokes her head around like a mole appearing from a hole before unloading on the sofa in the kitchen diner. Does she just have one of those faces, or is she looking for signs that something just isn't quite right? She stops looking around pretty quickly, though. There is nothing strange to find here. My house is meticulously clean and tidy - very minimalistic. It is the perfect example of how a normal, sane person should live. Of course, there is nothing accidental about that.

"Cup of tea, Melanie? Maybe something stronger?"

Melanie slaps the flat of both hands down against her thighs and releases a horsey laugh. Does relief drain from her body? Not only am I normal, but I'm *fantastic*.

"Wish I could have something stronger," she says. "Really, after the day I've had so far! But it's more than my job's worth. I'd love a cup of tea, though. Milk one sugar. And thank you."

The kettle boils and I open and close cupboards. From the kitchen, I comment that it can't be easy doing her job. Must come into contact with all sorts. I make it clear that I'm not one of them.

"Oh it *does* have its moments, as you can imagine. But it can be wonderfully rewarding when you help somebody."

Killers. Rapists. Paedophiles. And not forgetting their victims, of course. "I bet," I say, passing her the cup of tea and sitting down opposite her, close enough to touch her leg. I don't drink tea. It yellows your teeth. I join her now, though. Nobody likes to drink alone, do they? Taking a long slurp (and seemingly savouring it like a tug of a cigarette), Melanie tells me it hits the spot. She blows out air. The niceties are over. It is time to get down to business.

"So, how are you settling in to the town, Sheena?"

My face is overly enthusiastic. "Good. *Really* good. Much better than I ever expected."

Melanie scribbles on her notepad in cumbersome, messy handwriting. "That's fantastic news," she says. "Just what I was hoping to hear."

"It's not been easy, of course," I say.

Her face distorts with sympathy. I must be doing good if *she* feels sorry for *me*. "Of course not," she says. "Breaking away and making a fresh start never is. Especially in these circumstances. But I do admire your bravery in doing so, Sheena. I wholeheartedly think it was the right thing to do. You needed to get away."

"Become innocuous?"

"Maybe." Her eyes narrow. She isn't sure about my choice of words. "So how are you getting on in the town? I imagine this is a massive culture shock from London. Have you made any friends yet?"

Suddenly, I'm five-years-old and my mum is asking how I got on at school. I look to the ground. My mum is dead now. When I told her I'd made plenty of friends after that first day, she told me not to lie. Sent me to my room. I wasn't lying then, but I will lie now. I tell so many lies that sometimes I forget what is true.

"I've joined a group," I say. "Nothing fancy. Just a group of women who meet up every Saturday morning and share our problems. We went out the other Saturday, nothing major, just a few drinks down by the river. I'm cautiously getting closer to a few of the women. I hope you understand that I need to make sure I can trust people. It is difficult for me to share things with them until I know they're on my side. There are two sides to every story. I can't be judged."

My fingers twist the hem of my skirt. The fabric rolls a few inches higher. My sun-kissed thighs are smooth to the touch. *Result.* Just as I suspected, Melanie's eyes widen. They look high inside my skirt.

"Absolutely," she says, blinking and pushing around papers. "Of course I understand. You've had a huge shock to the system, Sheena. You need security. You need to surround yourself with people you can trust. This group sounds like a fantastic step. Well done."

I expand my smile to show her I appreciate her endorsement.

"So do any men attend this group?" she asks.

My pinched expression tells her that no, men do not attend the group.

"And...have you met any men in the town?"

She shifts her weight forward. She wants me to feel comfortable telling her everything. What she wants me to tell her is that I've left him behind, that I'm no longer in touch, that I've moved on. After all, if I were an alcoholic then she'd want to ensure I wasn't drinking. In her mind, *he* is my poison.

"I've been trying not to," I tell her.

"Oh."

"Don't think I need them in my life right now."

"Oh, I *get* that."

"Don't you think they're the cause of all trouble and disruption?"

"All trouble and disruption? Oh, you mean in your life? I guess you could say that with your individual situation. Yes..."

"No. I mean the cause of *all* trouble and disruption. Its best I stay away. Don't you think?"

Her heads arches to one side, like she is trying to read between the lines. "I guess that might be advisable in your circumstances."

I don't persist. I can tell she wants to deflect what I'm saying. I take her cup and head to the kitchen, pushing out my arse as I walk. When I return, I can tell that she 's been hit by a thought, one that needs scratching. The softness of my face tells her to go ahead, that she needn't worry. She can ask me anything. I won't be offended.

"I was just wondering," she says. "Do you think anybody in Pontbach knows who you are?"

I don't miss a heartbeat. "No," I reply. "Nobody knows who I am. I plan to keep it that way."

She continues writing, then closes her folder with a bang. She runs through some formalities, says it is great that I am doing well, tells me to look out for another appointment in the post.

I escort Melanie to the front door. "Come around again any time you want," I say. "Even if it is just for a chat. Or *something*."

As my eyes flicker down to her heavy bosom, my guest desperately scrambles inside her handbag for her car key.

I close the front door. Jesus, I think. This is going to be even easier than I imagined.

Tuesday 9th October 2018

Katherine

Sometimes I wonder about my epitaph, what the priest will say about me to the congregation at my funeral, what I'll be remembered for.

She was content with her life.

This is definitely the impression I give. Why wouldn't I be? I have a loving husband, a beautiful home, a son that has graduated and progressed his career in London. I don't have money worries or work demands. The cakes I bake are the talk of the town. I have my friends from the group. When I want to relax, I embroider and piece together jigsaws. You could say (with some right) that I'm a privileged, pampered, middle-class suburban housewife.

And yet today (and many other days) the black clouds have fallen from the sky and engulfed my entire body. I'm too tired to sleep. I'm too tired to stay awake. I don't want to be here, but I don't want to be anywhere else, either. I feel trapped, but I have nowhere I want to escape to.

Ray left for work early this morning, like he did yesterday and the day before. Ray is lucky. He is straightforward. He does not over-think. He does not contemplate the pointlessness of it all; he never sees himself as a hamster going round and round just to stay still. With my wet cheek sunk into the pillow, my half-opened eyes watched him pulling on the same grubby jeans as yesterday, watched him sniff his faded white tee-shirt to check it didn't smell too bad to pass for another day. The thought of pulling my own feet out of bed saddened me. The thought of staying in bed all day terrified me.

And so, a few hours later, and with the rest of the day lying ahead, the spitting rain sticks to the living room window. The room is dark even with the curtains drawn and the lights on. All I can hear is the humming of the fridge, the tick-tick-tick of the clock on the wall and my racing, rebounding thoughts. I experience every passing second of my life. I can almost see it, like an upturned egg timer; my life - what is left of it - disappearing before my eyes.

Why did I *choose* this life? Why did I let him choose this life for me?

Picking up the remote control, I point it at the 60-inch plasma TV screen. Daytime TV? I throw the control onto the carpeted floor, like a hot coal threatening to scold my hand. I don't want silence, but I don't want noise. I wipe the underside of my eye, reminding me of Rose leading a meeting. Not only have I sucked out my tears, but my emotions, too. What about a quick lie down, to gather my thoughts? It is never quick though, is it? I imagine springing from my bed, revitalised and recharged, a squirrel with its tail upturned. Sheena would be like that. That never happens though, does it? I always wake like a cardboard box left out in the rain. Glancing at the clock that just never stops fucking ticking, I calculate the hours and minutes until Ray returns home. Jesus. That is just too many minutes, too many hours.

I shoot up from the sofa. My coat moves from my hand to my back. The front door opens and then shuts. My trainer sinks into a puddle, saturating my sock. The drizzle wets my cheeks and leaves a ball of moisture on the tip of my nose. I blow it away. Glancing over my shoulder, I squint before swinging open the car door. *That's* a bit odd.

The windscreen wiper squeaks. The heater doesn't clear the mist, but it does aggravate my sensitive skin. Green and yellow fields surround me on both sides. I've no idea where I'm heading, but that's the point. Wherever I'm heading, it isn't here.

I glance in the mirror. That white van is still there, joining me down the winding, twisting roads. My neck juts forward, my eyes try to see through the haze. I'm compelled to peek back in the mirror. What is it I fear? The van has edged closer, despite the rain, despite the slippery road. A man is behind the wheel - of course - and the eyes are set too close together, the forehead hangs over the brows. Of course, I know serial killers don't always look like you'd expect them to. Turning the heater off and blowing out my own hot air, I dab at the windscreen with my sleeve. Ray is not here to tell me off, to inform me that it does more harm than good. I go to change gear, but my wet foot slips from the clutch to the brake. The car slows, nearly halts to a stop. I put the car in first. Slamming my foot on the accelerator, the engine revs, sounds like a hair dryer, like it is about to blow.

I don't need to look in my mirror to know the van is right up against me, virtually kissing my bumper. He is deliberately trying to intimidate me, to suffocate me. I slam my foot on the brake. This time, the car halts to a stop. One. Two. Three. Strength seeps through my body. In my own time, I push the gearstick into first, press my foot against the accelerator.

Blowing air from my plumped cheeks, it feels like I'm blowing away the tedium and monotony of everyday life. Fuck *you*. Fuck *men*. I'm bigger and stronger than any of you.

My bravado shrinks the closer I get to the junction. An overgrown hedge lies in front of me. Where am I? How do I get home? Is this *really* liberating? What if I get lost? What if Ray's tea is late? Glancing in the mirror, at least the white van has gone.

I try to ignore the dark shadow engulfing me from the right. Pretend it isn't there, like a red bill on the doorstep. It doesn't go away, of course. It merely grows bigger, more engulfing.

The white van stops. It takes up the whole other side of the road. The driver peers down at me with swollen cheeks and hair in tufts. Thankfully, there is no trace of anger, just a glimmer of a smile. He lowers his window. His pointing finger indicates for me to do the same. The breeze is refreshing. He looks like he wants to say something. Maybe apologise for getting too close? Perhaps ask if I am okay, if I need anything?

I watch in slow motion as the man pulls back his head and sucks in air through his teeth. I know what is coming. I watch it unfolding.

The dirty green phlegm covers my face.

Through my sleeve, I hear his laugh, hear the engine of his van. I'm glued to my seat, my body numb. And then, I almost visualise the red mist forming before my eyes. Gripping the gear stick, I thrust the car into gear and slam my foot down on the accelerator.

The car stalls.

Turning the key in the ignition, I start again. The car moves away, in the direction of the van. My breathing is thick and heavy and full of moisture. The window steams up. I cross the white line as I turn a corner, no idea what is round the other side. I glance down at the pedometer. 60.70.80. The roads are narrow and curving. There he is. The white of the van appears in the distance. 90.100. The rear of the van grows bigger, wider. I get close enough to take in the dust, the grime, the moisture on the treads. The metal ladder on the roof rattles, looks like it may fling off as the van goes over bumps and divots in the road. I dig my teeth into my upper lip. Wiping with my forearm, I sneer at the trail of blood.

My eyes widen as I spot something on the back of the van.

A telephone number.

"You *fucking* idiot."

Thrusting my hand inside the glove box, I dig and paw like I'm searching for a pound coin down the slim crack of the sofa to slot into the electricity meter. I pull out my phone. Glance down at the screen. Tap with my finger. My leg appears in the screen, then the steering wheel, all out of focus. Looking up, through the tiny gap of clear windscreen, I'm on the other side of the road, heading for the hedge. Slamming my foot on the brake, I tear at the steering wheel. Road. Hedge. Road. The car spins, then stops. Facing the other way.

My first thought: thank fuck I'm alive. My second thought: turn the fucking car around.

What would the old me do?

I pick up speed at the same rate my hope of finding the van fades. It is nowhere to be seen. I try to remember the telephone number, then realise I didn't know it in the first place. I'm just putting random numbers together in any old order. I slam my fist down against the steering wheel. The horn blasts.

And then, just as the car begins to slow, as I start taking control of my breathing, the white flashes in my eye line, a boat bobbing on choppy waters.

"Got you."

Exhaling sharply, I realise I'm gaining ground, even though I haven't sped up. The van has slowed down. Reality hits me. I'm a mouse chasing a cat. What am I going to do if I catch him? Momentarily, I long him to speed up, to give me a way out, an excuse for not catching him.

The beautiful green and yellow fields are replaced by the shadow of houses. I can't do anything here. I'll be seen. I'll be caught. There could be witnesses. Cameras. Ray will tell you - in the old days you could get away with things. The flashing indicator is like a bulb in my brain. The van turns left. I slow down, keep at a safe distance. The van stops. The man gets out. Slams the door behind him. Kicks out his long legs.

He has no idea I'm here. Stupid, knucklehead men.

His narrow, sliding shoulders contrast with his belly which is inflated like a balloon. Shoes drag against tarmac. He enters a house. *His* house. Through the safety of my car window, I watch the man plant a kiss on the cheek of a portly woman. *His* woman, no doubt. His poor, insufferable wife. He disappears out of sight, into another room. And then, he returns. He sits on the sofa with his feet up, at peace with the world, with no regrets.

I'm in control from here. I can see him, but he can't

see me. I'm a sniper, taking my time, zoning in on my target. My finger taps away at my phone. Right now, this phone feels much deadlier than a gun. It starts ringing. I watch as the man digs inside his jeans, as he puts his hand to his ear.

"Hello?"

My breathing is heavy. I say no words.

"Who is this?" he asks. "Is anybody there?"

"Yes. Somebody is here."

"Who is this?"

"This is the woman who you just spat on."

The man rotates his head, looks around the room. I laugh. Make sure it is loud and clear through the receiver.

"Where are you?" he asks.

"What if I told your wife what you did to me?"

There is a pause. He sucks in air. "My wife isn't here."

"Fair enough. If your wife isn't there then maybe I should just wait here until your wife comes home, then I can tell her you've just kissed another woman in your own home. How does that sound?"

The man is on his feet now, of course. Looking through the window, he reminds me of a gorilla in a cage. Spotting me in my car, I wave, all nice and friendly. His face turns a darker shade of red.

"Listen, darling," the man says, "I don't know who you think you are, but you sure don't know who you're messing with-"

"You look really scary, with that little fat belly-"

"Do you want me to go and get my wife? This really isn't much of a threat, sweetheart. She knows what I'm like on the road, that I sometimes lose my temper. It's just a man thing, you know? She's seen me do that before. What she'll be more concerned with is some psycho woman following me. It's not me you need to be scared of, it's her. She'll come after you, not me..."

I pause, let the man's bravado subside, let him dwell in his cesspit. "So you *do* have a wife? I just want to check with you. What is it you think I'm going to tell her?"

The man glances over his shoulder. Looks back. "That I spat on you."

I laugh. Long and hard. "But that's child's play. Like you said, she already knows her husband is a dirty, filthy little bastard. What would be the point in telling her that?"

"But that's what I did. What else would you tell her?"

I push open the door and step out of the car. Start walking down the drive, my heels clicking. He is jumping up and down in his living room now, suddenly *very* concerned.

"What you going to tell her...?"

"I'm going to tell her that you got out of your van and you abused me. That you touched me up. Tell her that you really *are* a dirty, filthy bastard."

"Why would you say that?"

"Because I fucking despise you, and men like you, that's why."

I can no longer see the man. He is out of range because I am too close.

"I'm stood right outside your house. Ready to press your doorbell."

"No. Please. What is it you want?"

Pause. Good question. My hand hovers over the doorbell.

"I want you to tell me you are sorry."

"What? What else?"

"Nothing else. Just tell me you are sorry. That you did it because you have a tiny dick, that picking on women smaller and weaker than you makes you feel bigger and stronger."

"I'm sorry. Honestly, I'm sorry..."

"And?"

"I really do have a small dick, too. Tiny."

I press a button and the phone goes dead. The walk back down the drive feels longer than the walk up. I hold my head up, oblivious to the dreary drizzle.

I'm hit by a thought, one which thwarts my bluster somewhat.

This is exactly what Sheena would have done, isn't it?

Monday 22nd October 2018

Rose

Am I deliberately walking into a burning fire? Every inch of my brain and every ounce of my heart tells me to stop - to turn around - to walk back in the direction I came from and don't look back.

Naturally, I keep walking towards the burning fire.

Pontbach train station has but one platform; even that seems surplus to requirements. I imagine the station is fairly busy early in the morning, with villagers commuting via Cardiff Central to Newport, Bristol and Swansea, to cities actually offering employment. It is now mid-morning and I could lie down in the middle of the track and the first person to see me would be the driver of the train veering towards me. The wooden bench lies damp and uninviting. With my head bowed, my eyes scan the cracks in the concrete, soggy chewing gum and traces of spit. I walk up and down the platform. Up and down, up and down.

From the way Bernard spoke, it sounded like the ladies had a wild social at the river. Katherine did text me, asking how I was, enquiring where I was. I told her I had an upset tummy, apologised that I hadn't got in touch, that I'd been too busy running to and from the toilet. She was hardly going to ask any more questions now, was she? I didn't tell her the truth, that I could barely function, that I didn't have the desire to even bathe myself. She sent me another message the next morning asking if I was feeling any better, no doubt suffering with a hangover. I didn't need to lie the next day. I *was* feeling better. Truth be told, I sprung from bed that Sunday morning with more motivation than I ever have living in this town.

Katherine has always been good to me. I need to warn her of the threat. I just need to work out how.

I'm joined by a few other lost souls on the train, with hair sticking up at the side and blurry eyes staring at the passing countryside. The carriage rattles and shakes, stops and starts, seems in no hurry to get there. I'm not hygiene obsessive, but even I wonder who last sat in this seat, what they had on their trousers. Every time I board a train, I'm always reminded of Ringo Starr narrating *Thomas the Tank Engine.* Just how did a Beatle end up with that gig? Stepping off the train and onto the platform at the other end, I look around. Are there any old faces here from back in the day? If there were then they'd certainly be old. Don't be silly, Rose. Who am I kidding? That day was so *many* days ago. I've long been forgotten. Sure, the locals may still gossip about my family, but they won't recognise me; we are confined to folklore.

There is only one person in this town who really knows me.

The street sloping downwards from the train station is so much steeper than I remember. My thick thighs rub together; I can almost imagine blue veins popping out of my calves. Wiping a film of cold sweat from my forehead, I'm almost tempted to stop at the pub at the bottom of the hill, even if it is just for a coffee (or what about a nifty whisky?). I keep walking though, across the road. I have a purpose, for a change. I'm here for a reason. If I stop, the nerves will just keep growing. I may look like a sweet little old lady, but I'm a sweet little old lady who could easily spend the whole day in the pub drinking, hiding away from her fears.

It isn't a long walk. I just need to head out of town, across the bridge, towards the park. The memories are everywhere, though. I keep my head focussed forwards. I daren't look around. Nearly every street has a story, indirectly linked to me.

I stop outside the house. The square patch of lawn is only about ten feet by ten feet. It would only take a minute or two to mow. And yet my knees graze against the spiky tips of the grass. The grey paving slabs are stained at least three shades darker than their original colour. My body slants with each step, threatening to topple over. There is no doorbell, and no brass knocker. The blood has flowed to my head. I long to shovel some sugar cubes into my mouth, like a horse. Taking a deep breath, I knock the door.

Nothing.

I grab for the excuse. At least I tried, I think. What else can I do? But then I spot the outline of a hunched figure through the stained glass. Damn. Too late now. He'll see me, even if I *try* to run. The door opens.

The way he shields his red-rimmed eyes from the sun it's like he's been living in a cave. Black and grey hairs sprout from the top of his faded vest. It looks like he has dipped his hair in a frying pan. His eyes widen; his mouth opens.

"Rose?"

I think it is fair to say my husband is shocked to see me.

******

I follow him down the hallway, his tattooed arms hanging low like a gorilla. Maybe I *am* becoming a hygiene freak? Either way, I narrow my body, make sure my fingers don't touch the greasy walls.

"Take a seat," he says, before heading to the kitchen.

I wait until he shuts the kitchen door before I step over the newspapers scattered on the floor to open the window. Even the window seems to sigh with relief as a cold, sharp gust of wind enters the room. Sweeping aside some empty cans of Coke and Stella, I plonk myself down on the sofa. Warm fluid trickles down the cushion. Dear Lord, please let that be drink from one of the cans. Realistically, that is the least of my worries.

"Ta," I say, as he hands me a steaming cup of coffee. Milk and two sugars. He remembered. Just like Bernard.

Pressing the red button, the daytime TV disappears. Moments pass without either of us saying anything. Depressingly, it feels just like the old days.

"So, is this a social visit, Rose?"

My face breaks into a smile. He quickly follows. To a lesser degree, Bernard had the same thought. I know what it looks like. After years and years of *nothing,* I return to the house we lived in together, as husband and wife, and silently drink his coffee. I'm not one to swear - I'm a sweet little old lady, after all - but I'm aware my husband wants to know what the fuck is going on.

"I've just been thinking, that's all," I say. "I've had a lot on my mind."

"Such as?"

"I want to talk about her."

"Her?"

I cast him a look. *Don't you fucking dare.* He flinches.

"Our little girl. Our darling Marie," I say.

His head slants down. The thick tufts of hair bring focus to his bald crown, reminds me of a monk.

"But why now? Why after all these years? I don't get it..."

"Someone brought it all back the other week..."

"I don't buy that," he spits. "I know you. You think of her every day. We both do. Why do you want to talk about her *now*?"

"Don't I have the right to talk about my little girl anytime I choose, Mick? Forget why I choose now. I want to talk about her, that's all you need to know. I want to talk to you about her..."

He holds up his hands. "Okay, okay. Keep your hair on, woman."

"You always were a charmer," I say.

He shrugs his shoulders. They used to be so much wider.

"Has anyone visited you recently?" I ask. "A young, slim blonde woman, very attractive..."

"I fucking wish."

I ignore that. We're only married in name. We never bothered to get divorced.

"Does the name Sheena mean anything to you?"

"No."

"Anything seem strange recently?"

"Apart from you sat over there drinking coffee with me, then life has delivered the same old shit, day after day."

"Sure?"

"What *is* this?"

Inhaling deeply, I blow out the air I just sucked in.

Clearly, he knows nothing. My husband is an experienced liar, but he isn't an actor. This line of enquiry isn't worth pursuing. There are other things I want to say to him though, things that have simmered for years and only just risen to the surface; because of *her.*

"Marie should have been home with us," I say. "She should have been home with Mum and Dad. We should have been a family. She should never have moved out. She was too young to live on her own. She couldn't look after herself. Not really."

"That was her choice. We didn't throw her out. There was always a bed in our house waiting for her..."

"She was still a kid. What kind of parents were we...?"

"They were different times, Rose. She was over eighteen. What's to stay she wouldn't have gone out that night even if she was still living with us?"

"I don't know that she *would* have."

Mick shuffles forward in his chair. His hands are icy cold, like the blood stops at his wrists. "I know you, Rose. You've always looked for reasons to blame yourself. It is natural for a mother to do that, it is her instinct, but it doesn't make it right..."

I pull my hands away. "I don't blame me," I say. "I blame *you*. You killed her!*"*

Mick folds his arms across his chest. "Charming. Fantastic. So tell me Rose, *why* do you blame me?"

His back straightens. *I really want to hear this.* "You treated her like shit. What sort of a man calls his own daughter fat? You belittled her. She wouldn't have moved out if it wasn't for you."

"Here we go again. It doesn't really matter that she moved out, does it?"

I shake my head. His watery eyes brighten. "Maybe

not. I'll give you that. You want to know the real reason I blame you, Mick...?"

His upper lip quivers. He says nothing. "You made her feel so worthless that she would have gone with any man. And she did. She went with a killer."

His whole body trembles now. His white fists ball. I can't help myself. "You killed her, Mick..."

Standing over me with his feet apart and legs bent at the knee, he is suddenly my tall, strong husband from thirty years ago. Spit bubbles from his mouth. I pull my arms to my face as he lunges forward. My teeth gnaw as his knuckles crack. I long to drown out the screaming. I dare to peek through a gap in my arms.

"What did you do that for?"

Plaster crumbles from the dent in the wall. My husband holds his fist in his hand. His outstretched arms reach for my neck. He has aged, and grown weaker, but so have I. I am still no match for Mick. He could squeeze my windpipe and suck the life from my body. His bony fingers dig into the nape of my neck. He pulls me towards him.

My husband never embraced me so tightly in all our years of marriage. His shaking body is like a train passing through a station. His face dampens my cheek. Guilt cloaks my body like a dark shadow. What sort of a woman am I to make somebody feel this bad? His blubbering mouth pushes against my ear.

"Don't you think I have the same thought every day of my life?" he asks.

"I'm sorry," I say.

He pulls away. His hands cup my cheeks. "*You're* sorry? I'm so, so sorry," he says.

As my husband sobs, in my arms, my fingers graze

the cool sharpness of the blade in my pocket.

Sheena

So many days have passed since he last saw me, I feared that maybe the spark had disappeared, that maybe - just *maybe* - he no longer loved me.

It wouldn't be the first time he'd broken my heart, of course.

I had his name, and I had his (basic) credentials, but that was it. If you were so inclined, you could call it a blind date. I didn't even know what he looked like. Waiting for him, my tangled fingers whitening, I questioned what the fuck I was doing. Did it even make sense? Negative thoughts had welled in my mind, had grown and blossomed, and I just hoped if I met a stranger then I could maybe tell them about it without them judging me. And so what if they did judge me? I'd never see them again.

"Shall I see you again?" he asked, that first time we met.

The lure was too strong. I was helpless to resist.

"Yes," I said. Thinking back, I spoke too quickly, too urgently. He would say I wasn't in control of my emotions. "Are you available next week?" I asked.

We met the following week, and then the week after. Instantly, the rest of my life paled into insignificance. Before long, he totally consumed me.

"I think I'm addicted," I said. "It is totally out of control. On the one hand it shames me, on the other

I've never felt such excitement."

He didn't flinch. As a rule, his face remained placid. "A degree of shame can be positive," he said. "Sometimes it means you are challenging your underlying beliefs. And life is generally monotonous and predictable, Sheena. Excitement is like water to a flower. Emotionally, humans need excitement, otherwise they wither and die..."

"Oh God yes."

"So what is your addiction?" he asked.

"*You*," I said.

He only needs to look at me now, from across the other side of the table, and I know nothing has changed. I have been a fool to doubt him.

"I've missed you so much," I say.

His eyes penetrate my soul and undress me down to my panties, both at the same time. My leg crosses over the other. "I miss you with every fibre of my being," he says. His teeth are still so white, still so straight, even though he is no longer young. Time has been kind to him. "My biggest struggle is learning to live life without you. For now."

I look away. I can't face that reality. Not yet.

"Is the town as beautiful as I described it?"

Black and white stubble coats his normally clean-shaven chin, giving him a masculine, grizzled edge. He has a cut on his right cheek. I'd hate to see what the other guy looks like right now. Just how sharp is that stubble? Would it tickle my inner thighs? I'd love to find out. If only. Why have they kept us apart like this?

"It is paradise," I say.

His mouth slants upwards. "And what about the slower pace of life? I remember when I first moved to London it felt like the rest of the world moved whilst I stood still. You've always been a Londoner. Are you experiencing the world in reverse?"

"I've cherished it. Today is the first day in months I've been anywhere near a bus or a train. I always envisaged the countryside to be dull. But it's not. It's beautiful. It's mesmerizing. Sure, I struggled to sleep for the first week or so. But that was because I was excited. I lay awake with a burning sensation between my legs-"

"I've experienced that. With you-"

"But I've had my holiday. I intend to quicken the pace now..."

"Have you decided who you'll bring along for the ride?"

I smile. His face remains a trained blank canvas, but I know him too well. This is what he's *really* interested in. Everything so far has merely been pleasant foreplay. He respects me enough to at least go through the formalities.

"Now that *is* a decision," I say. "I've been watching and listening, just like you said. At first, I was like a dirty voyeur peeping through a hole in the bathroom wall. But now I've revealed myself. The tongues are wagging. I'm pretty sure I know who I'm choosing. I just need to decide which side they'll be on, what role they'll play."

"Perfect. So tell me about Rose..."

I smirk. "God, she's old and weak and pathetic-"

"The worst thing you can do is to underestimate somebody, Sheena."

"Do you think she is a threat?"

He looks away. "Everybody is a threat, Sheena. And the most dangerous people are those who don't have anything to lose."

Smiling, I glance at my wrist. "Don't worry. I'm pulling the strings. I've planted some thoughts in her mind. I've kept my eye on her. I caught her lingering around the train station this morning-"

"Where do you think she is going?"

He leans forward. I sense eyes on us.

"I *know* she's dangerous, Daniel." I say. "She is angry and bitter and sad. I just need to use that to my advantage, don't you think? I suspect she was catching a train back to Bridgend, to her old home-"

"To see her husband?"

I nod. "Her anger is immense, Daniel. It wouldn't surprise me if she fucking kills that poor man."

His mouth opens, just an inch. I flinch. What *is* that look? Awe?

"Nothing less than he deserves," he says. "People need to take responsibility for that poor girl's death. Regardless of who plunged the knife in her body, there is never only one killer."

His eyes trace the outline of my smile.

"What about Katherine?"

"Now, she *is* interesting..."

"Yes. She is."

"I'm already cracking that shell she's created. She doesn't quite realise it fully yet, but she's agreed to lead the group. So much more efficient to spread the message from the front, to an audience of willing listeners, yes?"

"Like Hitler..."

I smile. "Exactly. She just doesn't realise that the message she'll be delivering is mine."

"You're learning."

"From the best," I say.

"And do you think the women in the group - the

minions - will take in the message without questioning it? Do you think they'll help to spread the message?"

I sit back. I want to show him I've got it all under control, that this is all a breeze for me. Maybe I'm trying too hard? He can sniff out my insecurities. "They're vulnerable. They're open to any suggestion. Let's just say I've planted the seeds. Now I just need to watch them grow..."

He stretches out his arms and clicks his knuckles. "Fantastic," he says. "Always remember that you are the Queen in this game. You need to decide who will be your pawns...."

I hold his eye contact, then I roll my tongue around my lips, letting him know I'm thinking about my face nuzzling his lap. I've never known a man control his erection quite like him.

"Shall I see you again?" he asks.

I stand up, smiling. "You try stopping me, Daniel, " I say.

Saturday 27th October 2018

Katherine

The chatter begins to die down and the heads begin to rotate. They're bored of the warm-up and they want the main event of the evening (Saturday morning) to kick off. Pinched faces glance at their phones. The guests are here but the bride has yet to turn up for her wedding. I've run out of excuses. Whilst I'm stood at the front of the room, in the space normally occupied by Rose's chair, I'm not talking. They're beginning to wonder what exactly I *am* doing.

"Good morning, ladies."

"Morning."

"I've received a text message from Rose. Unfortunately she won't be able to make it. She is still not feeling great. We will have to make do without her today..."

Faces turn. Heads twist. Nobody says anything. I'm about to ask how everybody's week was, if anybody would like to share; I'm distracted, however, by the scraping of a chair at the back of the room. Sheena's heels click on the wooden floor. Her long fingers twist and unravel. Another actor has taken to the stage, taking the spotlight away from me. I seize the opportunity to grab a spare seat on the front row.

"I hope you don't mind me standing up and talking,

ladies? I've only attended a few meetings and usually I'm hidden at the back of the room. Pretty invisible. Believe me, that's where I'd rather be..."

Apinya's laugh dwarfs the muffled chuckles.

"My name is Sheena..."

"Hi, Sheena."

Sheena's darting eyes remind me of a gerbil daring to look out of the cage.

"I'm new to Pontbach, and to the group. You've all made me very welcome. Even though I've only been an observer, the group has already become a big part of my life. I look forward to coming here; it gives me a purpose..."

Some of the women look down, stare at their hands, smooth and soft from all that Fairy liquid. Maybe the thought has dawned on them that the meeting is the highlight of their week, too?

"I'm just picking up on what Kat said. I've actually bumped into Rose a few times in town. We've chatted. I think she finds it easier to talk to me because I'm not so close, I'm not so involved in the group..."

"Makes sense," one of the women on the front row says.

"I'm not sure if it is my place to say this, but Rose *does* seem tired. I recognise it because I've been there before. I'm sure we all have. I think she'll really benefit from the break. It will do her good. If you think about it, she has been running this group for twelve years, hasn't she? That is a long time. That is bound to take its toll. Can I be frank...?"

"Please do..."

"I also got the impression she was kind of worried..."

"*Worried*? What about?"

"That the group will fall apart in her absence..."

The women shuffle in their seats. I can almost sense them pushing their chests out. I know what they're thinking, because I'm thinking the same. We really *are* important, aren't we?

"We won't let it fall apart," one of them says.

"I believe you," Sheena says. "I just think we need to make it more apparent to Rose. Give her some reassurance. The human mind isn't always rational, is it? Imagine going on holiday and leaving your house to a neighbour to look after. The house normally looks after itself anyway, doesn't it? But suddenly you're terrified it will be burgled, it will flood, it will burn down..."

Knowing laughter fills the four corners of the room.

"And Rose sees this group just like that - as her home. I think we owe it to her to reassure her things are fine."

"What are we going to do about it then?"

"I think she'd like to know someone has taken the reins in her absence, that somebody is leading the group, taking it forward..."

My bowed head watches my knees knocking against each other. I'm a fish on dry land.

"Kat and Apinya have kindly offered to do this..."

I glance up, taking in the clapping hands. Oh my word, that feels faintly familiar. Attention. I'd forgotten how wonderful it can feel, how frighteningly intoxicating.

"And because I know this is a tough gig, I've agreed to help them out, if that's okay?"

The women nod their heads. If they had tails, they'd be wagging.

"Kat, would you care to say a few words?"

I'm treading in water as I move back to centre stage.

"Oh, hi again," I say.

Laughter is replaced by silence.

"I wanted to share. I don't often do this, but somehow it feels fitting. I think it is time to be brave, to go out of my comfort zone. I've already spoken to Sheena about the incident, and she hopes it will inspire some other ladies..."

The nods and the smiles are distracting, but they *are* encouraging.

"The other day I was in my car when a man in a white van pulled up beside me. He wound down his window and he spat all over me..."

I'm struck by the gasps from the front row. A lady puts her hand to her mouth.

"That's terrible. *Disgusting.* Why do men think they can get away with this? Just because they're supposed to be the stronger sex? They think they can bully and intimidate us?"

I wave away the concerned, aghast comments.

"The thing is," I say, "I took his telephone number from his van, and I called him."

"*What?* Weren't you scared?"

"Terrified. But that's the point. You know that book? Well, I felt the fear and I did it anyway. And you know what else I did...?"

"Go on, go on..."

"I threatened to tell his wife what he did unless he apologised...."

"And did he?"

"Yes. He begged for forgiveness."

The second round of applause is louder than the first. This one feels authentic.

"And you know where I got the bravery from? I knew

I'd have the backing of all you ladies if it did backfire, if it did go wrong. It felt like I wore a protective shield. I knew that - combined - we are so much stronger than any one man..."

"You better believe it, girl!"

Sheena wraps her sinewy, lightly muscled arms around me. Pulling away, her eyes are red.

"This is what men are capable of, ladies," she says. "And no, we don't let them bully and intimidate us. We need to be strong together. Do you know what will make our bond stronger?"

The open mouths can't quite produce any words. A few go to say something, but then pull the words back.

"Trust."

The heads swivel to a glowing Apinya.

"Exactly," a beaming Sheena says.

"But we *do* trust each other," a voice pipes up.

Sheena waves her hand. "I know. I know. But you know what would reassure us that little bit more?"

Sheena turns to me now. We'd discussed this earlier, before the group collated.

"Whatever we say in this room stays in this room, do you hear? We don't share it with our husbands or boyfriends or anybody else," I say.

Sheena gives me a high-five. "That way you can be sure whatever you say is confidential. How amazing would that be?"

Uncertain heads begin to nod.

"We should do this for Rose," Sheena says.

The approval is more vocal and assured this time.

"Right," Sheena says, "would anyone else like to share?"

For the first time in twelve years, I'm taken aback by the show of hands.

Sheena

Walking into the pub from the bright Saturday afternoon outside, it is almost as if I've put my shades on. The low ceilings and thick brick walls make the pub feel like a cave or an igloo. Wooden bookshelves pack the walls from floor to ceiling. Passing the occasional solitary punter staring into space or completing the crossword, I head to the back of the pub. With a half-emptied pint in his hand, his cheeks plump with smugness, he looks up at me like an inquisitive ferret.

"You sure made me work for my money," he says. "I wasn't expecting any of that shit!"

"Were you not able to cope?" I ask.

My teasing smile makes him look away. I sling the sealed brown envelope across the wooden table. There is no name on the front. There is no address. I pull out a chair and sit down.

"Go get me a drink," I say.

"What's the magic word?"

"*Now.*"

"I was thinking more of one beginning with a 'p'."

"I'm sorry," I say, wiping my mouth with the back of my arm. "Go get me a drink now. Prick."

He rolls his shoulders. He knows I'm not going to give way here, and neither of us have the time or the inclination to argue. Besides, men always want an easy life; that's why they always say you look good in that dress. Apart from Daniel, of course. Daniel likes to complicate things just to make life more exciting, more unpredictable. He thrives on confrontation.

My drinking buddy scurries off to the bar without asking what I want. Returning, he slides the glass across the table. Daniel likes to do that. Only, with him it isn't always a glass he likes to slide. I pull the glass to my nose. Vodka. Straight. Fair play. He made a good choice.

"So you pulled it off then? Well done."

He unravels his shoulders, buoyed by this apparent compliment. "Took the bait, hook, line and sinker..."

"You were the perfect man for the job. Daniel said you were."

He twitches at the mention of the name, like I spoke of Voldermort or something. The only people who want to be associated with Daniel do so for bravado, like a Kray twin. This man needs to be discreet, to remain oblivious. In my experience, the men who lead double-lives are the most dangerous types.

"Hey, I have my uses."

"So I take it you followed her from the house?"

He stretches out his body now, savouring the moment. "Hey, I was just playing the role. You know that I'm a charmer, really. Thought she'd never leave the house. Was sat there for hours eating the cheese and pickle sandwiches my wife made for me. Luckily, it was raining something rotten, so she probably couldn't see much through her rear window. She definitely couldn't see me leave her house. And then - typical woman driver - she stalled the car, and I took my moment like a professional..."

Part of me can't help but be impressed. I dig into my purse and slide a note across the table. "Call it a tip.

You sure did a grand job of convincing my darling Kat that men are the scum of the earth. And she's told *everybody...*"

His face drops as I slide the chair away from the table. Every man wants to spend their daytime with a pretty lady. "Can't stay," I say. "I'm off out with the girls tonight."

"Any more jobs for me?" he asks.

"I'll call you," I say.

Katherine

Sheena has popped to the shop to get, she says, some chewing gum. I press my body against the wall whilst Apinya walks around in circles, staring at her feet, humming a song. Sheena must have bought a shit load of chewing gum, because when she comes out of the shop, face alight with mischief, a plastic bag dangles from her wrist. Glancing down at the bag, I break into hysterics. Sheena ignores me and links my arm with hers. We skip along the pavement. I glance over my shoulder. Apinya is following us, like she's a dog on a lead.

Fuck knows where we're heading, and fucks knows if I care. I'm not sure whether Sheena is leading us, or if I'm leading Sheena. We could be heading through a black hole, for all I know. Apinya, bless her, would watch us drop into oblivion and then dutifully do exactly the same. At least I'd die happy.

"Hold on, you're walking too *fucking* fast..."

Turning around, Apinya reminds me of an elf or a dwarf, or whatever you call it. She looks so cute and tiny running after us barefoot, with her shoes in her hands, her cheeks pumped with air. Sheena bends forward at the knee, pushing her tiny arse out, like she's riding a horse at the Grand National. I'm sure her skirt has ridden up so any lucky guy behind us probably has a view of her pants. Oh my God, does Sheena even *wear* pants? She seems the type who wouldn't, the dirty, *wonderful* girl. She slaps her bare thigh with her hand.

"Come on girl, you can do it!"

Apinya's smile broadens as she edges closer to us, as she realises she's catching up. The smile turns upside down. Her eyes dangle on stalks. She knows where she's heading. She has stumbled on the crooked pavement. I put my hand to my mouth, gasping.

Apinya lies flat on her front on the pavement.

Crouching over her, I shake her body with my hand. "Apinya! Apinya! Are you alright?"

The whole world is rotating, going round and round me, but Apinya remains still. Completely motionless. Oh my *fucking* God, maybe she banged her head? I look up at Sheena's creaseless face. I decide to shake Apinya's body harder and faster, to shock her back to life.

Apinya lifts her head. She's alive. That's *something*. Her long, dark, luscious, *gorgeous* fucking hair covers her face. I sweep it to one side. Her face looks fairly normal, from what I can remember.

"What the fuck happened?" she asks.

Her laughter erupts. She bangs her fist down on the pavement. Holding out my hand to help her up, Sheena doubles over with hysterics, too.

And then the three of us are arm in arm, with me in the middle, skipping along, heading God-knows-where. I'm too absorbed in the talk and I'm too high on life to notice where we're heading until it's too late to do anything about it, to try to change the direction.

"Why are we here?" I ask.

Sheena shrugs her shoulders. "Why not? Not like I know many places. Thought it would be nice to sit down by the river. And I got us a few treats..."

Sheena's teeth glisten in the darkness as she dips her hand inside the plastic bag and pulls out a pack of beers. Apinya dumps herself down on the grass so that, momentarily, both her legs rise up in the air. She holds out her hand and grabs at a beer. Sheena doesn't know my history, but *surely* Apinya does. Does she say nothing because she doesn't care, or because she's too drunk to notice?

"You're a *star,*" Apinya says.

I take a beer, too, and plonk myself on the grass next to Apinya. I'm aware that I *should* be uneasy, but that's all it is - an awareness.

"God, it was like the men in the town have never seen a woman before. Did you see the way their jaws dropped every time we entered the room?" Sheena says.

I *did* see that, but then I dismissed it as an illusion, as the shots going to my head, giving me ideas of grandeur. But their eyes *definitely* lingered; they definitely outstayed their welcome. But then that was the problem. I *did* welcome the hungry looks. It excited me. It made me feel alive, like I'd awoken from the dead.

"The men in this town are just peasants," Apinya says.

"Apart from our husbands?" I ask.

Apinya hesitates for a moment too long. Maybe the drink slowed her reflexes. I doubt it. "Of course," she says.

"Ever wanted to do something crazy?" Sheena asks.

All the fucking time, I think, but then I usually curse myself for having these thoughts, for not acting my age, for not being content with all the wonderful things I have, for not living the life we agreed.

"Like robbing a bank?" Apinya asks.

"Something like that," Sheena says, looking ahead.

"Like sleeping with another man?" Apinya asks.

I sense Sheena's blue eyes looking at me, her lips moistening. "Yes," she says. "Like sleeping with another man. Or a woman."

Apinya scoffs. "That *is* crazy," she says.

From the movements next to me, I can tell what Sheena is doing. My head hopes I'm wrong. My heart hopes I'm right. I dare not turn to look at her. I don't know what will be stronger - my fear, or my excitement.

My suspicions are confirmed by the sight of her naked, upturned arse running away from me. The splash makes me jump. Sheena disappears beneath the surface. I glance at the neat pile of clothes to my side. Apinya squeals like a girl at a concert. Sheena's face reappears, glistening with moisture.

"Who's joining me?"

Apinya pulls down her skirt and kicks off her heels and - again - I flinch at the splash. Sheena dived into the water; Apinya was much less graceful. She raised her knees to her chest like a kid at the swimming baths.

"Come on," Sheena says, floating in the water.

I laugh. "I'm alright. I'll just watch."

"Pervert," Sheena replies. "Can't swim?"

"I can swim," I say.

"Maybe she's scared?" Apinya says, her teeth chattering. "You know? Maybe she has reason to be scared."

"I'm sure Kat isn't scared," Sheena says. "Kat isn't a baby..."

I *should* be scared. I *should* be terrified. After all, my parents drowned in this river twelve years ago. This river *killed* my parents.

But I'm not scared.

With my abandoned clothes at my feet, I long to

disappear within the water as quickly as possible. My naked body feels huge and horrendous next to these slim, beautiful specimens. Closing my eyes, I jump feet first into the river.

My head sinks below the surface. Water pours inside my open mouth. I kick and flail with my arms. The water is suffocating me. I keep going down, deeper and deeper.

I'm going to drown. This was meant to be.

My head shoots up from out of the water. I cough out the water.

"Are you okay?" Sheena asks.

I'm aware of her tender hands around my waist, moving to my hips. Blowing air out of my mouth, I open my eyes. I look up at the bright stars in the dark sky. A weight has been removed from my ankles.

"It's been years since I felt this good," I say.

Sheena smiles. I glance down at her lips. For a fleeting moment, I think she is going to kiss me. I have no idea what I'd do if she did.

"Good. From now on, Kat, things are going to get a whole lot better. Do you hear?"

I nod. I really *do* hear, loud and clear.

Tuesday 30th October 2018

Ray

Shuffling around in the seat, I flick on the full beams and squint through the steamy windscreen. I'm tempted to give the screen a quick wipe with my hand, but I tell Kat off for doing that; I do try not to be a hypocrite. Pushing a mint into my mouth, I jolt the van into first gear.

"The mornings are getting colder," I say, aware of the steam emitting from my mouth, aware I'm not sounding too cheerful. I rub my hands together, balancing the steering wheel on my knee. "Fucking darker, too. I wish they didn't put the clocks back on Sunday."

Rob stretches out his arms, a bear waking up in the woods. "Tell me about it," he says. "The alarm clock was taking the piss when it went off this morning. I thought it was the middle of the night. Turned it off by mistake, didn't I? Mum had to get me out of bed. Told her to fuck off. She didn't like that too much. Reminded me that she brought me into this world, that she carried me in her belly for nine months. I said that I thought I was adopted. My mum really doesn't get my sense of humour. Felt like I'd only just got in bed, let alone out of it again..."

I smile. Weakly. Thinly. It felt like he'd only just gone

to bed because he *had* only just gone to bed. It was only a Monday night in October; it wasn't New Year's Eve, for God's sake. The boy was making me feel old. When I'd knocked on the front door, his old dear appeared in her dressing gown, flustered and apologetic, cursing her good-for-nothing-son; he'd been out late again last night, stumbled up the stairs drunk as a skunk. Of course, I told her not to worry, assured her it wasn't her fault. Truth be told, I felt sorry for the old buzzard. I sat in the van and waited; flicked through my phone. It grated me that I'd dragged myself out of my bed at the crack of dawn just to sit on Rob's drive until he sorted himself out. I did the boy a favour giving him a job. He didn't have any qualifications, no real experience. I just wanted to give a local kid a chance. I inhaled deeply when Rob pulled open the passenger door, his eyes glued together, hair sticking up in a tuft at one side. I questioned whether I was being reasonable, whether I was just being a grumpy old man. The boy was young - twenty-two - just a year and a bit older than that girl I found drunk on the pavement. Honestly, I was a tearaway at that age. Rob is only hurting himself. I was hurting others.

Glancing to the passenger seat, I see that things haven't improved. With his eyes closed, Rob rolls a joint as fluently as brushing his teeth. My smile broadens. Think I've been harsh. He's a good kid really. Harmless enough, I guess. Just lacking in direction, in ambition. He's just been brought up in the wrong generation, where it's normal to be glued to the phone, cackling at videos of dancing cats and singing dogs. How the fuck is that productive? Spends most of his spare time down the gym, admiring his 'guns' in skin tight vest tops. Only, because all his mates have biceps, just as big they don't have any novelty factor. Clearly the kid has no interest in his future. None of my business, of course, but I long to put my arm around his shoulder and have a quiet word; I'm just no good with that sort of thing. Kat is the talker. She's a woman, after all. I just feel bad knowing that, unless the world miraculously falls on his lap, he'll be doing exactly the same shit in ten, twenty years, only then he'll be bitter and twisted and hating the world, too.

"God, there were some women out last night, Ray. They weren't wearing skirts; they were wearing belts. You'd have loved it. Must take you out sometime, drag you away from that gorgeous wife of yours, if she'll let you..."

Staring intently at the road, I grin and say nothing. I try not to give him any further encouragement. Kat was out with Sheena and Apinya on Saturday night. But for a few days, she could have been one of these women he's talking about. I remind myself – again – that I was young once. Can't ever remember talking about women like that but – *hey* – times change, and I was no saint. Something gnaws at me: my boy is grown up now (luckily I didn't have a girl - how could I have coped with that?) and I can't help but think that these women are somebody's little girl.

Rob's eyes widen as the black, metal gates slide open. I park the dusty, trusty white van next to the polished Jaguar E-Type on the drive.

"This is a bit fancy," Rob says, bobbing up and down in his seat. "Must remember this place next time I go out on the steal. Rob goes on the rob. Get it? Cracking."

I jerk my head, pretend to be shocked; I know the

boy is only winding me up.

Rob's ashen face lightens when a woman in her early forties opens the front door wearing a knee length black dress and high heels. Somebody's little girl. It is eight in the morning and I'm barely out of bed, yet this lady is ready for a ball. Very easy on the eye. I nod my head and try not to look too menacing; the painted red lips widen.

"Right on time, gentlemen. This is a good start. Come on in," she says, angling her body so we can push through the door without brushing against her.

I know from my stiff back and damp forehead that I'm out of my comfort zone. I'm a prostitute in a church in this gaff. I'm more at home in a place I can get my hands dirty and not worry about the consequences. I can smell the money. My feet sink into the deep burgundy carpet. I offer to take my dirty work boots off.

"If you don't mind; that is very kind of you," the woman says.

She glances at Rob, indicating, without saying anything, for him to follow suit. Next to him I'm fresh out of the bubble bath. Rob hops on one leg, pulling at a boot. Thrusting out his hand and pressing it against the wall, he only just misses a marble dolphin statute. This is like a comedy sketch. I raise an eyebrow and snigger. *What are young people like today, hey?*

The floor space in the hallway is as big as our lounge. Could have a decent kick around in here. The family portrait is up on the wall, there for everybody to see. Her husband is maybe a few years older, with grey hair and a soft, intelligent face. Reminds me of Richard Gere, which I guess can't be a bad thing. All the women love Tricky Dicky, don't they? The three children are all boys, probably all under ten, with beaming, colourful smiles. I can't help but compare; something heavy and unpleasant lingers in my throat. I look away but there I am, staring back in the monumental mirror; my bulky shoulders slumped, face worn and forlorn, my torn, dirty jeans unwelcome and out of place in this meticulous, beloved home. I catch my apprentice's reflection in the mirror, rubbing his red eyes, stumbling around like a drunk. I don't have a chip on my shoulder, but I'm aware of the class divide here. What must she think of us pair?

Passing door after door, the woman leads us to an emptied room at the back of the house. I'm not sure what the room is used for – possibly a library or a play area – and she doesn't volunteer the information, either. She shows us what needs to be done – just extensive painting, money for nothing, really, something the husband could do if he didn't have cash to burn – then she dutifully offers us tea and biscuits.

"If it's free, then I'm in," Rob says, holding her smile.

"That's cracking," I say.

We're prepped and ready for work by the time she returns with the goods. "I'll come back with sandwiches later," she says. "Need to keep your strength up."

"That would be grand," Rob says.

I can't help but glance at the shapely, gym-toned legs as she disappears from the room, leaving us two brutes to it.

We work fast and quietly, Rob probably because he has no energy to talk and me because I just want to get the job done. We paint the underlay in no time. If we keep this up then we could complete the job before the sandwiches arrive, and we'll be on our way home, with cash in hand and a possible recommendation to some well-to-do-friends.

"What the *fuck* you doing?" I ask, woken from my trance.

I'd kind of forgotten he was in the room; I'd been lost in my mind, thinking of going home early and surprising the wife, of possibly jumping into bed with her for an afternoon fondle, before the tiredness kicks in. I'm not keen on doing anything later (after ten at night) when all I can think of is sleep.

"What's the matter? You said I could smoke."

"Did I *fuck*. I said you could smoke in my van, with the window open. You can't go around lighting up in somebody's house, you idiot. Look at this place. What if you set the fire alarm off? Or set light to an antique painting? She probably already has you marked as a potential arsonist."

"Why? Cos' I'm under twenty-five? That's ageist, that is..."

My face must redden - I feel the burn - for Rob smirks; he's playing the class clown. He covers his chest with his hands, suddenly the victim.

"Alright, keep your hair on, Granddad," he says. "I'll go outside and have a fag. I'm entitled to a break, Ray. This isn't slave labour. Regulations state I can have a break. You need to be aware of these things to make sure you comply with the national minimum wage."

I take a step closer, laughing. "I'll give you a break. I'll break your fucking legs, you numpty. Now go outside, take your break and then hurry back. We're on for an early finish, and the wife will be waiting for me."

Rob blows a kiss, skips out of the room. Enjoying the solitude, I kneel down and get to work on the skirting boards. Time passes. I turn to Rob. He isn't there. I remember he'd popped out for a fag. He was taking the piss now. How long had it been? Where *was* that little prick?

Pressing my back against the wall, I pull on my boots. It was drizzling in the van this morning and I don't fancy damp socks. Gently, I shut the front door. I trot down the drive, between the parked vehicles, then venture onto the grass. Nowhere to be seen. I consider calling his name, but then, he isn't a dog and besides, I don't want to alert the owner he'd gone missing. Something wasn't right, though. The boy had taken the piss before, but not like this. Was he alright? Maybe he'd had a reaction to last night's excess?

Kicking off the boots, I tiptoe around the house in my socks, hoping and praying I don't bump into the woman. I know exactly what I look like to her, despite her pleasantries. I scare her. I'm wide. High. Rough. *Dangerous.* What excuse would I give for loitering in the corridors on my own? She told me where the toilet was. I haven't shouted for her attention. I pick up my pace; my breathing quickens. I complete a full circuit, a complete tour of the downstairs. Beautiful house, I think, but still no sign of Rob. I look up. I have no choice.

I climb the stairs, grimacing every time the floorboards creak. I reach the landing.

There he is.

He seems okay. His eyes are open, and he is standing up. The relief is replaced by a dull punch to the chest. I narrow my eyes, peer through the tiny gap in the door. I hope I've got it wrong. But no: that *is* the bedroom door. *Her* bedroom. The master bedroom. I look down. My face crumbles. Rob's dirty jeans are in a ball at his ankles. Both hands are down by his midriff. I inhale deeply.

Pulling open the door, I grab the boy's shoulders and drag him out of the room. Rob trips and stumbles, falls to the floor. He kicks with his feet like he's an infant riding a bike, his face red and flustered.

"Get your trousers on. Meet me outside."

In the front garden, boots back on for the second time, I pace in circles with my head down. I only look up when *he* appears in my eye line.

"Sorry, Ray, it isn't what it looked like."

My neck muscles tighten. "My mistake. Must have got it all wrong. Silly me. So you didn't sneak into the woman's bedroom? You weren't watching the woman take a shower, with your cock out?"

Rob shrugs his broad shoulders. Grins. "Okay. It *is* what it looks like. Can you blame me? She is smoking hot."

Don't you fucking dare smirk at me.

The boy holds up his hands, keeps me at a distance. "She wanted it, Ray. You're too naïve to notice, too wrapped up playing the happy husband. But she gave all the signs. You heard the way she talked to us. The way she looked at us. She probably planned for me to watch her, was most likely getting off on it..."

I shake my head. This kid watches too many adult movies. "She fucking *smiled* at us, Rob. She made us tea because she was being *fucking* nice. Just because I'm married, and just because I love my wife, it doesn't mean I'm a complete idiot. I see the signs, just like everybody else. And she gave no signs she wanted you to play with your cock in her bedroom, you dumb son-of-a-bitch."

"Her type are all the same..."

"All the same?"

The boy pumps out his gym-hardened chest. Spittle coats his front teeth. "Yes, Ray. They're all the same. They all fucking want it..."

I turn my back on him. I'm taunted by the memory of pinning that guy from the pub, Tony, down on the pavement and pummelling his face. Had to stop myself from killing him. Brought back my blood-filled past, something I've tried hard to forget. Can't let that happen again. Just can't.

His hand is on my shoulder, twisting me around. In my face. Teeth bared. Hands clenched.

"Go on, Ray. Hit me. I know you want to. Only, I don't think you're as tough as they all make out. You're an old man these days, all soft around the middle..."

I clench my fist, pull back my arm. The boy flinches, closes his eyes. I don't punch him. Instead, I caress his forehead with gentle fingertips usually reserved for the wife.

"Got a hair out of place there, sweetheart," I say.

Retreating towards the house, I shout, "I want you off the job. This job and the next job and every job. You're fired. You hear?"

Turning around, I stop dead. Damn.

The woman stands in her dressing gown on the doorstep, her big blue eyes staring me down, her face like thunder. How much had she heard? Was she going to call the cops?

Then, her face creases. "Thank you," she says.

Wednesday 7th November 2018

Katherine

Apinya works the aisles, filling plastic cups with wine. This was Sheena's idea, and Apinya lapped it up. Coffee and tea were still available, but it was only optional. We want loyal women to come here, Sheena said, and we want them to enjoy it whilst they *are* here. A glass or two of wine won't do any harm and besides, it may lower their inhibitions, get them to tell the truth. I hadn't heard any of the ladies complain.

We've made quite a few changes to the meetings over the weeks. For starters, we now meet on Wednesday evenings, too. Sheena has talked about increasing this to three meetings a week next year. We only want committed members. And why not? We're sharing our darkest secrets and we need to know we have total trust. We all agreed that, apart from authorised annual leave and sickness, if a member misses two meetings in a row then they're out. We're all in this together, after all. There are no passengers. Listening is not participating. Every woman needs to share on a regular basis.

The door opens and all the heads jerk – in unison – to the right. A newcomer. The girl is young – maybe early twenties – and her pretty, plump cheeks look hot to the touch. Blue, watery eyes twinkle momentarily as she looks up at me; the smile is brief and forced. Head staring intently at the floor, she locates a chair at the back of the hall - the one I'd vacated -no doubt hoping to disappear into the background.

We all know what it is like to be here for the first time. Sheena had made the need to make every newcomer feel welcome crystal clear - to acknowledge their arrival, make them feel important, like they actually existed. Like many things Sheena suggested, I wasn't too sure. Surely it was a big enough ordeal to pluck up the courage to come to the group for the first time anyway? Sometimes you just want to dip your toes in the water, test the temperature. Sheena made another valid point, though. We need to know who the newcomer is. We need to know we can trust them. We can't risk them spreading our private conversations with outsiders.

I glance at Sheena. Her eyebrows expand into rainbows. The eyes are expectant. I suck in air, puff out my cheeks, then blow the air right out again.

"Welcome to the group," I say, standing on tiptoes and looking to the back of the room. My voice is an octane too high. "It's *fantastic* to have you here. We were all newcomers once, weren't we ladies? I'm sure we all remember how difficult it was, don't we?"

The guffaws of approval make our little group sound like the House of Commons. Sheena nods her approval. The poor girl's cheeks redden, look so scorching you could fry an egg on them. The girl smiles. Says thank you.

"I'm Kat. Is it okay to ask your name?"

"Tess. Hi."

"Hi, Tess," the whole group says. Feels like I'm back

in kindergarten.

Glancing at the floor, I count to three. It is as though I am gaining courage and strength from somewhere. When I look up - address the room - I speak louder and clearer. "We're all here for a reason, Tess. Something - or some *things* - have happened in our lives to bring us to seek solace. We've all made the brave decision that we no longer want to suffer in silence. We think of ourselves as a little community. A family. We want to speak up, and stand up. Seek support from others who've suffered the same, or similar. Would you agree that's the reason you're here today, Tess?"

There is a pause as Tess takes all of this in. She leans forward in her chair, face red and hands white. Slowly, she nods her head.

The room is alight with smiling, approving faces.

"Well, congratulations for finding the strength and courage to be here today, Tess," I say.

"Congratulations, Tess," a chorus of voices say.

I wait a few seconds, wait for the applause to subside.

"We all know how difficult it is to share in the group. It can be terrifying. But we find the longer you leave it, the more it grows and builds in your head, until it becomes a dark, fretful cloud, like the Boogeyman at the bottom of the bed..."

The room laughs at this, especially Apinya, who snorts wine from her nose.

"I've had a few Boogeymen in *my* bed," one of the older ladies says. The laughter becomes hysterical.

"But am I right, ladies?" I ask.

One of the women turns around, holds Tess's gaze. "She's right, babe," she says. Tess nods again.

"With this in mind," I continue, a peacock with its tail up, "we normally offer newcomers the opportunity to share their story as soon as they join the group. There is no pressure, of course, and you can say no if you're not quite ready..."

Tess bows her head. Silence. My eyes flick in the direction of Sheena; they just can't help it. She raises her eyebrows. In her mind, there *is* pressure. She's challenging me to pursue it. If I don't today, then Sheena will have a quiet word with Tess in the next meeting. She'll be disappointed if she has to, though.

"So what do you think, Tess...?"

When Tess looks up, her eyes are wide and childlike. I wonder just how old she is. Twenty? Twenty-one? Her hands press down against her knees, maybe to stop them shaking. The faces in the room - generally wrinkled and creased - turn to zone in on her. She is a bird with a broken wing that just can't fly away. Just tell them all to fuck off, I think.

"Okay," the girl says. "I'll share."

The smiles in the room are an advert for Colgate.

"Well, that's just *fantastic,*" I say. I long to climb over these vultures, hungry to feed on a story, and give the girl a motherly hug, squeeze her real tight. "Just go ahead. In your own time. If it becomes too much, then - *please* - just stop."

Of course, nobody else wants it to become too much; nobody wants her to stop. This girl is new; she is fresh blood. Everybody in the room has heard the same stale old stories from all the other stale old women.

"I think I was molested," the girl says.

There are shakes of the head, pitying murmurs around the room.

"Think?"

The eyes turn from the girl, to Apinya. The glazed

eyes, the way her head sways unsteadily on her neck, like it might topple off, has become more and more familiar. No doubt, Apinya has drunk more than a glass or two of wine.

"Sorry, I'm just curious..."

"Curious about *what*?" I ask.

"Why she only *thinks* she is molested. Why doesn't she *know*?"

"Isn't *think* enough for you, Apinya?"

I'm aware of the tremor in my voice, of the rising anger. That was the type of question a man might ask, not a fully-fledged member of the group. Apinya looks away. Even she must know she's overstepped the mark.

"It's okay," Tess quickly says. "I've been asking myself the same question, again and again, every day..."

Silence fills the room. We wait for her to continue.

"I was drunk. My memory is vague. Sometimes it feels like my mind is playing tricks on me. Sometimes it feels like I'm making things up. But deep down I don't think I was molested, I *know* I was..."

Fat droplets trickle down her puffy cheek.

"Tell us what happened, Tess. It sounds truly awful. Only if you feel up to it..."

"It was my fault..."

"You were molested. How on earth was it your fault?"

The faces turn back to me. Their lips are pursed, the eyes narrowed. They have a point. I sound angry with this poor, brave girl. How dare I? I *am* angry with this poor, brave girl, but not in the way they think. I want to shake her, tell her that there is no way it is her fault.

"Kat is right. You are the victim, Tess. The only person at fault is the man who did this to you."

Tess looks up. She holds Sheena's eye, stood at the

back of the room. Sheena smiles at Tess, and then she smiles at me. My fairy godmother, fighting my corner.

I want to stab her with a pen.

"I know it wasn't my fault," Tess says, "but it kind of *feels* like it, you know? I was so drunk. If I wasn't drunk, then it wouldn't have happened. So I keep blaming myself. Does that make sense?"

I speak softly, breaking up myself. "It does, sweetheart. We all have these thoughts. But you need to listen to what Sheena said. You are *not* at fault..."

She holds my look. "I know. I've been dwelling on it for weeks. That's why I didn't come forward straight away..."

"You're here now, and that's the important thing," I say.

"Well, I got drunk, and I can't change that now. My friends left me, were nowhere to be seen. So much for girls sticking together, looking out for each other. That's partly why I thought this group might help. I have no idea how I got there, but I ended up sat on the pavement, surrounded in sick. Some man came to help me-"

"How did he help you?" I ask; the words spit out of my mouth fast and urgent, bullets from a machine gun.

"Asked how I was, what he could do to help. I'm sure there were two of them. They seemed to care-"

"They're the worst types," one of the women shouts, venom in her voice. "They gain your trust and then they attack-"

"Let the girl talk," I say.

"One of them left. The nice one. But he came back, I'm sure. And then it felt like they were no longer on my side, that they were no longer looking after me. I remember there were hands on my body, in places I didn't want them to be. I was too scared to push them away. I just closed my eyes, waited for it to stop..."

"Where did the nice man go?" I ask.

Tess looks to the ceiling. Is she trying to remember? "Oh yes. He went to get tissues. For the vomit."

"Did both men touch you?" I ask.

Tess looks down. The seconds pass slowly. She looks up, seems to hold my gaze.

"I honestly don't know," she says. "At least one of the men touched me. Maybe it was two. Does it really matter?"

"I guess not," I say.

But the room is spinning, and my legs feel like they are giving way. I hope the women in the room, who now look to me as their leader, don't notice the film of cold sweat on my forehead, or my shaking hands.

To me it matters more than anything else in the world.

"Thank you for sharing, Tess," I say.

The voices in my head are silenced by the sound of clapping.

Friday 9th November 2018

Ray

That's him in his dirty, outsized joggers, looking like he lives in a cardboard box. We're coming from opposite directions, but we're both heading to the same destination; two ships on a map. His sunken head is oblivious to the surroundings, to the people passing, to those brushing up against him. I slow my pace so that we join at the same point. Looking up, he catches my blank face. I let him wait. Nod. He jerks his head. I open my hand to let him into the cafe first.

"What do you want?" I ask.

What is that dumb expression? He's not sure if I'm offering to buy him food or just a drink. He's a greedy son-of-a-bitch, and so if he can get some free grub out of me then he will. On the other hand, he really doesn't want to piss me off, does he? He stoops his head forward, tries to work out the best way to raise the conundrum.

"Er- what you getting, Ray?"

"Full English for me," I say. "Can't be beaten."

His face brightens into a smile. "I agree. Same for me, please."

I open my body to him. My expression must be as I intended, because he takes a step back. "You cheeky little bastard," I say. "I was only offering to buy you a brew. You want food from me, too? After what you did?"

He holds out his calloused hands. "Not at all, Ray. I just thought you were offering, that's all. My bad. Just a black coffee for me please, mate. And I proper appreciate it, you know."

I hold his look just long enough for him to twitch. Shaking my head, my face breaks into a smile. "You always were a daft bugger, Rob. I'm fucking with you. Now go and sit down you silly sod and I'll get the order in."

With his hunched shoulders and tiptoed steps, he reminds me of a dog caught shitting in the garden (not my garden because he'd be scarpering). And to think, this is the clown who thought he could take me on. Maybe I'm a hypocrite - I've always despised bullies - but I'm getting a kick out of having the upper hand, of making him pay. After making the order, I sit down close enough for my leg to brush against his, daring him to move away. I want him to know that, if I wanted to, I could reach down and squeeze his balls. The drinks arrive. I pour some sugar in, stir the cup, blow cold air on the coffee. Rob wriggles next to me. He'll be waiting a long time if he expects me to talk first.

"So I just wanted to say, Ray, I'm really sorry about what happened at that lady's house. I was well out of order, and I know that now."

"You need to treat women with respect. That was somebody's daughter. Somebody's mother. Somebody's wife-"

"I know. You're right. I'm sorry."

"Is that all you have to say?"

"Er-yes. That I'm sorry, like."

"Apology accepted."

I lean over to the next table, grab a copy of The Sun, browse the cover. I start whistling the Jaws theme tune.

"So are we good?" Rob asks, turning his body so his stale coffee breath wafts against my cheek.

I keep looking forward. "We're good."

"So I keep my job? I can keep working for you, Ray?"

I turn to him now. We are so close that if I puckered my lips, I could give him a kiss. I raise one eye. "You said there was one thing. You apologised. You never mentioned anything about your job."

"Right. It's just I was hoping if we were good then there was no reason I couldn't keep working for you."

"So you only said sorry to keep your job? Is that the game you're playing? You're not really sorry?"

"No! I mean, I am sorry, Ray. I'm not playing no game. I just want to work for you, too. I love you, Big Man."

Raising an eyebrow, I open the gap between us. Turning away, I pretend to be deep in thought. This is a mistake. Two gorgeous women walk into the cafe. My jaw literally drops. One of them is Kat's friend and Bernard's wife, Apinya. She returns my nod with a smile.

I have never spoken to the second woman, never even been in the same room as her before, but straight away I know who she is.

I turn back to Rob. My thoughts are scrambled. "I'm sure we can sort something out," I say.

Sheena

I've never known anybody quite so giddy with her
husband's credit card clasped in her hand as Apinya,
and I've known some pretty formidable gold diggers in
my time.

Of course, the high street is nothing compared to
Oxford Street or Mayfair. In a way, though, it is quite
splendid. I always did get a thrill out of dirtying myself
in grubby, dimly lit pubs and seedy sex shops. The
shops here are tiny and compact; I'm a slip of a woman
but occasionally I have to walk sideways to navigate the
aisles. Apinya is determined to depict the pampered
wife. Whilst the brand names are laughable, she still
manages to buy the most expensive shoes and
handbags. The shop owners have palpitations when she
enters. They recognise her as Bernard's wife. They look
me up and down too, sharks circling a turtle or (and
this always makes me laugh) a surfer they mistake for a
turtle. My initial excitement begins to wane (and I'm
just stifling an almighty hippopotamus yawn) when I
spot them entering the cafe. With that scalped skull and
wide shoulders, it can only be one man. Instantly, a
piece slots into place. Idling for a few moments by
admiring my reflection in a shop window, I give them
time to settle.

"Fancy a drink, Apinya?" I ask.

Apinya's eyes glaze over as she takes in the flaked
paint and the cracked window. I grab hold of her hand

to stop her running in the other direction. She crinkles her adorable nose, like she whiffs the sewers. Swinging her arm, I take a skip.

"Come on," I say. "It will be fun. Who knows what - or *who* - we'll find inside..."

Apinya stops mid-step when she spots Ray huddled close to another guy in the corner. His heavy chin drops. Apinya's smile and fluttering lashes undress him. I'd already figured this was one of her weaknesses. That poor husband of hers must be worn out. She has an insatiable eye for the men. I wanted to test her, and she passed with flying colours. No man is off the radar, even if he belongs to one of her best friends.

I turn to Apinya.

"Why don't we ditch the coffee? Have something exciting?"

Apinya's smile broadens. "The pub?"

Oh my, I think; I could easily take advantage of her sense of adventure. I smile to the shapeless lady behind the counter. "Why don't we try one of their delicious milkshakes? Now that *would* be fun..."

Apinya deflates. She'd like nothing more than to waste away the afternoon sipping champagne. The girl has been watching too much *Sex in the City*.

Milkshakes in hand, Apinya makes no pretence of sweeping the plastic chair before sitting down. Just what lowlife does she envisage sat there before her? She *does* make me giggle. She is great fun.

Damn it, I'll probably miss her when she's gone.

She sniffs her upturned nose. How long has it been since she lived in the slums? Too long. The glass flute filled with strawberry milkshake is nearly as big as her elfin face. Like a kid, she bends the plastic straw to use it. No wonder her mind is a frazzled mess - nothing but fluids ever enters her body. Ironically, she looks like she'd swallow rather than spit. If she swallowed her chewing gum it'd be her meal for the day.

Her glass flute slides across the table. She smiles. She's resigned to the fact we aren't moving anywhere else any time soon. She may as well enjoy it.

"This *is* fun," she says .

I nod, showing her I'm impressed she understands my thinking. I decide to stencil an imaginary halo above my head. "I'm *so* bored of the whole coffee culture," I say. "It's just so untrendy these days. So pretentious. All these wealthy people sipping overpriced coffee in chains stores that get away with not paying taxes. It's good to support your local establishments, that's what I say."

I can tell Apinya has never even contemplated this before. "Oh yes, I *so* agree," she says.

I take the opportunity to drown out the sound of Apinya slurping milkshake through her straw. I lean forward, my elbows sliding on the damp table.

"So tell me about this husband of yours, Apinya. He sounds fantastic. I gather that he is very wealthy."

Apinya sits up straight, seemingly growing in stature. Does she sense admiration? Or is it envy?

"He is very rich. I don't like flaunting it, but I can't deny that."

"So how did you two lovebirds meet?"

"Oh I wouldn't ever say we've been lovebirds, Sheena. Certainly not from my side. I'm not really into all that romance crap. We met on the internet, on a website for singles seeking similar things..."

I don't need to ask what kind of website. Of course, I didn't need to ask how they met, either.

"How very modern," I say.

She raises both her eyebrows.

"So who was the guy you smiled to when you walked in?"

She slaps her forehead with the back of her hand.

"Oh, I'm sorry, I should have said. That's just Ray, Kat's husband."

I lower my tone, make it a whisper. "Kat needs to keep that one on a tight leash."

Apinya nearly spits out the milkshake. "Seriously?"

I nod. My face is a blank canvas. "He's handsome. A big guy, too. Bet he could do some damage in the bedroom. Maybe I underestimated her."

Apinya shrugs her shoulders. The smile on her lips is sly. "Guess so."

"There's one main problem with that, though."

"What's that?"

"All good-looking guys are the same. They think they can get away with whatever they want."

Apinya looks at me intently, absorbing this revelation.

"The other problem is that Kat doesn't really do much to stop him getting what he wants, does she?"

We huddle close now, like a half-time team talk. "What do you mean?"

"Kat is a beautiful girl. I'm so jealous of her pretty face. But let's be honest, she carries too much weight, doesn't she?"

Apinya's jaw drops. She can't believe I've said something so outrageous. She is so glad I said it first.

"She can be so frumpy," she says.

"It's not fair on Ray, is it? I bet she didn't look like that when he married her. That's not what he signed up to. It's not fair on him."

Apinya shakes her head, struggles to hide her glee.

"I sense troubled waters ahead," I say.

Apinya smiles. She'd love some drama.

"So what about you?" I ask.

"Me?"

I move aside our milkshakes. I can see her properly now.

"Is the marital bed still as vibrant as when you first got together?"

Apinya gasps. "We do have sex, just not as much as I'd like. We are married. It is hard..."

"He gets hard? That's a good start..."

She puts her hand to her mouth, giggling hysterically. "You know what I mean, Sheena. *Marriage* is hard..."

"Does he ever initiate sex?"

She thinks for a moment and then shakes her head. I look away. Let her sweat.

"In my mind, Apinya, you're the opposite of Kat. You obviously look after yourself for him. You're a wonderful wife..."

"I am..."

"Too good. You're not a mug..."

"What?"

"You need to think of yourself for a change. Be more selfish."

Apinya's eyes widen. "Oh yes?"

"You cook. You clean. You have sex with him. I'd say Bernard has done very well out of this transaction, wouldn't you?"

"Transaction?"

I slap my hand down on the table. Apinya flinches. "Oh come on," I say. "I thought we were being open and honest here. I thought that's the kind of friendship we have now? Bernard paid for you to come here, didn't he? I'm just saying you've fulfilled your side of the bargain..."

"Yes. I have."

"But you want sex and he clearly doesn't. That doesn't sound fair."

"It isn't."

"You have needs, Apinya. All women have needs."

She nods her head. "I have my toys."

"*Toys?* That's pathetic, girl."

"Uh - don't all women have toys, Sheena?"

"Only the women who can't get a man. Listen, if your husband doesn't want sex with you, Apinya, then there are plenty of men who do..."

"I couldn't do that to him..."

She is almost asking. Pleading. She wants reassurance that - *yes* - she can do that.

"It's only fair on Bernard, Apinya. Think how awful he feels for not giving you what you need...."

"Well, I did make him feel pretty bad the last time he didn't perform very well," she says.

I stifle a laugh. An angry Apinya is probably a sight to behold.

"What about Ray? He looks like he could sort you out..."

Apinya gasps. She is *so* melodramatic. Has nobody never suggested she fuck her friend's husband before? What sort of a town *is* this? She vehemently shakes her head.

"Okay. Spoilsport. Leave him for me..."

Her eyes widen before she bursts into hysterics.

"What about that young guy with Ray? He looks like he knows his way around the female body. And let's be fair, his eyes haven't left *your* body since we sat down..."

Apinya glances over. She doesn't say anything, but this kitten looks as though she's just been given her milk.

Yes, I think, considering that chess board.

The pieces are really beginning to slot into the right places.

Monday 12th November 2018

Katherine

My heart sinks when the doorbell rings.

Surely, it is never good news when somebody unexpectedly rings your door? What are the chances that it is - for example - the smiley Postcode Lottery crew, here to tell me I'm now a millionaire? Very *unlikely.* That's why it's called a lottery. I haven't ordered anything, and Ray never does; he worries that I'll eat it. It is probably somebody selling something I really don't want or absolutely can't afford. Or, God forbid, it is somebody delivering terrible news. Is Ray okay?

I'm surprised and relieved when I pull open the door and Sheena stands on my doorstep, blonde hair impossibly shiny and pale skin annoyingly flawless.

"Oh, hi. What are you doing here?"

"Charming."

We both laugh. I stand to the side to let her in. "Sorry! I didn't mean it like that. Just surprised that's all. Didn't realise you even knew where I live. Is something wrong?"

Sheena stretches her long legs out on the sofa. How does she enter somebody else's home and instantly be so relaxed? I *never* feel comfortable in somebody else's home. Do they want me to put my cup on their dining table? Should I take my shoes off? Should I be telling them their home is beautiful? Am I telling them too many times that their home is beautiful?

"Why on earth should something be *wrong*, darling?"

I shrug my shoulders. "Nobody ever visits unless something is wrong."

Sheena purses her lips. I know what she's thinking. *How pathetic does that sound?* I stifle an embarrassed laugh. "Oh God, listen to me! I don't mean *ever*. Just usually..."

Sheena slaps her thigh, laughing. I can't help but notice how long and lean and tanned her legs are. I bite my lip. How does she do it? I never hear her talk about exercising.

I sort out the drinks and then sit down opposite her. I'm not too sure if I'm too close, or too far away. Sheena raises a knee to her chest. She doesn't seem to have any insecurities. I'm aware that - if I dared to look - I could see all the way to the top of her thigh. I focus on her eyes, like a man talking to a woman with big boobs.

"I just came for a chat, Kat. I do so enjoy your company, you know. You have been on my mind a lot recently. This sounds terrible to say, and I'm not sure how to say it, but you do worry me sometimes."

"Worry you?"

"Nothing to worry about. Hold on - that doesn't make sense, does it? It's a few minor things."

"A few? Oh fuck."

We both laugh.

"What was going on with you and that Tess girl?"

I look away. Does she miss *anything?*

"What do you mean?"

"Come on, Kat. Don't treat me like an idiot. Show me some respect."

I can't tell her everything. Just enough. For now. "I don't know. It's probably nothing. Just something she said sounded familiar..."

"You don't trust Ray, do you?"

I tried to say little, but I've said too much. I try to shut the box. "Well, he's a man, isn't he? Can any of them really be trusted?"

Lines form around her lips. This was the right thing to say. "There's one other thing, darling..."

My curved eyebrows tell her to continue.

"I'm just worried about your self-esteem, that's all..."

"*What* self-esteem?"

"Exactly!"

"But why would I have any self-esteem?"

"Oh for *fuck's* sake, Katherine."

I look away now. I don't want Sheena to see my watery eyes, to take in the flush to my cheeks.

"You know the first thing I saw when I met you?" Sheena asks.

I shake my head. My fingers twist.

"Why-oh-why is this beautiful woman hiding?"

I laugh. Is she ridiculing me? It has been years since anybody thought I was beautiful.

"Why is she covering herself up? Why is she making herself look dumpy?"

"Nobody wants to see my flabby body, Sheena. I feel terrible for people when part of me accidentally pops out. I think they'll need counselling..."

My smile fades when I turn and spot her face, utterly expressionless. Surely she knows I'm joking? Surely she knows I'm at least *partly* joking? Sheena shakes her head. What is that look? Disgust? Contempt? I pull my arms over my chest.

"You do know you're gorgeous, don't you?"

"Don't be ridiculous. I used to be nice looking. Not anymore."

She pulls her head back at the sharpness of my words. Her incisors look sharp.

"Why don't you love yourself, Kat?"

"Is this a counselling session?"

She ignores the creases in my cheeks, my attempt to deflect her questions.

"Men like skinny girls," I say. "They might say they don't but they're lying. And what do I care? Ray is the only man that matters, and he likes the way I look..."

"Does he even notice?"

How fucking dare she? I dig my nails into my hand. Am I pissed with her, or am I pissed because she's right?

"So you're a little overweight. If it makes you unhappy, why don't you lose it?"

I blow out air. "If only it was that easy, Sheena. Have you ever heard of comfort eating? I've tried losing weight. I get fed up. And then I wonder why I'm bothering, because nobody gives a shit. So to cheer myself up, I eat some crap. Not surprisingly, this approach doesn't help me lose weight."

Sheena grins. The lines disappear. Her face softens. "I understand comfort eating, girl. But people only do it because they're sad. It's like I said in the river. Things are going to get so much better for you, girl. So we need to work on adding some fun to your world-"

"Again, easier said than done..."

"We'll work on it together. You hear? I'm sorry if I sound harsh, Kat. I've played it over and over in my mind how to raise the issue. I decided it was best I just play it straight. That way you know I'm being honest-"

"I appreciate your honesty," I lie.

Sheena shuffles her body forward. "Seriously though, I think you'll feel fantastic if you lose a bit. We'll get healthy together. I think part of the problem is you haven't given yourself a real reason for losing weight. I think you need a reward, something that makes the effort worthwhile..."

"Such as?"

I look away, but her eyes are so fixed on me I have no choice but to look back.

"I don't care what you say, but Ray doesn't give a shit what you look like. I can just tell from the way you speak about him. And that's wonderful when you think about it, isn't it? He loves you whatever you look like. But there are plenty of guys out there who really do care."

"So what are you saying? I should do it for other guys? Why? And besides, I couldn't live with the guilt..."

"I'm not saying you need to fuck them, Kat. Just get them to notice you. Let them make you feel alive. I assure you, it will make you feel amazing, and if you feel amazing..."

"I won't need to comfort eat."

Sheena gives me a high-five, just like she did in the group. My heart beats fast. I try to ignore it. I know it is because I'm excited. I know it's because I'm turned on by the thought of other men noticing me, by the thought of other men *wanting* me. God, how long has it been since that happened? Nearly thirty years, that's how long. His eyes were all over me when we first met.

"You *are* terrible," I say, slapping Sheena's wrist.

She laughs outrageously. "That's why you love me."

I nod. I'm not sure if I love or hate her, but I

definitely feel *something*. I think I could cope with hate right now so long as it evokes an emotional reaction.

"Let's do this," I say.

Sheena doesn't say anything. She just pulls her body close to mine. I inhale the subtle, feminine perfume.

Both our heads jerk up when the front door opens. The movements down the hallway are so heavy, so rapid, we both flinch. Is somebody breaking in? My fists tighten.

Ray appears in the living room. His wide shoulders barely fit through the door. His fists are balled, his jaw is tight. I could just imagine him saving children from burning fires. *I need a hero.*

"Rose has been arrested," he says.

We both gasp.

"They think she murdered her husband..."

Seven months later

Thursday 6th June 2019

Katherine

The troubled, choppy waters of winter are a distant memory. Now it feels like the tantrum has passed; the river lies quiet and exhausted. Only, I was always told to worry when it was quiet. Why was the world silenced? Was it the quiet before the storm?

Winter has gone. Spring is passing. Summer awaits us.

Pressing my hands down flat, I'm aware of the dryness of the grass. Just months ago, my hands sunk into the dark, sodden mud. My shoes lie abandoned next to my outstretched legs, just metres from the river bank. I wouldn't have done that so long ago, either; who doesn't deplore soggy socks? I consider protecting my face from the sun; don't get carried away, Kat. The breeze cools my face like a fan in a doctor's waiting room. Inevitably, my mind wanders. My memories appear from behind the rock.

My gaze is instinctively drawn to a spot in the water, a circle, maybe two metres wide. That's where it happened. All those years ago. That's why the villagers pity me, the reason they understand my dour demeanour, why they allow my gloominess. You'd be sad if both your parents drowned, years after your older brother was brutally murdered, wouldn't you?

I can pinpoint when everything changed. Ben must have been sixteen, because he was hiding away in his room studying for his O Levels. We assumed he'd pass the exams with flying colours, move on to A Levels before heading off to university. Hooray! I didn't share everybody's excitement. I missed my big brother. His room was my room; I floated between the two. As we moved to Easter and the examinations loomed, however, the colour faded from his sun-deprived cheeks and he demanded we knock at his door before entering. At first I thought he was joking. Okay, Big Brother, that rule can apply to Mum and Dad, but surely it doesn't apply to your little sister? But it did. He was pushing me away, too.

I knocked on his bedroom door one Saturday morning.

"Who is it?"

"Kitty Kat."

"Come in."

The stale air instantly dried my skin. Ben sat on his bed, a text book lying on his lap with his legs outstretched. Perfect rings circled his eyes. When was the last time he had a shower? He pulled at the bed sheet as I perched on the edge of his bed. This no longer felt like our bedroom. He was protective of his territory.

"What's up?" I asked.

"The same old. Studying."

"Why don't you get a break? We could go for a walk. Head into town. Buy some cassettes."

"Maybe later. Just want to get this finished first."

My brother no longer felt so big, he no longer looked

so handsome. He appeared shrunken and dishevelled. I wasn't sure if I'd feel proud or embarrassed walking the streets with him now. My heart dropped. Running out of options, I reached out and tickled him under the armpits. This was our thing. Squirming, he kicked out with his legs. His body shifted to the edge of the bed, up against the wall. The bed sheet moved with him. Something cold grazed against my cold leg. My brother's face froze, like I'd pressed the pause button on the remote control. His eyes pleaded for me not to look down. How could I resist? I looked down.

"What's this?" I asked.

"It's not what it looks like."

I knew what it was, and I knew it was exactly what it looked like. My fingers thumbed the pages of the magazine, bringing a welcome breeze to my hot cheeks. Unclothed men smiled at me. One poor man had a stapled midriff. A couple of pages stuck together.

"How long have you felt like this?" I asked.

"Like what?"

I didn't say anything. My look said it all.

Ben scraped at his knee with a nail. "All my life, I guess. I can't ever remember feeling any different, I know that."

My older brother responded to my outstretched arms. His chest shook against my shoulder. My hand patted his back. This was the first time I ever recall looking after him. It was always the other way around.

"It feels so good that you know," he said. "It feels amazing that you don't mind."

I pulled away so that he looked deep into my eyes. "Why would I mind? What difference does this make? You're still my amazing big brother, Ben."

The dimples in his cheeks reminded me how long it had been since he smiled.

"I just hope Mum and Dad feel the same way."

I looked away. His eyes followed me.

"What is it?" he asked.

"Nothing."

His hand gripped my wrist. I'd forgotten how strong he was. "What *is* it?"

"Why are you telling Mum and Dad?" I asked. "What good will that do?"

"Should I be ashamed?"

"No! Of course not. But you know what they're like. They come from a different generation to us. You know they're deeply religious. Remember the line from Leviticus-"

"'You shall not lie with a male as with a woman; it is an abomination'. I know it all too well, Kat. Do you think the words haven't taunted me all my life?"

"Why don't we just keep this a secret? Between me and you. Just like the old days. Just for now?"

I kissed his lowered head. We did keep it a secret. It wasn't just for now. We never told Mum and Dad. And then - just like that - my brother was gone.

Looking out at the loping, green and brown water now, my mind doesn't rest. The images of twelve years ago are as vivid as if it happens right in front of me. Right now. My parents' outstretched arms flapping above the surface. Their whitened, flat hands slapping down against the water. The life draining from their pinched, anguished faces. The desperate shrieks fading. And then - most deafening of all - the silence.

"Thought I'd find you here."

I flinch. Rocking back and forth, with my arms hugging my knees (pulled tight to my chest), I feel exposed. Not exposed because of my body, but because of the rebounding thoughts in my mind. She must notice my surprise, for she holds up her upturned hands. Her figure casts a shadow over me. The villagers have excitedly gossiped about her over the last six months or so. I know more than anyone that nothing sells better than bad news. I know what they've said; I've heard it often enough, from friends, from the women in the group, from my own fucking husband. I picture her now as the whole town has pictured her - standing over a dead body, gripping a blood-stained knife.

"Rose," I say. "This *is* a surprise."

She quickly replaces her grimace with a forced smile. "I think people are surprised to see me *anywhere* these days. But I am beginning to emerge from behind the shadows, Katherine. Could I take a seat?"

There *are* no seats, just miles and miles of open, bumpy ground. My middle finger circles an imaginary space. I stand up as she sits down; my open arms catch her halfway. This is more awkward than my tear-soaked hug with my brother. I can't remember the last time I hugged this woman - this *friend* - I've known for so many years, but surely the last time her body felt softer, was layered with more cushion?

"It's so good to see you, Rose, so good to see you looking well, you know, all things considered..."

Her silence unrests me. I need to fill the void. My words fire from my mouth.

"Where have you been? I texted you and called you and knocked on your door. I've been worried about you, Rose. We've all been worried about you."

Rose bares her teeth. Who am *I* to seek sympathy?

Her smile is too wide. Her cheeks plump up too much. "*You* were worried. Oh, and Bernard was worried. But come on, we both know the rest of the town weren't worried about me. They were the Ku Klux Klan hunting a black man. They were calling for my head..."

I'm compelled to protest; I know it's pointless. We both know she's right.

"But I'm sorry I didn't get back to you. I just wanted to hide away for a while. Christmas was pretty miserable. January was bleak. I couldn't face the world. Not then, anyway."

"So what happened? You know-"

"They locked me up. Took away the key-"

"But they let you out?"

The words are projectile vomit. Of *course* they let her out. She sits next to me, a free woman. I am not visiting her in a prison cell. Thank goodness.

"They arrested me, but they couldn't charge me. They haven't charged anyone. Yet. It's an open case. They couldn't prove I did it-"

"Why?"

She turns to me. Darkness circles her eyes. Her jaundiced skin is dry and flaky. She has aged since I last saw her. Back then she was the head of our group, leading from the front in her own understated way. At first the group covered her absence. We ran the sessions in her honour. Then we disowned her. She is an outsider now. We only met on Saturday mornings then. Now we meet three times a week. It has all changed. If she ever tried to come back, then she sure as Hell wouldn't be welcomed.

"Because I *didn't* do it, Katherine."

My teeth dig into my upper lip. "I know, I know. I'm sorry. But sometimes - legally - these things aren't so straightforward..."

She knows I've heard the rumours. The police found a return ticket to Bridgend in Rose's house. The ticket was dated just a few weeks before they found her husband's body. Dead. That was something else the villagers had to untangle - Rose had always maintained her husband died *years* ago. If she was capable of lying about that, then what else was she capable of?

"Well, he's dead *now*, isn't he?"

Her smile is mischievous. She knows exactly what I'm thinking. I can't help but laugh.

"They *wanted* to convict me. You better believe it. *They* didn't believe me. They thought I killed him. But they didn't have the evidence. God wouldn't allow it. Listen, I never denied that I'd visited him. But there is no crime in that, is there? He lay dead for weeks. It was impossible to confirm the exact date and time of death. Somebody killed him-"

"What do you think happened?"

Her eyes burn into me like a laser. "*Somebody* killed my husband-"

"Why would anybody kill your husband?"

She looks down, explores the grass, fading yellow. "He wasn't always a good man, Katherine. He wasn't liked by everybody. Heck, *I* didn't like him. But I can't say he deserved to die. Who deserves to be killed?"

My anguished face tells her - hopefully - that nobody deserves to be killed. We sit in silence. I tear at the grass, throw it into the wind. "I'm so sorry, Rose," I say.

"I'm sure *you* don't have anything to be sorry about, Katherine," she says, brown eyes watering.

"No. I guess not. But I'm still sorry. And it *is* good to see you. You *will* keep in contact now, won't you?"

"Oh yes. Of course, dear. You'll be seeing a lot more of me now. Plenty of people will."

Does she intend to return to the group? I should warn her off, for her own good. I decide she doesn't mean that. She *can't* mean that. I don't mention it.

"So what next?"

"I'm going to find out who killed my husband. Who set me up..."

"*And?*"

"And I'm going to take revenge, Katherine," she says. "That's what I'm going to do."

Sheena

We sat in this same dreary cafe, four or five months ago now, the first time she told me.

Apinya's scarf twisted around her neck like a snake on a stick. The winter cold gave her cheeks a healthy glow, offset by the cutest Rudolph nose. The way she carried on, you'd think we were on an expedition to Antarctica. In contrast, I felt like I was experiencing a premature hot flush; the burning radiator next to my thigh made my skin feel dry and flaky. With my chin sunk into my upturned hands, I watched with fascination as Apinya sucked vanilla milkshake through a plastic straw, an excited adolescent keen to tell her best friend that the captain of the rugby team had asked her to the Prom.

"Do you remember that guy we saw in here? Last year. Way before Christmas...?"

Of course I remembered. I planted the seed. Naturally, she is oblivious to this.

I shrugged my shoulders. Narrowed my eyes. "No. Don't think so. There are so many guys around. Frankly, I don't take much notice."

She shrunk; a bird caught in the rain.

"You *know*. He was with Ray, Kat's husband..."

"Oh, *that* guy? Rob*?*"

"Yes! So you *do* remember?"

"Barely." I took a long slurp of milkshake. "What about him?"

Her cheeks plumped and, I swear to God, her tiny, child-like tits perked up. Who needs plastic surgery when you have gossip to share? "I've been seeing him..."

"You dirty little bitch," I said. "I'm so proud of you."

Naturally, she'd been worrying about my possible reaction. She'd worried about all the things she *should* have worried about. *What about your husband? How do you feel about cheating?* I planned to dismiss these thoughts so quickly she'd feel paranoid and ridiculous for even contemplating them. My approval had begun to mean everything to her, like a thousand Likes of an *Instagram* post. It was official. We were now Best Friend's Forever (BFF). Apinya was my Bestie. What the *fuck* was that about? I smiled at the effect I had on her. I could almost sense the relief escape her diminutive body.

"Honey, why are you proud of me? I'm married. I'm cheating. Surely it's not a good thing...?"

I brushed my hand across the table as if to indicate her sacred vows were just surplus red tape. Bureaucratic nonsense. My eyes admiringly scan her figure. "Oh *come* on. Can a woman like you really be expected to stay with just one man?"

Her ruby red mouth widened into a perfect circle. "You dare to be different, Apinya. You're ballsy. I love that. The people in this town - and you know how much I adore them - well, they're just a bit fucking boring, aren't they? They all play perfect happy families. Probably plot their weekly shag - just after Match of the Day - on the calendar with cat pictures pinned to the fridge. How can doing the same things day after day not drive them mad?"

"Well, when you put it like that, Sheena-"

"You've got guts, darling. How many other women in the village can say they're fucking another - *younger* - man behind their husband's back? Not many. Sure, they probably fantasize about it, probably when their husband is actually inside them, but do you think they'll do anything about it? Of course not. They're all too busy staring at the walls, too busy waiting for their lives to drain away. But as I said - you're different, sweetheart. You know what drives you...?"

Her raised eyebrows encouraged me to tell her.

"You're driven by excitement."

Apinya brushed away this compliment with the cutest, dimpliest smile.

That was back in winter. The soggy yellow and brown autumn leaves had dried and were curling at the corners, like a party sandwich left on a plastic plate for too long. Now the daffodils and snowdrops have outstayed their welcome. Summer is already peeking through the clouds, checking to see if it's too early to join the party. When Apinya leans forward, fluttering her painted eyelashes, I know she has another revelation to share. Lucky me!

"Rob is so lovely," she says. "The sweetie bought me flowers from the petrol station the other day. Darling, they were so cheap and pathetic looking - I swear they were already dead - I had to put my hand to my mouth to stop giggling. But at the same time, I nearly cried. How sweet was that? He doesn't have much money - he's always complaining that Ray pays him peanuts and he works so hard - and he chose to spend it on me, to show how much he loves me..."

"*What* did you just say?"

"He loves me, Sheena. I truly think he loves me."

Leaning back in the plastic chair, I glance over both my shoulders. I knew this was coming. It was scripted. Apinya is gorgeous - and *thin* - how wouldn't this boy fall in lust and confuse it for love? And Apinya, bless her, well she doesn't have much going on in that life of hers - of course she'd be flattered by this young man's attention, by his adulation. Regardless, I still need to give the impression I'm absolutely astounded by this latest revelation.

"Listen here, Apinya, and listen good. This is not about falling in love. You have a husband at home for that. Do you hear me?"

Her flinch tells me the message hit home. Nodding, her chin disappears into her neck. Our hierarchy has shifted. Suddenly she is a little girl trying to make sure the school bully doesn't steal her dinner money. "I'm sorry, Sheena. I didn't understand what you meant about having fun with him..."

"Oh you can have fantastic fun," I say. "The whole thing is fantastic, Apinya..."

Her face brightens. I sense her skin tingling. Her nose crinkles like a bunny rabbit. She's confused. "Oh good."

"See it as the dirtiest, most exciting fun you've ever had in your life. See it as a forbidden fruit. Outrageous fun..."

"Oh yes. It really is."

I look away before leaning back in. I whisper my words. "But frankly, dear, this is all getting rather boring now, don't you think?"

"Oh." She tangles her fingers together with such force I worry a bone might snap. She looks down. "Why do you think it's boring?"

I fold my arms across my chest. I'm not wearing a bra, and momentarily I'm struck by the hardness of my nipples. "It's your life. I'm sorry. You shouldn't take any notice of me. Forget I said anything-"

"No, please..."

"You sure?"

"Please."

I release a tired sigh. *Okay, you've forced me into this.* "It's just all this romance talk. Like I said, you have a husband for that-"

"What should I do?"

"Make it more exciting."

"How?"

My darting eyes pretend to check nobody is listening. There are only a few old dears in the cafe, shopping trolleys pulled up close to their tables; I don't think they can hear anything anyway.

"Has anyone seen you together?"

A shadow reappears. "No. God, I hope not. I've been careful."

"Good. Make sure nobody sees you, otherwise this will *all* be ruined. But does he tell Ray anything? And does Ray tell Kat? We both know Kat has a mouth on her-"

"He swears he tells Ray nothing."

Is she convinced by that any more than I am?

"Great. Nobody can know. Apart from Bernard. Of course, he needs to find out at some point..."

"What?"

I wish I could take a picture, hang it on my wall.

"Okay, so this isn't all about me, Apinya. But you know what excites me the most about this little adventure of yours?"

"No. What?"

"The thought of you nearly getting caught, of you

doing it in places where you might just get caught..."

"Oh yes," she says, twirling her long dark locks. "That *is* exciting."

"Can you do me a favour? For me?"

"Yes. Anything."

"Get a thrill out of nearly getting caught. Then get a bigger thrill out of *getting* caught."

She gasps. I could slot a penny in the dimples that appear in her cheeks. "Then what?"

I smile. "Then we'll see just how much that husband of yours really loves you. Then we'll see how much of a man Bernard really is..."

Saturday 14th June 2019

Katherine

Sheena fires compliments at me. Is she on a mission to make my head explode? Stop it. Oh, keep going...

"Can't believe how many men were checking you out tonight, darling. I felt invisible..."

"Don't be silly."

"Honestly! But you *are* looking hot. You always *have,* of course. But now you've lost a few pounds, those wonderful curves have really come out to play..."

We both know I've lost more than a few pounds. My old size eighteen clothes hung from my body like a shapeless tent. I bagged them up and dropped them at the charity shop. It felt like I was offloading not just worn clothes, but an old life. Tonight I sucked in my belly and squeezed into a - wait for it - size 12 top. Twirling in the mirror, I checked from every angle, tried to view it as objectively as I possibly could, through the bitchiest of eyes, and - *definitely* - the top was *not* too tight. My boobs on the other hand, well they looked *fantastic* - soft and round and delightfully big. I imagined him looking at me, shaking his head; I allowed myself a sly smile.

I always knew, deep down, that I could lose weight. It didn't make sense that I couldn't. I'd never tried. I've always worried what he'd think. What others would think. They'd no longer view me with those sympathetic eyes. He always worried about me drawing too much attention to myself. It was part of the plan. Logically, if I moved more, and ate less, something remotely like I did in my late teens, then I'd stop expanding and start shrinking. There has been no magic formula. No scientific eating plan. I've just cut out the treats (which I realised I didn't really crave after all), eaten smaller portions, and walked, first a mile or two every day and now some days up to ten miles. It's not just about the weight, though; it's about the attitude.

I no longer worry what he'd think. Now I think *I'll show you.*

My bare forearm is wet and clammy against the burger bar table. Everything here is slippery, including the freshly mopped floors. Outside, the orange street lights flicker in the receding darkness. A few months ago I would have been snug in my bed like the rest of civilised society. Within a few hours the birds will wake, and shortly afterwards alarm clocks will ring across the country, officially bringing in a new day. We're the only group here. There are no other females. The other tables are occupied with singletons, some nursing sore heads after a night out; others with crumpled bodies that look like they have nowhere else to go.

I have a home. A bed. A husband.

Sheena sucks a fry into her mouth as elegantly as if it were a cigar; she could so easily belong in a black and white movie. "I really adore this new you," she says.

My cheeks widen. My dimples are probably on display. "Thank you," I say. "Although I didn't really realise there *was* a new me."

She looks away. She thinks I'm fishing for another

compliment, and she's all out of those. "The thing is, though, I'm still not sure whose side you're on..."

She has struck a match. Now she is ready to throw it on the fire.

I turn to Apinya for support. Why do I bother? They are as thick as thieves these days. Apinya only repeats things Sheena has already said, or thoughts Sheena planted in her mind. They've stripped off the sheep's clothing; now the two wolves circle their prey, noses pressed forward, foaming at the mouth.

"*Side?*"

"Are you with us, or with them?"

I know who the 'us' is. We started meeting on Wednesday evenings before Christmas. Now we meet on Monday evenings, too. Unless you have a good reason for not being there, you're excluded after missing two meetings in a row. Why? It is all about commitment. We are a family, and we work on total, unequivocal trust. Sheena is testing this trust and commitment with me now.

This morning's meeting was an eye-opener. After welcoming the ladies, I quickly retreated to my seat at the back of the room, allowing Sheena to take centre stage. This, I've gathered, is her preferred role. Sheena bypassed any greetings, forfeited any niceties.

"We all trust each other don't we, ladies?"

The room responded to the affirmative.

"I trust you ladies with my life," Sheena said.

"Me too," Apinya chipped in. A few women raised their eyebrows.

"Prove it to me. I'd like one of you to share your darkest secret. Something you wouldn't dare share with the outside world. I yearn for you to test just how much you trust the women sat in the room. Do you view them as your family?"

Predictably, silence filled the room. I examined my fingernails. I suspect I wasn't the only one. From the corner of my eye I spotted a raised hand.

"Yes, Moira?"

"I slept with my husband's brother," she said.

"Jesus Christ, woman," Apinya yelled. "You don't mess about do you, sister?"

A few women exchanged glances. Moira is a sixty-something-year-old grandmother who sometimes passes idle minutes by knitting. "I know it sounds shocking," she said.

Sheena's face remained expressionless. That one isn't easily shocked. If anything, her eyes softened. "These things happen, Moira. We all make mistakes. Only the self-righteous, the deluded or the judgemental would be shocked by your brave revelation."

"We'd only just got married-"

"The early years are often the most difficult-"

"No, you don't understand, dear. We'd *literally* just got married. I slept with him at the reception after the ceremony-"

"Holy Mother of God, Moira, you're some sort of freak!"

Sheena's narrowed eyes silenced Apinya's outburst. I had to press my legs together to stop myself from wetting my knickers. I daren't look at Moira for fear I might burst into hysterics.

"I never wanted to marry him. A dark cloud suffocated me when I walked down the aisle. I wanted to run away, but I didn't want to humiliate him. So I went through with it. My brother-in-law saw that I was upset, and he consoled me. And one thing led to another..."

"Where were you, Moira?"

"In the cloakroom."

I put my hand over my mouth.

"And how is your relationship now?"

"I'm happily married, thank you. I haven't looked at another man in a desiring way since the day after my wedding day. Well, maybe Gerard Butler, but I'd say that's perfectly natural, wouldn't you...?"

After Moira's contribution, plenty of other ladies raised their hands. Whatever my personal thoughts about Sheena's approach, I can't deny that the women in the group trust her unquestioningly.

Dipping my middle finger into an opened sachet of tomato ketchup, I suck it into my mouth, savouring the sugar (God, maybe I *have* missed the sugar rush?). Gives me some time to think. Sheena doesn't know it, but I do have my own tricks; they just aren't as obvious. Sometimes I even repeat questions back whilst my mind works out the answer.

"Who is '*us*'?"

"The group. The women."

I tut. Why didn't you *say* that?

"I'm with the women," I say. I hold my voice. Hold her eye. "I've always been on their side. I was the founding member of the group, remember. With Rose, of course."

We don't really mention her name anymore.

"I've never been quite sure why you joined the group," Sheena says.

"Don't I have enough reasons?"

Sheena glances at her reflection in the window. Even after hours of partying, after hours of drinking, she still looks flawless. Apinya's open-mouthed face moves back and forth, back and forth, like she is watching the final at Wimbledon.

"You know and I know that, if anything happened to any woman in the group, each and every woman would support the other with no questions asked. Would you?"

"Of course."

"I really want to test your commitment to the group, Kat. I don't doubt any of the others. Do you know that I've been mingling with the men in the pubs-"

"What? Why?"

"To find out what they're talking about. To check what the potential threats are. And you know why? Not for me. For the group."

"Which men?"

"The usual suspects. Dave. Geraint-"

"Ray? Bernard?"

Sheena smiles. "Sometimes. They tend to be less regular, don't they? Although Bernard does appear to be morphing into his idea of what it means to be a bloke. So tell me. Will you be on our side against *all* men?"

I flinch. Of course. Sheena doesn't really give a damn if I despise a drunken leach in The Oak, or if I scowl at the postman; Sheena wants assurance I'll support her in favour of Ray, in favour of my own husband.

"I'm married to a man, Sheena. A man I love. How can I be against *all* men?"

Sheena releases a long, deep sigh, like she's exhausted from all this nonsense. "We've been through all of this," she says.

I turn to Apinya. Straightening her back, she seems to expand, both in stature and self-righteousness. "I'm married too, remember. And I think all men are fucking savages."

Sheena's tapered eyes suggest she doesn't believe Apinya any more than I do.

"How can you say that about your husband?" I ask.

"Bernard is just like all the others. Only he is too weak to act on his carnal instincts. He is a hypocrite. The worst kind."

"Then why don't you just leave him...?"

She shoots me a look. I keep an eye on her fists; they're rolled into miniature balls. Apinya is tiny, but I expect she could be vicious.

"Listen," Sheena says. "Let's not argue. We're on a night out..."

Apinya folds her arms across her chest, sinks her chin into her neck. I know what she's thinking - you started it.

"I would like to prove my point, though. Just not in this way. We're best mates. We shouldn't argue. Shall we have some fun? Play a little game?"

Apinya springs to life, like she's been stabbed with a needle. "I love games," she says. "And fun."

"It's been a long night," I say. "All I can think of right now is my bed."

"Don't be a chicken," Apinya says.

My feathers ruffle. Sheena spots it.

"Dare to play our game, Katherine?"

I do *not* want to play the game. Or, maybe I *do*?

"Let's play."

Sheena nods her approval. Apinya is a rabbit on coke. "Who's first?" she asks. "Can I go first? *Pl-ease*..."

"Kat's first." Sheena's unflinching eyes fix on mine.

I shrug my rounded shoulders, deliberately

indifferent.

"Sure. Whatever you want."

Sheena gazes around the plastic restaurant, searching for something that takes her interest. Her smile tells me she's found something.

"See that guy there?" She points with her middle finger. "Go up to him. Be the sexy minx you've been all night..."

"And..?"

"Dance with him, girl. *Provocatively-*"

"*Sexily,*" Apinya adds, clapping her hands like a sea lion.

"Yes. Sexily." Sheena winks at Apinya. "We both know how sexy you can dance, Kat..."

"What on earth for*?*"

Sheena doesn't answer. She just smiles.

My clicking heels trot like a horse on match day. Drunken bodies unravel from their slumber. There is something for them to see.

Me. How long has it been?

"Go, girl!" Apinya shouts.

Blue, watery eyes look up at me. Judging by the lines on his forehead and the grey peppering his hair, he is probably in his forties. God, that's *my* age. Not bad looking, though. Bending at the knees and shuffling my hips, I resemble a surfer.

Sheena's shouting interrupts my momentum. "I said *sexy,* goddamn it! Dance like you mean it. Get closer to him!"

With my thighs (and my crotch) inches from the edge of the table, the guy's smile broadens. He scans my body - up and down, up and down - zoning in on my curves. He isn't offended by my attention. Far from it. He likes what he sees. He thinks I'm sexy. I half expect him to slip a ten dollar note inside my cleavage. Now, this *is* fun. This is what I would have done thirty years ago.

I shuffle back when the man stretches out his arm, attempts to touch my thigh.

"Hands off her, you beast...!"

The voice isn't mine. The room spins. I press my hand against the smooth edge of the table to keep my balance. What is going on? Sheena's finger stabs against the man's chest.

"You dirty little bastard!" she says.

The man holds his hands up, protests his innocence, says he thought I wanted him to touch me. Saliva coats his mousy, foamy teeth. He says sorry, again and again and again.

Back at our table, it takes a few minutes for the excitement to die down.

"Prove our point...?" Sheena asks, smiling wolfishly.

I slump in my seat. I'm not sure *what* she proved.

"I'm not really interested in that guy," Sheena says.

"Who *are* you interested in?" I ask, knowing the answer. Apinya's broadening smile indicates *she* knows what's coming, too.

"That darling husband of yours."

I blow out air. "Not *this* again."

"We all know something happened with Tess, that sweet, young girl that came to one of our meetings. How old was she again? Twenty? Twenty-one? You said as much yourself. That time I came round to your house, when Ray came home and told us about-"

"I really didn't say that."

"I'm not saying it's a bad thing. It *excites* me..."

"What...?"

"We're all doing our bit, Kat. Apinya here has her own little challenge..."

"And you...?"

"I told you I have my own game going on with a few guys from the pub."

"With *our* husbands-"

"Not just them."

"What exactly is it you want me to do with Ray?"

Sheena leans forward, like a shark with an open mouth, teeth bared. "I want you to see if he does have another, more exciting side..."

"And if he does...?"

"Happy days, Kat."

"And if he doesn't...?"

Sheena glances at Apinya. "Then life is passing you by. And I don't think you should let it..."

"Just what are you saying?"

"If your husband isn't prepared to give you any fun, Katherine, then I think you should seek some elsewhere..."

Glancing away, I'm sure I spot a smile on my face in the reflection.

Saturday 22nd June 2019

Bernard

Apinya was at her group when she told me. Coincidence? In retrospect, of course she timed it that way. She waited for her to leave the house, waited until the coast was clear. I remember the day. The windows rattled from the wind outside. Rain spitted against my luscious green lawn. My jaw dropped when I opened the door, for it *did* feel like I'd seen a ghost. She appeared on my doorstep like a drowned rat. Her body was huddled together so she looked shrunken. Her darkened skin looked ingrained with dirt.

"Rose! I thought-"

"They let me out, Bernard."

I was the first person she told. That meant something. She'd hidden for so long, like a fugitive running from the law (which, ironically, she *had* just escaped from).

She slipped past me, into the hallway and through to the kitchen, without waiting to be asked in. Following her metaphorical tail, I found her in the kitchen, boiling the kettle. Was she moving in? Rose perched on the edge of the sofa, her sizeable buttocks hanging over the edge; she rocked back and forth, staring into space. I had questions to ask her - of *course* I had questions to ask her - and I craved answers but, right at that moment, she looked so delicate, so *incapable,* I managed to tie my tongue and keep quiet.

"You're a good man, Bernard," she said.

I didn't know what to say. I didn't feel good. I felt useless.

I remained silent. We barely exchanged a word for the twenty or so minutes she stayed. Whilst, for me, there was an air of awkwardness, it did feel appropriate.

Rose finished her coffee. Took both cups and saucers to the sink. Washed and drained them. "Can I come again?" she asked, turning to me, heading for the door. "Have another chat?"

I reassured her that she could come any time. And she has come, every week, always coinciding with Apinya's Saturday meeting.

I told Apinya about that first visit. I haven't told her about all of the others.

"What did you let her into the house for?" she asked.

"Why wouldn't I? She's my friend."

Apinya shook her disbelieving head. "You crazy? My husband is crazy. She was arrested for killing somebody. Murder! What is to say she won't kill you?"

I didn't mean to laugh. Apinya's eyes quickly quietened me. "She didn't kill anybody. They let her go, remember..."

"Only because they couldn't prove she did it. They couldn't prove OJ Simpson killed anybody. They haven't arrested anybody else, have they? The killer is still out there. That poor, dead man. And Rose remains the prime suspect, Bernie..."

I left it there. Apinya is a stubborn mule. Especially so when she has a point.

This morning Rose greets me with a hug. She has lost weight, but it feels healthy. The combed hair and the perfumed scent indicate she is (hopefully) looking after herself.

"My usual please, Bernard."

Passing the steaming cup of coffee to her (milk and two sugars), I sit down and wait. She, on the other hand, sits and slurps. I raise an encouraging eyebrow.

"I've been following her," she says. "I've been piecing together her movements, getting familiar with her habits."

I tighten my lips. I think back to what Apinya said. First, she waits for Apinya to leave the house, and now she is following Sheena. Are these the actions of a sane woman? There is another reason my teeth grate together, however. Has Rose spotted me in The Oak with Sheena?

At first I mocked the control Sheena had on Dave and Geraint. They listened to her every word like she was a Messiah sent to correct the world. Why else would such a beautiful woman land unexpectedly in our dreary town? Ray, on the other hand, sat rigid in her presence, with his flat, calloused hands planted firmly against his thighs. What was he thinking? Was he fighting some urges? I stopped mocking Dave and Geraint when Sheena leaned closer to me one evening, her stocking-clad leg grazing against my knee, and whispered that I was looking handsome tonight. I'm certain she felt my leg shake, the wooden table rattle. I cursed myself for the effect she had on me.

Remove the fake, superior pretences and I was just like all of the other men.

"I know she visited him after I did," Rose says. I blink away my spiralling thoughts.

"So you have evidence she did?"

"Not evidence. I just know."

We've had this conversation before. At first it was muffled, like she was thinking aloud, struggling to control what was bouncing around in her mind. Now she is convinced. It is an obsession. Personally, I'm not convinced it is a healthy obsession; I fear where it could end. We all have unhealthy obsessions, don't we? I know how deadly they can be.

"Have you been to the police, like I told you to?"

Her grunt is dismissive. She didn't respond when I first suggested it; her turned back told me everything."They don't want to know, Bernard. They want *me* to be the killer. I'm convenient. They want to stick a square peg into a round hole-"

"I'm confident that's not how detective investigations work, Rose-"

"And besides, like you said, they need evidence. Even if they did listen, I have nothing tangible to tell them, merely theories and my gut feeling. They'll think I'm a crazed conspiracy theorist, like that David Dyke-"

"Ike..."

"That's what I said. Anyway, it is irrelevant that I just happen to be right..."

"Can you *get* evidence? Maybe find some rail tickets? Like they did with-"

Her constricted eyes cut me off. "I don't think she'd leave rail tickets hanging around, do you? I only did because I had nothing to hide. It wasn't a mistake, like the rest of the town seems to think."

"What about CCTV? Maybe footage of her at both train stations?"

"I thought about that, Miss Marble. But I don't even know what day she travelled. They couldn't confirm the date and time of death. And besides, she could have travelled some other way. And, who knows? I'm not saying she actually held the knife. She may have hired somebody else to do it..."

I try to keep my face neutral. Placid. I *want* to tell her that she is answering her own questions; what good would that do? It is a lost cause. Move on. She never liked the man anyway, but he *was* her husband, and besides, we both know this isn't really about him.

"Do you know what I'm going to do?"

I look at her. My blank expression tells her I don't know.

"I'm going to hunt her down myself..."

She has implied this before. This time, I believe her.

"The thing is, I may need some help, Bernard..."

I take the empty cups to the kitchen. Standing at the sink, my hands feel cold, they feel numb.

I have no idea if I feel this way from fear, or from excitement.

Katherine

"Somebody looks nice tonight," I say.

A crimson flush crosses my husband's freshly-shaved cheeks. He brushes a hand down his ironed shirt. Raising both eyebrows, he flashes a Colgate smile.

"Not *you*," I say. "The barman that served us."

I playfully slap his arm as the colour drains and the smile disappears. "I'm joking. You look better than nice. You look edible."

His nod is uncertain and suspicious. Do I really not pay him any compliments? Just how much did I change over the years? Just how far have we drifted? Were we ever that close? Where do the secrets end, and the truth begin? Ray has never told me that he sometimes drinks with Sheena, but then, I guess I've never asked. I wonder whether he's ever imagined her when he's with me?

"So what do you think about the group meeting three times a week? I'll cut back if you like."

I can't cut back, of course. He doesn't know this. Another secret.

"I don't mind," he says. "Gives me a bit of space."

Space to go to the pubs with your mates, I think. Rob has been joining them, apparently. They've become quite close over the last few months, despite the age difference. And Bernard has become quite the regular, too. How outrageous is that! God, I think, looking at my husband from across the table, Sheena has no idea how keen I am to complete her challenge, how desperate I am to break free of this life of tedium and drudgery.

"Are you going to let me taste you tonight?" I ask. "Back at the hotel room?"

He says nothing. His smile tells me in no uncertain terms that he will. Leaving my black heel on the floor, I stretch out my leg, snake my foot along his calf.

"I'm not the only one who thinks you look nice tonight," I say.

His eyes narrow. He suspects I'm playing a game. "*What?* What *are* you talking about?"

"The waitress. Didn't you see the way her eyes lingered? The way she smiled...?"

"That's her job, Kat."

"If you say so. Not sure she learnt those looks on some customer service course."

"You jealous?"

"Far from it. It excites me."

"*Excites* you?"

My smile widens. My foot circles his knee. His legs part maybe just an inch wider. His fingernails dig into the meticulous white table cloth.

"Why?"

"I've always liked the thought of you with another woman, Ray. I guess you could call it a fantasy. I think about it when I play with myself. But maybe I'm tired of living life in my mind? I'd like to watch. Maybe join in..."

"What the *fuck* is going on with you...?"

I release a long sigh. "Don't you ever get bored?"

"With?"

I hold out my upturned hands. "With *this*. With

everything. With everyday life."

He looks down. Examines the fingernail. "I have a beautiful wife I love. The most fantastic grown-up boy I could ever ask for. My own business. Friends. Isn't that pretty good, Kat? I'm content. I thought you were, too..."

"I get all that. And you're right. Of course you're right. But don't you ever want more?"

"More?"

"Don't you ever crave excitement?"

Ray looks away. Examines the room. My foot massages his muscled thighs. All the other dignified diners remain completely unaware.

"If I gave you a pass to do whatever you want, with whoever you want, maybe just for one night, would you take it...?"

My husband explores my face for clues, searches for a punch line. "No. I wouldn't."

I pull back my neck and laugh. "Of course you would."

My husband's face remains blank.

"Why wouldn't you?"

"You're all I need, Kat."

We both look up.

"How was your meal?"

The waitress gathers our plates. She is probably in her twenties. There is a pink streak in her long blonde hair that falls to her slim waist. My husband dares to hold her eyes. His ears burn red. "It was lovely. Thank you."

Her smile is bright. Her eyelashes flutter. "Care for dessert?"

"Oh I'm sure my husband would love *something* for dessert."

My laugh is suggestive. I massage my husband's

crotch as I discuss the dessert options with the young, pretty waitress.

"Don't blame you," she says. Her look passes from me, lingers on my husband. "Sometimes you need to be naughty, don't you?"

My eyes follow her backside as she leaves to get some menus. I turn back to my husband.

"You don't want me to ask her to come back with us?"

He shakes his head. His restless hands and his watery, hungry eyes tell me that he'd *love* me to ask her to come back with us, but I also know he wouldn't do it. My husband is too faithful, too doting.

"Okay. But you promise me something?" I ask.
"Yes?"

"Promise me you'll take me back to the hotel room and fuck my brains out?"

My husband stands up. My feet drop to the floor. He smiles. "Now *that* I can promise."

Sunday 23rd June 2019

Sheena

Even though the rules society imposes on us are amended on Sundays, it is still, by any stretch of the imagination, a reasonable time to call. Still, I lie naked on my bed, the duvet rolled in a ball next to me.

I'm aware of the vibration on the bedside table next to me. Still, my eyes focus on the still blankness of the ceiling. My arms remain in a straight line by my side. The phone stops vibrating. I smile from the corner of my mouth.

I know who it is. I'll let her phone back. She will. She desperately wants to let me know what happened.

Minutes later, when the phone rings again, I stretch out my arm. Put the receiver to my ear. Don't even bother to check the screen.

"Hello, my darling," I slur. "How did it go?"

"It didn't work."

She breathlessly told me about her plans after yesterday's meeting. It took quite a while for the women to disperse, for the room to empty, for us to be alone. Excited chatter echoed around the room. We needed to drag chairs from the kitchen to seat the twenty-two attendees. I stood at the front of the room, in my element, talking to the masses.

"We're all agreed that we do not share anything we

discuss in this room with anybody outside of this room?"

"Absolutely. Agreed."

"And what should you do if you can't commit to that vow?"

"We should stand up, walk out of the door and keep on walking."

"Good," I said. "So we can trust each other."

With my head bowed and my hands clasped behind my back, I paced up and down in a straight line. "That's the difference between us and them..."

Closing my eyes, I sensed them glancing at each other. A woman on the front row - I'm not sure which one - plucked up the courage to ask what I referred to.

"*They* can't be trusted. You never know what they're scheming..."

The women muttered their hearty agreement.

"But you need to *try* and find out what they're up to, what they're planning..."

"How do we do that?" Apinya asked.

We have an unwritten agreement that Apinya asks probing questions when she suspects nobody else will. This was probably the first time she got it right, bless her.

"You should check their phone on a regular basis. I say regular because they'll delete most of the messages because they're worried you'll read them. Check for suspect names in the contact list. Is your husband getting all flirty with a George? Don't worry, your husband probably hasn't turned gay. George is most likely a Sharon or a Tracey..."

A couple of ladies released a knowing chuckle."But I don't know the password on his phone."

"Me neither. God knows I've tried enough times. The bastard didn't choose our wedding anniversary or my birthday, I know that."

The laughter spreads.

"Do they sleep with their phone next to them?" I asked.

"He's glued to it. He'd much rather sleep with his phone than with me."

A few others nodded.

"Wait until they're asleep and then tap the screen with their thumb. You won't need the password that way."

I allowed this to sink in. The women agreed that it was a fantastic idea. However did you think of that? I jerked my head up; one of the ladies on the front row flinched.

"But don't go thinking they won't try exactly the same thing. People are, by nature, possessive and paranoid. Katherine, you'll back me up on this, won't you, darling?"

Kat, staring at the dusty floor, nodded her head.

"Just leave your phone around for them to pick up. Don't put a lock on it..."

Predictably, a few women appeared aghast at this suggestion. "I don't want my husband checking my messages!"

"Let him," I replied. "After all, he won't find anything. That way, he'll trust you more than ever."

"He'll find plenty on my phone," one of the loudest protested. "And not just all the topless photos!"

With my hands on my hips, I thrust my pelvis forward. "Delete all messages. Delete all provocative photos. Delete anybody on your contact list who shouldn't be there. We discuss everything here. If you make private plans, then do it in person. Don't leave any traces. We can't afford the risk of ruining what we've got going here. Are we able to make this commitment for the sake of the group? Speak up if you're not."

I looked around the room. I could have stuck an apple in the open mouths. None of them dared utter a word.

"I'm in. Makes sense to me. If it's for the good of the group."

I looked up at Kat's smiling face. My lips parted. Apinya added her commitment. The rest quickly followed; none of them wanted to be the last to commit.

Once the room emptied, a flushed Kat told me about the posh restaurant she'd booked, about the hotel room, about her plans to seduce her own husband.

I don't say anything to her now. I let seconds pass. Ensure that all she can hear down the line is my slow, steady breathing.

"How hard did you try, Kat?"

"Believe me, I tried. Pretty much offered another girl on a plate for him. Offered him a threesome. That's a male fantasy, right? She was serving us at the time."

"Did he know you were genuine, darling? Or did he think it was a trick? Did he think you were trying to con him into saying he'd sleep with another woman? These men are shrewd."

She thinks about this. Problem is, *she* isn't sure she was genuine. I'm not sure dear Katherine is aware of her limitations, is aware of just how far she has progressed. Before I met her, she was a frumpy housewife. Does she really envisage that she has suddenly transformed into a sex vixen? What would she have done if her husband upped and left the table to go shag some other woman? Realistically, did she *want* him to fail her challenge?

"I made it pretty clear, Sheena."

Clipping at a fingernail, I let her know I'm distracted, that she does *not* have my full attention.

"Did you book the hotel room, like you said you would?"

"Yes."

My friend has impressed me. If what she says is true - and, let's be honest, she wouldn't lie to *me* - then she really has come a long way. My hand drifts. The tips of my fingers circle my pink, stiffening bud. "So did he take you back to the room and fuck you, darling?"

There is a gulp down the line. "Yes. Harder than he's fucked me for years, Sheena..."

My fingers pinch harder. "Then the thought of fucking another woman *did* excite him, Kat. He was probably thinking about her when he was inside you. You realise that, don't you?"

I hear her throat tighten. I wonder whether this thought repulses her or - more likely - thrills her.

"Maybe-"

"So he is like all the other men, Kat..."

"No. He has urges. We *all* do. But I offered an opportunity to him on the plate and he didn't do anything about it, did he?"

Of course he didn't. Nobody had a lower expectation of Ray than I did.

"So what are you going to do about it now?" I ask.

"That's the thing. I've made a decision-"

"Decision?"

"It's like you said."

"Remind me what I told you, dear. Sometimes I have

an awfully short memory..."

"Put it this way - part of me was relieved when he didn't take the bait-"

"And another part?"

She blows out air. "Another part was gutted. It made me realise, Sheena, that I really *am* bored. I'm brain-numbingly bored. I don't think I can keep living like this for much longer..."

"So I repeat my question. So what are you going to do about it now?"

"What you told me to do, Sheena. I've decided that if my husband doesn't want any fun, then I'm going to find my *own* excitement..."

"Good girl," I say. "I'm proud of you."

I end the call just as my hand drifts lower down my body.

Wednesday 3rd July 2019

Bernard

Hippocrates said that walking is man's best medicine - well, for me, his prognosis is spot on.

Walking helps me think. That doesn't tell the full story because - *God* - I don't need any help thinking. I dissect and ruminate and reflect about anything and everything - my dead dad, Apinya, and now, more and more frequently, about Rose. What I should say is that walking allows me to think logically, to crystallise my thoughts, to actually find solutions rather than more and more problems.

Apinya's lips tasted so deliciously sweet when I kissed her goodbye; I was tempted to stay a while longer, but she ushered me out of the door. A pleasant chill filled the air when my sturdy walking boots dug into the grass at the bank of the river, but as the miles passed my calves pinched and I held up my hand to protect my eyes from the sun. Looking down at the village from the peak of the mountain, I was struck, once again, by a single, comforting thought - *does any of this really matter?*

The drawn curtains of our house bat away the sun. Shutting the front door behind me, the coolness in the hallway soothes my sun-kissed cheeks. My body deflates as it disappears within the depths of the sofa. The eerie silence tells me that Apinya must be out.

*The magic thing about the home is that it feels good to leave,
and it feels even better to come back.* Again, this is true of me.
I love my home - my palace - but I appreciate it even
more when I've gone out and come back.

I didn't deliberately deceive Apinya into thinking that
my beloved wife, Diane, had passed away; I just never
corrected her. Written words are often misconstrued,
aren't they? Apinya asked if I was still married; I said
my wife was no longer around. Strictly speaking, we
were still married at the time - the divorce papers were
still in transit. Apinya flooded me with sympathies; I
didn't push them away. Frankly, I didn't have the
courage to tell her I returned home from the office one
day to find a Dear John note left on the kitchen table.
Diane had already packed her bags and moved in with
her personal trainer. It went without saying, of course,
that Mr *Fucking* Motivator had younger, bigger muscles.
Diane really *had* upgraded to a newer, superior model.
The main reason I didn't correct Apinya, though, was
because I was ashamed to tell her I didn't do anything
about it. I didn't fight to keep my wife. By now Apinya
must know that Diane is still alive, of course; we've just
never discussed it. It gives me hope, in a way. Apinya
must have a heart - somewhere - for allowing me to
hang the family portrait on the living room wall.

What was that?

Despite the clarity of my thoughts this morning, I
haven't been able to shrug off this feeling of impending
doom. I fretted that something was going to happen to
Rose; she's certainly keen to venture into the lion's den.
Maybe it isn't Rose? Maybe it's me?

My eyes rise to the ceiling. What was that noise? Is
Apinya actually in? Maybe she's just having a sleep. But

then, she never takes daytime naps. My forehead furrows. This doesn't feel right. I push my hands flat down against the sofa. I'm already on tiptoes as my socks sink into the thick, carpeted living room floor. I move out into the hallway, flinching when the pine stairs creak. With each passing step, as I move higher, the noise upstairs grows louder. Clearer.

Standing in the hallway, I consider scurrying back down the stairs, a mouse disappearing into his hole. Nobody knows I'm here. I could pretend I never was. My father's crinkled face invades my mind. He shakes his head.

I push open the bedroom door. *Our* bedroom door.

Somehow, I'm not shocked. It is *exactly* what I expected.

My wife has a house guest, of course. Only, he isn't here for tea, biscuits and a chat. This isn't a fucking coffee morning. My wife's knees dig into the silk, burgundy bed sheet, freshly washed on the weekend. Her guest has made himself at home - he is buried deep inside my wife from behind. Apinya jerks her head to the side. Judging from her flushed cheeks, she is getting quite the workout. Her quivering upper lip says nothing. Her wide, unblinking eyes are (have I *possibly* got this right?) accusing. Turning her head forward, she no longer looks at me, but instead stares at her reflection in the mirror. She doesn't utter a word.

Her deep, unadulterated moan tells me I've outstayed my welcome.

I turn. Leave the bedroom. *Our* bedroom.

I grip the wooden banister as I climb down the stairs, threaten to rip it from its hinges. I plunge back into the sofa; this time my face sinks into my upturned hands. I can hear myself, though I'm desperate not to. I'm

quietly sobbing, just like I used to in the privacy of my
bedroom after Dad scolded me for being weak, for
being too feminine. When I remove my hands, my
vision is blurred and dotted; it takes a while for the
portrait on the wall to stop moving from side to side.
Maybe I'm imagining Diane's pitying look? That isn't
sympathy. That look says oh you poor, pathetic old
man; no wonder I left you.

I spring from the chair. Stomp towards the back of
the house. Unlock the garage door. Turn on the light,
introducing a whole realm of possibilities. I start
opening and slamming cupboards, pulling and shutting
drawers. I'm not sure what I'm looking for until I find
it. Perfect.

I know there is a smile on my face as the palm of my
hand massages the smooth, angled length of the
wooden baseball bat.

My dad always condoned me for being shit at sport;
he said it was a waste of money buying me a bat if I was
never going to use it. Well, fuck you, old man! I'll make
sure you get your money's worth from the purchase,
alright?

The house shakes like an elephant on a rampage as I
charge up the stairs. This time, I don't hover in the
hallway like some sort of dirty voyeur. Stretching out
my leg, I kick open the bedroom door.

I recognise the young man (and *he* is young, probably
half my age. Why do they *do* this to me?). He works
with Ray. Is it Rob? Who is this punk? I really don't
care. He slowly turns. Casually. I'm an irritant. I'm
interrupting him. Getting in the way of his session.
With my wife.

He starts taking me seriously when his eyes drop and

he takes in the baseball bat, firmly gripped in my right hand. I bare my teeth. Raise my eyebrows. His jaw literally fucking drops. He removes his hands from my wife's snake hips like suddenly she's contaminated, holds them up in the air instead to show he means no harm. The man with his dick in my wife means no harm? I shake my head to tell him that simply won't do, squire.

I turn to Apinya. The colour has seeped from her cheeks. Her brow is covered with another layer of sweat. She fucking says something *now*.

"No, Bernard! Don't do it!"

And I *don't* do anything for a while. I just stand there, in the middle of the bedroom, my legs slightly parted (not as wide as my slut wife), my feet pressed hard against the floor. I just let the lovely couple wait. I let them suffer. Let them squirm.

The wooden baseball bat drops to the floor with a loud crank. It bounces a few times before rolling on the laminate floor, rests against the fitted wardrobe, away from harm. Both bodies on the bed deflate. Both bodies on the bed release an audible sigh of relief.

It's all over.

I take two rapid steps forward. My clenched fist strikes the man on the side of the jaw. His open mouth spits out blood and dirty phlegm. A woman screams. I take a handful of hair and pummel the man with a barrage of uppercuts. Grabbing his kicking feet, I pull him off the bed and then drag him down the wooden staircase, his bruised head banging against each step.

I sink into the sofa for the third time. For the first time, though, I have a bloodied, unconscious body lying at my feet. I glance at Diane on the wall; I can't help but notice her smile. I push away my father's image from my mind, but I know he is no longer embarrassed, he is no longer ashamed.

Pulling my phone from my pocket, I dial a number. The voice on the other end of the line is deep. Confused. I don't think I've ever called him before; I don't belong in his social circle, not really. I'll always be an outsider in one way or another. I fire out the words quickly and concisely. I ask if he can help.

There is a pause, and then he says yes. He can help.

"Thank you, Ray," I say.

The line goes dead.

Thursday 4th July 2019

Rose

After months living like a prisoner within my own home, these days I like to be outdoors, hitting the streets, listening and watching. It keeps me busy. It keeps me sane. I know my enemies. I *think* I know my friends.

The events unfold almost in slow motion; clearly he is oblivious to what is about to happen. It is like observing a motorway collision from six cars back.

Pushing open the door of his dusty, white van, he slams his crusty boot down on the pavement. He turns around. Stops dead. I feel like popping out my tongue. Surprise! Curly, salt and pepper hairs break free from the cut of his vest, just like a young Sean Connery. His five o'clock stubble came out to play before lunch. His eyes look round, like he is weighing up his options. He realises it is too late. I've nearly walked into him. *Oh, young man!* I may have lost a few pounds (the wrinkled loose skin hanging from my neck reminds me of a turkey), but you can't miss me from fifty yards away, let alone five.

"Rose," he says. Lines stretch from the corners of his mouth; they're not sure which direction to head.

"Ray."

The poor man isn't sure whether to embrace me or

shake my hand; instead he leans close and smooths a sprinkling of dandruff from my right shoulder.

"Where's that young apprentice of yours?" I ask. "Have you two fallen out?"

The black shadow circling Ray's eyes suggest it was a late night, last night. I wonder if that vixen wife of his kept him up. He looks over my shoulder. Forces a laugh. "Nothing like that, Rose. He's just under the weather today, that's all. Don't think he slept too well."

"And young Bernard says he's been seeing plenty of you in the pub? I bet you chaps get up to some proper mischief, don't you?"

Ray's squint suggests he wouldn't use this expression to describe what they've been getting up to. Bernard and Ray are like chalk and cheese. "You've been talking with Bernard?"

I smile. "Of course. He's one of my oldest friends. There aren't many of those left."

His creased forehead implies that maybe he's remembering that the two of us used to work together. That does feel so long ago. That does feel like a completely different world.

"So how have you been?" he asks.

I don't mean my laugh to be so loud, so mocking. I wish it didn't escape from my mouth. None of this is *his* fault, I don't think.

"Sorry," he says, shrugging his huge shoulders. "Stupid question."

Bunching his hands inside his dirty blue jeans, his body rocks back and forth on the spot. Whilst I'm more into the intellectual type of man, like Barack Obama or Denzil Washington (come to think of it, maybe I'm just into black guys), I can see why women might fall for this hulking specimen. Squinting, I try to push the thought from my mind. This is my friend's husband, for God's sake.

"It's okay," I say. "It's the obvious and honest question to ask. What can I say? It's been a really shit time, Ray. But I think I'm over the worst of it. Onwards and upwards, as they say."

He nods. A thought passes through his head. "Why did you lie, Rose?"

"Lie?"

I'm not being deliberately awkward - I'm just not sure which particular lie he's referring to. There have been so many.

"Why did you say your husband had been dead all these years? Don't you think that's odd?"

"Oh I never pretended I wasn't *odd*, Ray."

He laughs with me, but his laugh is awkward. Embarrassed. So is mine.

"I *was* in mourning. But not for him. For my little girl. I just couldn't face telling anyone that. It was too raw. Too brutal. People didn't need to know that Katherine and I had this connection, that her brother, and my daughter, were both killed by the same *man*..."

He lowers his head. Nobody ever talks about that monster. Not anymore. He stares at the pavement, at the weeds sprouting through the cracks. He knows how difficult this is to talk about. It is difficult for him, too.

Seconds pass before he nods.

"In my own warped thinking it somehow felt less of a lie to tell people that somebody had died. My husband was the obvious choice. He *was* dead to me."

"Didn't Kat deserve to know the truth?"

Part of me has always admired the way Ray protects his wife. So old fashioned. Reminds me of that Bonnie

Tyler song. *I need a hero. He's gotta be strong and he's gotta be fast and he's gotta be larger than life.*

"Did you move to Pontbach because of Kat? Because of what you had in common?"

I grimace. The truth hurts. "Yes. Katherine and her parents."

His lowered head nods.

"I planned to tell her. I *wanted* to tell her. But when I met her parents, who were exactly the same as me, I just knew I couldn't-"

"What?"

I take a step back. Suddenly his large frame is intimidating. Suffocating. Right now he definitely looks strong and fast and larger than life. "I knew I couldn't tell Katherine after I'd met her parents..."

"You met her parents? But you arrived in the town after they'd passed away..."

"No, Ray, I didn't. It took me a few months before I really ventured out, became part of the community. I met them in church only a few days after I moved here. They appeared to have finally found peace with the world. I just couldn't break their hearts, bring up horrific memories."

His puzzled face tells me he has many more questions.

"I must have got it wrong," he says.

He manages to hold my eye. "The way the town treated you was wrong, Rose."

"I know that. But what can you do...?"

Hesitantly, he leans forward and finally gives me that hug.

Tuesday 16th July 2019

Sheena

Apinya sits cross-legged next to me on the wooden bench, hands clasped together on her lap, an obedient child in assembly. We're in the shadow of the beautiful pine trees. Apparently Rob took a few days off work. Thought it was best to let the dust settle. Not only was his body bruised; his ego was, too. He has been quiet over the last few weeks.

"And how has Bernard been?"

Apinya looks to the blue, cloudless skies for answers. "He's a changed man-"

"He's turned into a bitter brute?"

Apinya shakes her head quite vehemently. What is this? Is she offended when somebody speaks ill of her darling husband? "Far from it. We've never spoken about what happened. He's been charming."

"Are you sure he's not playing a game?"

"Aren't we *all* playing a game?"

Jesus, where did that come from? I take a double look. When the fuck did she turn into Plato?

"Things have gotten better," she says. "He's actually making moves on me in the bedroom. He's pleasing me. He's hurting me, but in a good way..."

I lick my lips. "So how did you feel when Bernard caught you and Rob fucking...?"

Her eyes squint. "Ashamed. Humiliated. But-"

"But?"

Those almond-shaped eyes widen. Her teeth sparkle. "It made me feel like a dirty little slut. And that made me feel-"

"Fantastic?"

She pulls her hand to her mouth and giggles. "Yes."

Craning my neck, I look at her like Victor Frankenstein evaluating his monster. What *have* I created? I tangle my long, wiry fingers together. The possibilities are endless.

I lower my voice. She likes it when we conspire, when we discuss matters *so* important the rest of the world absolutely cannot overhear. Sometimes we do this when we discuss the group agenda. Does she think the trees have ears? *Now* who has a God complex?

"And how did it make you feel when Bernard hit him?"

My questions are getting progressively harder. If I keep this up, then Apinya will be answering for the million-pound jackpot. Her teeth dig into her nails.

"Honestly? I was proud of him, Sheena. I know I'm supposed to be a feminist-"

"*Are* you?"

"Aren't *you*?"

Really I just bend the rules to my advantage. I play whatever game antagonises the opposition the most. "Sometimes," I say.

"It felt good when my wimpy husband stood up and acted like a real man. The thrill was more powerful than any fucking. But then-"

"Yes...?"

She studies the lopsided concrete floor. "Then the

excitement vanished. I felt ashamed. Exposed. I just wanted to cover myself up. Hide."

So my little monster does have a conscience after all? I nod. Keep my face neutral. She needs to know that none of this is a surprise to me. My hand rubs against her smooth, hairless arm. "You know what I think, Apinya?"

She looks at me with an open face. "Tell me," she says. "I need to know. I really don't know what to do..."

My knee brushes against her thigh, just like I'm prone to do with her husband in the pub. I suck in air.

"You need to end it, Apinya. With Rob..."

Her beautiful, unlined face cracks, like she is staring at her reflection in a broken mirror. Her upper lip quivers, like she goes to ask a question but thinks better of it.

"I've been watching him," I say.

"*Who?*"

"Rob."

"What? *Why?*"

"Because you're my best friend, Apinya. Best friends look out for each other."

Her uncertain face smiles.

"I've been watching him watching you. Does he tell you that he follows you, Apinya?"

"What do you mean?"

I repeat the question. Just slower, like I'm ordering wine at a bar in France.

"No. No, he doesn't."

"Did you know that when you go for walks - for runs - he is often lurking behind you, hidden away...?"

Apinya's hand stifles her gasp.

"He's obsessed, Apinya."

Apinya smiles. "I've never had a stalker before."

"This isn't a fucking *good* thing," I snap. "It isn't a

badge of honour to have a stalker, you silly girl..."

She shrinks and shrivels, a dog caught pissing on the carpet. I suspected she might react like this, that she'd surmise she must be absolutely irresistible if a man is so infatuated that he wants to follow her everywhere.

"He's dangerous," I say. "He's out of control. And - don't forget - he's wounded. He's going to want revenge-"

"On Bernard?"

I wait a few moments before replying, before I shake my head. "Maybe. But most likely, he won't blame Bernard. Rob knows that Bernard had no choice. More likely, he'll blame you. He knows you set him up. Bernard was bound to come home, catch you two at it. And in Bernard's bed. What *were* you thinking, Apinya?"

"You said I should let him catch us-"

"Not in his bed!"

Apinya shakes her head.

"He'll want to revenge you..."

She shrieks. "Oh God. What will he do...?"

I pull Apinya close to me, put an arm around her. My soothing voice, my protective arm, tells her that she'll be fine with me.

"He won't do anything to you Apinya..."

She sighs with relief.

"That is, not so long as you get to him first..."

Katherine

This mirror is a snarling, taunting playground bully.

Sticks and stones may break my bones but words will never hurt me. I, better than anyone, know this is bullshit. I know that words can cause much greater harm, both psychological and physical, than any sticks or stones. And the (imaginary) words the mirror hurls at me hurt more than any other.

Except for *his* words, of course.

Naturally, I try to spend as little time with my nemesis as possible. The harder I try, the more the mirror follows me - I cannot pass one without grimacing, without taking a second, or a third, glance. Does he ever make me feel good? Does he ever provide the reassurance I crave? Of course he fucking doesn't.

This morning, however, the bullied and the bully made friends. They kissed and made up. This morning the mirror paid compliments, told me I looked real good. The words were warm and soothing and syrupy.

Of course, I've been here before. The mirror has done this countless times. The mirror has paid me compliments, made me feel good about myself, and then - just when I actually start believing it - it has started laughing, quietly at first and then building to a crescendo. I was ready for this. I waited. And there was no laughing.

I so wanted to be my worst critic, the Simon Cowell of the judging world, but I couldn't help but agree that my calves looked shapely in the white floral skirt. I *did* go in and out at the waist. Did the frilly, loose blouse display too much cleavage? Probably. Was it likely to make people point at me in despair? Unlikely.

Walking down the high street with my handbag dangling at my side, I'm more self-conscious than usual. I'm not usually self-conscious. This is deliberate. For years and years, I've hidden. I've become oblivious, just morphed into the background. Now, after months and months of eating healthily and exercising, I'm wearing clothes that *show* me rather than *hide* me. There is some resemblance to the teenager that was ready to take on the world, before my brother died.

All of this is *his* fault.

I want to slap my wrist, tell myself off for being so ridiculous, so utterly and disgracefully disrespectful to the dead; I can't help my burning resentment, though. If he hadn't died, then my life would have been so different. I would have remained that vivacious, energetic, gorgeous, *slim* girl I remember at seventeen or eighteen. I've *always* wanted to be her again.

Ben scraped through his O Levels, despite the distractions, despite the thoughts constantly invading his mind. Some colour returned to his cheeks and some vibrancy returned to his personality during that long summer break. He started coming out of his bedroom more. We started getting closer again. We never discussed his homosexuality; we were just aware of it.

Ben was there by my side the day I fell in love, too. I woke restless one morning; kicking off my bed sheet, I realised I couldn't face yet another long day of nothingness. I had to do *something*. I knocked on my brother's door, entered without waiting for his approval.

"Let's catch a bus," I said, talking to a bumpy mound underneath his sheet. "Go somewhere. Anywhere. Just to get out of this town for the day."

Even he could tell, through sticky, sleep-crusted eyes that, despite the darkness in his room, a glorious day existed outside. His dazed head nodded. His mouth didn't even open.

With plastic shopping bags packed with towels and suntan lotion, we ended up huddled together on a sweaty bus twisting and turning towards the coast. My arms prickled from the heat, from the excitement.

That was the day I met him. Stripped to the waist, he stood in the sea with the gentle waves slapping against his thighs. With his broad shoulders and narrowed waist, I thought he was majestic. My arms hung low, self-consciously covering my exposed flesh. He looked up, and smiled at me. No boy had *ever* smiled at me like that before.

That was the moment my life *really* changed forever.

I enter *Robsons,* the largest clothes shop in the town. A young girl leans over the counter, fingers manically typing on her phone; her lips mouthing the words of the background song - *You are Always on my Mind.* I'm not expecting a red carpet, but it would be nice for someone to acknowledge my existence. My fingertips brush over the metal railing. My old sizes call out for me like a three-legged dog at the kennels. A ceiling fan fires cold air over my body, drying a sliver of sweat from my chest.

Two young girls skip into the shop holding hands. I smile - I was like that with my brother at their age. Perfectly straight blonde hair falls to their chests. God, I think, their dad is going to have problems fighting off

the boys in a few years' time. If the one girl wasn't a
foot or so taller than the other then they could be
twins. I spot a few missing front teeth in the younger
girl; if I had to guess, I'd probably say they were about
six and eight. Disappearing from my eye-line, they're
replaced by their two straggling parents.

It is as if the two little princesses have sucked all the
vitality and vivacity from their poor mother. Mum's
greased-back hair is pulled so tight I'm surprised it
doesn't raise her eyebrows a couple of inches. Blue-
rimmed square glasses magnify her heavy-lidded eyes.
Whilst her skinny frame probably prompts envious eyes
from other mums at the school gates, her body is so
void of any bumps and curves that, to me, it resembles
an ironing board.

Her face brightens when she catches my smile; she
recognises my look - *I've been there, and it will get better.* I
don't recognise her. This is unusual, but not unheard of.
We do get visitors from the neighbouring villages, often
just looking for a change of scenery; additionally, I'm
not yet familiar with everyone from the new build
development that the villagers vehemently protested
against a few years back.

I'm aware of the outline of another figure, probably
Dad; I don't look, and I don't acknowledge him.

My hand lingers on a hanger. I glance around. Am I
being ridiculous? Nobody is looking. I unhook the
hanger. Subconsciously, I pretend I'm merely curious,
like I'm eying the Porsche at the showroom with no
money to buy one. I hold the size 10 strapless red dress
up against my size 12 body. The hem falls mid-thigh. It
would look sensational on the right woman, on a
digitally-enhanced catalogue model. Surely that right

woman isn't me?

I glance up. Somebody *is* looking. I address Dad for the first time. My eyes lock with his. Jesus, even *he* appears to have sucked the energy from the mother. *His* eyes aren't red-rimmed; they are sky blue and sparkling. Do my own eyes *voluntarily* wander? His white tee-shirt tightens at the shoulders and loosens at the waist and then dangles seductively at the crotch. I can't help but think that - naked - his body probably forms a beautiful v-shape. I imagine fine dark hair forming a line from his belly-button downwards.

My eyes dare to flicker back up. He is still looking at me. His eyes drop. They take in the gorgeous red dress, held up tight against my body. He smiles.

"Daddy, we're going..."

The man is pulled from the shop by his two gregarious daughters. I return Mum's wave as she skips to keep up with them. The automatic doors open and then close.

"Hold up, Grant," she says.

I glance out of the window; they headed in the other direction. I look over at the young assistant; she still stares at her screen. Did she even notice them come in and out of the shop? She looks away from her screen. Looks directly at me. Raises her two painted eyebrows. Flashes perfectly white teeth.

Maybe she saw more than I thought?

My lips curl as I move to the counter with the dress still in my hand. I avoid the assistant's eyes. The hairs on my arms prickle with excitement.

I'm short of breath as I hurry out of the shop with the bag in my hand. I want to get home. And I know what I'm going to do when I get there.

I'm going to strip off all of my clothes and throw

them in a pile on the floor. I'm going to lie naked, on the bed, and I'm going to watch myself in the mirror as my fingers explore my body. And when I orgasm - harder and more powerful than I ever have before - I'm not going to think of my loving, loyal and protective husband.

No, I'm going to think of the young, handsome guy in the shop and his approving look as I held the beautiful size 10 red dress close to my body.

Tuesday 23rd July 2019

Sheena

I've always loved being the centre of attention. Who says men are the stronger sex? I gain power from their weakness, from the vice-like grip I have over them.

The door swings open and the heads turn. Their smiles broaden, their dicks probably twitch inside their jeans, hidden away under the round, wooden tables.

Daniel knew. He was able to see through the words I spoke, through the lies. He discovered my unspoken fantasies. He got me to use a part of my imagination I never even knew I had. He'd pull a strand of hair from my ear and start whispering to me.

"Imagine you walk down a metal spiral staircase, down to the basement. You're straight from work, in your knee length pencil skirt. Sickeningly prim and proper and professional. Your heels click against the steps, so everyone in the shop is aware of you, knows you're coming..."

"What sort of shop is it?"

"The dingiest sub-basement sex shop in town. Sawdust lies on the concrete floor. The shelves are stacked with hideous videos. Women moan on the screens up on the walls. Only men dare to go in this shop..."

"Oh God. Won't I be out of place? A woman,

wearing a smart pencil skirt?"

"Of course you will, sweetheart. You look like you've accidentally walked into the wrong shop on the wrong street. But they see through your pretence. They *sniff* it out from beneath your wet panties. The men turn to you, straining in their trousers. The owner of the shop bolts the door..."

Daniel described how the men treated me like a whore, how they used and abused me. I'd absorb the words, take in their meaning, and caress myself until my body shuddered and I screamed obscenities at the top of my voice.

Daniel *knew,* though. Daniel knew that *I* was the one in control, that really the men were the weak ones, the ones who - obliviously - were under my spell.

Their eyes widen now as they glimpse the skirt that has ridden high up my thigh.

"Put your tongues away," I say, smirking.

The five of them shut their mouths. Geraint. Dave. Ray. Rob. Bernard. My hands drop to my hips. One knee thrusts forward.

I've grown close over the months, particularly with Dave and Geraint. They are the two that have no direct link to the group, but indirectly they have so many contacts. I tended to open up more when it was just the three of us. I chose my opportunities with the other three. Originally, I gained Dave and Geraint's trust by showing no talk was off bounds; it was impossible to offend me. Plenty of the talk revolved around Geraint's wife. Clearly, despite pretences to the contrary, the sappy guy adored her. He doted on her. The pub was merely his retreat from reality. The guy was doubtless unrecognisable inside his own home.

"She was going nuts at me on Saturday afternoon-"

"What happened?"

"Patience is a virtue, Dave. Patience is a virtue. She stood in the kitchen holding the freshly washed bed sheets. She asked if I could go upstairs and make the bed. At first - naturally, like - I thought, what did your last servant die of? Have your legs fallen off, darling? But then I sniffed opportunity. You know these women. They don't like any half-arsed efforts, do they? Everything has to be done properly-"

"Weren't you just putting sheets on the duvet, Geraint?"

Geraint's look silenced Dave.

"So, as I was *saying*, I smelt an opportunity. I quickly put the bed sheets on and then dived into bed for a quick nap before she noticed anything-"

"Do you need approval from your wife to take an afternoon nap?" I asked, smiling.

"I just want an easy life, Sheena. We both know who wears the trousers in our house. Anyway, two hours later I'm still snoring, and she storms into the room shouting and screaming-"

"Oh you poor man," I said.

Over time, of course, they felt comfortable sharing more and more. And it was only natural that I shared with them, too.

"I'm glad Ray and Bernard aren't here tonight," I said. "Something has been playing on my mind."

Two wooden chairs scraped closer to the table. "What is it, Sheena?" Dave asked. "You know that whatever you say doesn't leave this room..."

My squinting face indicated that I wasn't sure. This encouraged them even more.

"You won't tell Ray and Bernard?" I asked. "Or Rob?

I know Ray is one of your best friends..."

"What you tell us is in confidence, Sheena. It goes no further."

"Okay then," I said, raising my head. "I appreciate that. It's just that, obviously their wives are in the group. I don't want to upset them-"

"Quite understandable, Sheena. You're just thinking of them."

"I'm not comfortable with some of the things the women are saying in the group. It just isn't right. For example, one of the women said she slept with her husband's brother. And you know what the women said? They supported her. They said *she* was the victim, that he must have pushed her into it. I'm just not sure what these women are planning..."

Both men blew air from their cheeks. They shook their heads.

"There is more," I said.

"Go on," Dave said.

I picked up my glass. Downed my drink. "I really shouldn't. I really don't want to create a divide between you..."

"Between who?"

I glance around. Nobody is listening. "Between you two and Ray and Bernard."

Geraint rubbed his hands together. "You're just giving us the heads-up, Sheena. And, like I said, nothing leaves this room. We won't say anything to them. It won't cause a rift."

"If you insist. All I'm saying is that there is no way Kat and Apinya don't tell them things we discuss in the group-"

"Of course they do. They're married..."

"Exactly. Ray and Bernard know things. And, of course, the same applies the other way around..."

"The other way around?"

"Ray and Bernard tell Kat and Apinya things you discuss in the pub, too..."

"You think?"

"Why wouldn't they? Like you said, they're married. All I'm saying is, be careful what you say around them. And keep your eye out..."

They both shook their lowered heads at the enormity of this information.

"Of course," I said. "*We* can trust each other with everything..."

Geraint is the first to welcome me into the pub now.

"Can I get you a drink, Sheena?" he asks.

I can tell by the slowness of his movements, by the way he drags his words that, whilst he'd love me to stay, to grace them with my intoxicating presence, he'd prefer me to do so without him spending any money. He'd relish one of the other men volunteering to buy me a drink. None of the other men move. None of the other men say anything.

"I'm not staying," I say.

I look at each man in turn, from left to right, from right to left.

"Can I have a quick word?" I nod to the door. "In private, if you don't mind...?"

Katherine

My husband rests his hot, glistening cheek against my naked chest. My open hands cup the back of my head, the long greasy hair tangling within my fingers. The orange streetlights outside allow me to just about make out the white of the ceiling amidst the darkness of our bedroom.

"Oh my God," Ray says. "That was amazing. What came over you?"

Aren't I *always* amazing? I remove my right hand, start stroking my husband's head like he is an outstretched dog. His words are drowned out somewhat by my heaving cleavage. Should I tell him that what came over me was the thought of fucking another man? Would that add an extra thrill to proceedings?

I decide to leave that line of communication.

"You just drive me crazy sometimes, Ray," I say.

He twists his head. I feel compelled to pull a stray hair from his eyebrow. I can see his golden filling, right at the back of his mouth. I could ask the same question of him. Sex no longer appears like a chore to him, something that he needs to do to keep me happy. Ray has noticed a change in me, too, and not just a physical one. He has noticed that I'm more outgoing, more confident, more social. My husband gives the impression that the world passes him by, but really he quietly takes it all in, like a hawk. He has upped his game because he knows he needs to work harder to keep me satisfied. I am no longer so easily contented.

"I forgot to tell you, I bumped into Rose."

What reminded him of her? I bet he hadn't forgotten.

"Oh yes. How was she?"

"Good. All things considered, of course. Seems like she's fighting back. I did always think she was a tough old bird."

"You did?"

Rose has always appeared so unhealthy she could drop dead at any moment.

"Yes. Underneath that haggard exterior is a strong woman."

"Sounds like you fancy her, Ray."

His head moves closer, like he is trying to work out if I'm joking. My smile tells him I am. God, there are plenty of other women I could worry about before Rose. One of them is blonde.

"Strange thing is, she told me she met your parents. I never knew that, or I must have forgotten-"

"What?"

"Rose met your parents."

"No she didn't. Why would you say that? They were already dead when she joined the town."

My voice must be high-pitched, for Ray shuffles around under the duvet. He always pays extra attention when he is concerned about me. Sometimes his concern can be suffocating. Thank God we never had a daughter.

"That's what I thought. But she'd lived in the town a few months before we met her at the fete that time. She met them in church. Apparently."

"Don't you believe her?"

"It's not that. Guess I was shocked, that's all. I just

didn't know. "Shocked?"

"Yes."

"Don't you think it is a bit crazy, Ray? We've known her all this time and she never mentioned she met my-"

"Think about it, Kat. It kind of makes sense, in a backwards way. She didn't want to bring up old memories. She didn't want that to be what linked you..."

I twirl his chest hairs around my middle finger. He returns his cheek to my chest. He likes it there, and not for the obvious reason - he feels protected. Talk about role reversal. Can he feel my heart beating? It feels like a fist is punching me.

"This is all beginning to add up, Ray. First, she lies about her husband. Then her husband is found dead. Now we find out she has kept this secret-"

"What are you saying, Kat?"

My husband looks up at me again. His warm breath, tainted with my own feminine scent, blows in my direction.

"We need to be careful of Rose." I take a deep breath. "I'm not sure I trust her anymore."

Thursday 25th July 2019

Apinya

Sheena has a saying. It is something along the lines that people tend to walk around with their eyes shut and even those with their eyes open only see what they want to see.

That's the thing! The majority of the town walk around with their eyes shut. Open those eyes! They believe everything they are told without asking any questions. Because their damn eyes are shut, they don't see the lies. I feel sorry for them. But the women in the group? We're different. We have our eyes open. We see the truth. We think for ourselves. We're not sheep.

But my affair with Rob? That's partly why it's so exciting! That's partly why it's so exhilarating! Not even the women in the group know about this. The group is not supposed to have secrets. We trust each other with absolutely everything. And we don't - apart from this one thing. This is my dirty, wonderful little secret I share only with Sheena. Nobody else can know about the affair. Nobody else can know what is about to happen.

We arranged the time and the place the last time we met. We're shrewder than the rest of the world. We no longer text. We deleted our old texts. Rob - bless him - didn't ask any questions; he just assumed it was to keep any evidence away from Bernard. My hand cupped his crotch as his finger tapped away at the phone - he found it exciting, too.

As my feet tiptoe across the dry, yellowing grass, I remember the time Bernard took me to Stratford one weekend to watch a play. I dressed in expensive clothes and we sat in the gallery. I recall looking down at the rest of the audience and smiling, thinking just look how far I've come! I didn't understand much of the play - but who does? As I edge closer to where I'd agreed to meet my lover, I'm reminded of that play I watched holding my husband's kind hand - Romeo and Juliet - and I'm struck by the thought of how that love story ended.

I rotate. Look around. How fucking *dare* he leave me waiting? He was supposed to be here first. That was my plan. That was how I pictured it in my mind. My breath quickens. Does this feel right?

I pull my two arms to my face, stifling my scream. My whole body stiffens, unable to move.

The hands at my waist are large and strong. The noise rattles between my ears. It becomes louder, more deafening.

Opening my eyes, I peek through the gap in my arms. His teeth are bared. His lips are open. The laughter quietens.

"Thought I'd surprise you," Rob says, grinning.

"You idiot," I say, laughing. "Jumping out from behind a bush? You nearly gave me a heart attack. You could have been anybody!"

His open, puckered lips accept my kiss. My eyes wander to the bruise on his temple, red and shiny like a cricket ball. He took that for me. Who said romance is dead? My fingers entwine with his and our linked hands swing in the air. We haven't discussed where we're going; we just instinctively go there.

Can he read my mind? I hope not.

His body lies flat next to mine on the hard, bumpy grass. My eyes fix on the white moon. Why is it sometimes visible even before the light has faded? I twist to my side, cupping the back of my head in my upturned hand. Although his arms and chest are lean and well-muscled, his soft belly rises. He drinks too much beer, I think.

I am fascinated as I watch him roll a cigarette. There is something beautiful about the way he does it, with his long, mud-ridden fingers working in tangent. I love that he is always so calm, always so content. I may give the impression I'm fancy free, but I'm riddled with doubts. This guy? He is the real deal. Such a silly, gullible boy. It doesn't matter that his life is a cesspit, that it is heading nowhere, that he may possibly be about to die. Who cares!

"How was your day?" he asks.

He's not one for small talk. Besides, how can he ask about my life? Oh, I did this and that with my husband. Did you know I was married? Yes. And you still fucked me? Naughty boy! He doesn't really need to ask though, does he? Of course, I knew he was following me before Sheena told me. She thinks she knows everything, but she doesn't really. Not quite. The question is - who was following who?

"Same as yesterday. Same as tomorrow."

His flared nostrils suggest he's impressed with my candour, my witty ways.

"But it wasn't too bad," I say. "It's not like anybody died, is it?"

His brow hangs over his eyes. What did I mean? He thumbs my cheek, like he is trying to line my face with paint. "That's what I like about you, Apinya. You're always so cheerful about everything. The glass is never half-empty with you. Oh, and I like your arse, too. I *really* like your arse."

He tickles my midriff, just like my dad did when I was a child. My legs kick in a bicycle motion. I laugh uncontrollably.

"Stop it!"

His fingers straighten. He plants his head back down on the ground. The energy drains from his body.

"Do you love me?" I ask.

His head jerks to the side, but then it quickly twists back again. "You know I do," he says. "I told you I did."

"Tell me again. Tell me now. I want to hear it."

His smile is strained. "You're a bit demanding, aren't you?"

"Tell me."

"I love a controlling lady."

"Now."

His eyes focus on the sky. "I love you," he says.

My heart sinks. He couldn't even look at me when he said the words. I've sacrificed so much for this man - put my marriage at risk - and he doesn't really love me? Everything that has happened and everything that will happen - how was it possibly worth it?

Turning, he hovers over me, purring like a helicopter, placing his lips just inches from mine. Stretching out my arm, I grab hold of the back of his head, pulling the bastard closer to me. Pushing my head up a few inches from the ground, I poke my tongue out, slip it inside his mouth. My two hands press against his chest. His eyes widen at the strength of my wiry arms. Pushing him down onto his back, I straddle him, my bare knees grazing against the spiky, rough grass. I can feel him digging into me, pushing me upwards. His arms become straight lines. He tries to cup my breasts. I slap them away.

"You need to earn those," I say.

The white of his eyes tells me he is more than prepared to work hard for them.

"Take off your clothes," I say. "I want to ride you. You need to make me cum before I'll do *anything* for you."

What an offer! Unbuttoning his jeans, he wriggles out of them. He folds his tee-shirt into a neat pile on top of the jeans. I'm surprised he is so conscientious - I assumed Mum folded his clothes for him. His glaring eyes fix on me. They demand answers.

"I told you," I say. "You're not getting anything from me until you've made me cum. And that includes my clothes. I'm not taking off anything yet. Not until you've shown me you're a man. Not a boy."

Glancing down, the evidence is already there that he is a man. I've never seen it look so big. Bernard is bigger, of course. He is a dark horse. Heck, Bernard is *like* a horse. Nobody would expect it of him. But still, this will do. It is already a pole, straining so it doesn't explode. He rests his body next to the folded clothes. I merely pull my panties to one side and then I lower myself down onto him. His body trembles. This isn't going to take long.

"Fuck me, you horny bastard," I say, writhing on top of his youthful, naked body. "Don't stop until I tell you to. Do you hear me?"

Moisture from his upper lip trickles down into his mouth. His eyes stare into my skull, like he is reading my mind. His wonderful hands grope and thumb my buttocks. They slide over the fabric of my blouse. I'll let him cup them this time. I'll let him have one last, cheap thrill. His arms straighten. His hands open. Up to my breasts. They move past them. They move higher.

His beautiful, delicate fingers grip my throat. The stupid little bastard *does* stop before I tell him to. He flips my fragile body off him like I'm a ragdoll. Pushing my head down into the depths of the ground, his spare hand grapples with his clothes. Staring down at me, his white smile taunts me. From the corner of my eye, I'm blinded by the reflection of the blade he holds above his head.

"You silly little bitch," he says.

He lunges down with the knife. Both my hands reach up, grip his wrist. The blade sinks into the grass, an inch from my ear. His dumb face pauses for just a moment. I reach down and cup his naked balls. My teeth clench; I squeeze hard. Raising my knee to my chest, I push out with the sole of my foot. He stumbles back, placing his flat hands on the floor. His beady eyes don't move away from the knife.

I'm not interested in the knife, though. That would leave evidence, wouldn't it? Momentarily, I turn my back to my attacker. I take quick, assured steps away from him. Then, kneeling down, I lean forward and drag a heavy device from underneath the bush. I removed it from our garage a few nights ago, and I carried it here in a black, plastic bag. For once, I didn't want to draw attention to myself. It is just one of Bernard's gadgets that he never uses. He won't miss it.

I'll try and return it when I find the right moment to do so.

I turn around, eyeing the knife.

"You call that a weapon?" I say, smiling. Holding the handle of the chainsaw with my left hand, I pull the chain with my right. The engine growls. "*This* is a weapon."

Rob isn't interested in the knife now, either. With both his feet and his hands flat against the hard, unforgiving ground, he scurries backwards, reminding me of a crab. He moves towards the edge of the river. Perfect. His eyes don't move for one moment from the metallic, jagged edges of the chain saw. The noise is so thunderous, so empowering.

"Put your head under the water!" I shout.

Just for a fleeting moment, he jerks his head towards me. *What?* I don't say anything. I merely lower the vibrating, metal cutter a few inches from the pulsating, blue vein in his neck. His eyes become perfect circles. Lowering the back of his head into the water, he stares up at the beautiful, fading August sky. I read his thoughts; he weighs up his options.

Which is the better way to die?

His face disappears underneath the surface of the water. Bubbles float upwards from his mouth and from his nose. His flailing arms and his kicking legs are soundless beneath the surface of the water, drowned out by the vibrant howl of the chainsaw. His movements slow. Pressing a button, the noise dies down. I place Bernard's gadget safely down on the grass behind me. So it *did* have a use, after all.

Squatting, I push both of my hands down against Rob's chest. I hold his fading body underneath the water until I am sure it is completely motionless, until I am sure it is utterly lifeless...

Sheena

I'm not used to waiting. I don't like waiting. Call it a power thing, if you want. This time, however, I have to accept it is inevitable. I had to be here first. I have no idea how long it will take, how long I'll be waiting.

The light vanished an hour or so ago and an evening chill has descended. My cardigan is zipped to my neck. I wrap my arms around my legs; my knees push against my chest. With the street lights to the front of the church, the graveyard is just outlines and shapes. I can just about make out the church's sloping slate roof and the moss growing on the walls. The leaves of the trees outlining the yard shimmy in the wind. Apart from the dead bodies scattered underneath the ground, I'm alone with my thoughts.

From what people told me, I assumed I'd loathe Bernard. Who did he think he was - a character from *The Great Gatsby*? What a silly old buffoon! Once I did some digging, I discovered that he lived in an ivory tower on his dead father's money. But then reality struck. It was like looking in the mirror. I didn't earn any of my money. That was yet another thing I had Daniel to thank for. I considered myself better than the minions I surrounded myself with, too. Egotistical? Arrogant? In this respect, I felt I was merely acknowledging the truth.

I quickly realised Bernard was a man of routine. Most of the human race is. They like control. Some people are merely more organised and capable than others. I knew what time he'd turn up at the pub.

"Didn't think you smoked, Sheena?" he asked. His blue jeans were torn at the heel. Holes were dotted around his white polo neck shirt. His attempts to fit in were laughably transparent.

"Oh, I have plenty of dark secrets, Bernard," I said, blowing a ring of smoke from my puckered lips. "Seriously, though. I just treat myself every so often. Life is too short to deprive yourself of little pleasures."

His face broke into a nervous smile. He was just about to pass me and head into the warm, claustrophobic pub, when something caught his eye.

"I got this for you," I said. "I've caught you outside before. Thought I'd surprise you."

His blue eyes gleamed. His usually strained, programmed smile blossomed.

"Oh my," he said. "I don't know what to say. That's really touching. Thank you, Sheena."

He prodded my arm with his hand, wanting to get close but reluctant to appear inappropriate. Of all the men who touch themselves thinking of me naked, this one probably suffers the most guilt.

"I just wanted to say it was amazing what you did to Rob," I said.

His cheeks reddened. He stabbed at the floor with the tips of his shoes. Clearly, not many people had complimented his masculinity before. Maybe his was a childhood thing? Judging by the clothes he wore, the unnatural words he used, the way he tried too hard to fit in, he obviously had issues with this.

"Oh, it was nothing," he said. "I had no choice really, did I?"

He glimpsed me staring at him in wonder; he looked away.

"So she told you then?"

I flicked ash onto the floor and dabbed it with my shoe. "She tells me everything, Bernard."

He thumbed the pockets of his jeans. "So did you know about them? That they were engaging in a sordid fling?"

My hand gripped his arm. He needed to know that we were both victims. "I did. I'm *so* sorry. The more I got to know you, Bernard, the more I despised what she was doing to you. I wanted to tell you. You need to believe me. But how could I? She is my best friend..."

He shook his bowed head. "It wasn't your fault. You had no choice. Did she tell anyone else?"

I stared at the vacant road. "We don't have any secrets in the group, Bernard. We are like a sisterhood. Of course, they blamed you-"

"Blamed me? What did *I* do?"

"Nothing," I said. "Nothing at all. The women in the group have developed an unhealthy hatred of men, in my opinion. I'm torn whether to stay in the group or not. They were always going to be on her side. I try to tell the women to be more objective, but they just don't listen. Sometimes it is scary how much they seem to hate men. Jesus. Some of them see you as the enemy. I try to set the right example, tell them I mingle with you in the pub and everything, but they believe what they want to believe, don't they? Sometimes I long for them to open their eyes to the real world. It doesn't help that Apinya said you hit her-"

"*What?* Hit her? I've never hit a woman in all my life!"

"I know. I know. Don't worry, the women weren't shocked by that. They're of the opinion that all husbands hit their wives, that it is their divine right or something-"

"We don't! *I* don't!"

"I'm on your side with this one, Bernard. Maybe I shouldn't have said anything. I'm sorry-"

"No. You should have. Thank you."

"Believe me. I'm as mad about this as you are. The question is, what are you going to do about this mess?"

I absorb his bloodshot eyes. He holds my look. He says nothing.

"Well, you've taken revenge on Rob. But what are you going to do about Apinya?"

"Apinya?"

"Yes. She's got away with all of this mess really, hasn't she? And now the women in the group think you beat her. Because of her. That doesn't seem right."

"When you say it like that, Sheena, it really doesn't."

"If it was me then I'd be seeking revenge..."

My thoughts are interrupted by a shadowy figure heading towards me. This isn't a surprise. I arranged to meet here after it was done and dusted.

There was one question I didn't have an answer to, though.

Which one of them would meet me?

"Apinya," I say, standing up and taking her in my arms. Her icy cold body shivers. I remove my cardigan and unravel it over her shoulders. She barely seems to notice. I sit her down next to me on the bench. Planting her hands flat against her thighs, her back remains rigid and straight. Her unblinking almond eyes stare straight ahead. I could click my fingers an inch from her face and she still wouldn't flinch.

"How are you?" I ask.

"I killed him," she says.

I crane my neck. "*What* did you say?"

"I killed him."

"*Who?*"

She robotically turns her head. "Rob."

"What? Why?"

"You told me to."

I hold up my outstretched hands. "Hold on right there. I never told you to kill anybody. Just who do you think I am? What sort of a person do you think I am?"

"You said I should sort him out-"

"Yes. Sort him out. Not *kill* him."

She doesn't seem to listen. She digs inside her pocket. A metallic blade shines in the dark night. My throat tightens. I didn't expect to see the knife I gave to Rob again.

"Is that what you used to kill him?" I ask.

I lean closer. I look closer at the sharp edges. Where is the blood? Has she already cleaned it?

Apinya shakes her head.

"Then how did you kill him?"

"He drowned."

"But how? Why?"

"I forced him to."

I pull back my head. How deluded *is* she?

"Apinya," I say, "you couldn't possibly have forced him. Rob is bigger than you. He is stronger than you. How on earth did you overpower him?"

Apinya's tone remains perfectly neutral. A cold shiver runs down my body. What happens if the monster becomes more powerful than its creator? I dismiss the thought. Push it out of my mind. She'll never be shrewder than I am. "I threatened him with a worse alternative. I guess you could say he drowned himself."

Her hand unfolds. The knife drops to the floor. I glance at her accusingly. She doesn't move. Leaning down, I pick the knife up. Put it in my pocket.

"It was self-defence," she says. "He tried to kill me. He was a crazed madman. If I didn't kill him then he *would* have killed me. One of us had to die. It had to be him."

I shuffle closer. "Nobody will believe that, Apinya. What reason did he have to kill you? We need to think fast. Did you strangle him? Hit him? Did you leave any evidence that you killed him?"

Apinya shakes her head. She turns to me. "You do believe me, Sheena?"

I take hold of her hand. Her fingers are rigid. "Of course I believe you. You're my best friend. I love you. I need to protect you. We need to make sure you don't get in deep trouble. Clearly, this wasn't your fault."

She nods.

I release her hand. Rotate my right arm. Tighten my fist into a ball. And then I punch my best friend - the girl I love - hard in the face.

She squeals like a pig. She eyes me accusingly through the gaps in her fingers. I push her hand away and plant a soothing, wet kiss on the bubbling, blue bruise.

"What did you do that for?" Apinya asks. "You crazy bitch."

Ignoring her comment, my finger tilts the underside of her chin, so she looks straight at me. "Listen to me, Apinya. The detectives are going to come knocking on your door. Do you hear?"

She nods.

"We need to make sure that when they *do* knock, they're coming for Bernard, and not you..."

Monday 29th July 2019

DI Hunter

My black soles stick to the flimsy brown carpet, speckled with holes. Resting my elbows against the desk, my thumbs massage my temple. The rain outside spits against the rattling windows. I promised myself I'd go for a morning stroll, but the grey outside is even darker than the grey inside; I'm not sure I can face it. I look around the office. Is this my life after nineteen years on the force?

Gripping the levers on the side of the blue swivel chair, I raise myself about three inches. I sit still for a couple of seconds before lowering myself about two inches. In years gone by, my paperwork stared at me from an overflowing plastic tray. Now my work stares at me from my computer screen.

Glancing around, I unbutton my navy flares. Nineteen years ago I still had room to slip a hand inside my size eight skirts (my boyfriend at the time proved this point a few times). The men on the force joked that I had hollow legs, that the fizzy pop and fast food seeped out of me. Where does it all go, Debbie? Well, I disproved that theory good and proper, didn't I? Case closed. No suspicious circumstances. These days I don't put my legs on display, and I'm almost bursting out of my size sixteen trousers. The men don't joke about my hollow legs anymore. Whilst my Match.Com profile enticingly says I'm a Big Beautiful Woman (BBW), I don't feel beautiful. Just big. I used to be quite an attraction around this place. The men used to say my olive complexion and long black hair made me look exotic. Now they ask what time the kebab shop opens.

Poking my nose inside my empty coffee mug, my upturned eyes glance at the clock on the wall. Can I really justify a fourth cup before 11am? The doctor said the caffeine and Standard American Diet (even though I live in Wales) added to my anxiety. It was like pouring petrol on a fire, apparently, and I know all about arsonists. The doctor said boredom didn't help, either, so I'm caught in a cycle, aren't I? I decide to pass the time (and relieve the boredom) by pouring coffee straight from the jar into my mug. After all, I've already had three. One more won't hurt. Besides, I need something to counter my throbbing head (probably caused by too much caffeine). I'll make up for it by drinking a glass of water later, probably after lunch. My thought-process is interrupted by a dark shadow appearing at the side of my desk. Holding out my open palms, I roll my chair backwards.

"Welcome to my metaphorical office, DC Jordan," I say. "What's up? Whatever it is, I'm here to help."

I make it my business to run my eyes over his gym-toned twenty-four-year-old body. Why? I don't really have any interest in his hardened pectorals or abdominals or whatever they're called. It merely reminds me of long, wasted hours in the gym. I do so because that's what all the men did to me when I joined the force, when *I* was young and attractive. And slim. I make it my duty to ensure there is no fucking sexism in this office. I add a wink, just to ensure he is left in no doubt about my inappropriateness. What can he do about a wink? I'll tell HR I've developed a squint, brought on by too much caffeine. I glance at the cup. I hope he isn't going to be too long - I'm desperate for that coffee.

"Debbie," he says. "There's been a death."

Pushing my buttocks forward, I sit up in the chair. My hands grip the handles. This news is greater than any caffeine kick. "A murder?"

Jordan shakes his head. "No signs of anything suspicious at the moment. It is most likely a suicide."

I loosen my grip on the handles. My pumping heart slows. "What is it with this world? Do you know when the suicide rate is at its lowest, Phil? During a World War. Do you know why that is?"

His shoulders loosen. He looks over my shoulder.

"Because citizens are focussed on staying alive. In today's risk-averse world we are obsessed with staying alive. But do you know what I think?"

"No. I don't know what you think, Debbie."

"I think we're living longer, but more miserable lives. What is the point in that? Whilst we're obsessed with staying alive, more people than ever are killing themselves. Do you see the contradiction here?"

"I do."

I pick up my coffee cup. Stifle a yawn with my forearm. Whilst my metaphorical door is still open, there is a time limit. "So I'm guessing it's a man? Young. Usually is. Did you know suicide is the biggest killer of men under the age of forty-five, Phil?"

"It was a man. Under the age of forty-five. Under the age of twenty-five, by all accounts."

"Cause of death?"

My eyes follow Jordan's shuffling. He's on edge.
Maybe I should keep this door open a little longer?

"Drowning-"

"*What* did you say?"

Jordan takes a step back, stunned or bemused that
I'm suddenly on my feet. "I said that it was a drowning.
Could have been suicide or possibly just an accident.
The body was found in the early hours this morning by
a local walking his dog..."

"Where? Where did this happen?"

He holds up his hands, indicating for me to slow
down, to *calm* down. My heart stops beating, waiting for
him to reply. Please, please tell me what I want to hear.

"Pontbach-"

"The river?"

His eyes crease with suspicion.

"Goddamn it, Phil. Was it the river at Pontbach?"

"Yes. Yes it was."

His eyes follow my retreating back. "Get your coat," I
say. "We've got a murder to investigate."

Sheena

I so adore the woods.

Whilst sunlight slithers through the gaps in the trees, they protect me from the rain. The snap and the crackle of the leaves reminds me of the *Rice Krispies* adverts I watched as a child. All they need, I muse, are a pop. The air feels thick with moisture and nutrients. Raising my wrist, I check the time.

And then I wait.

I can see him coming from nearly a mile away. The straight track slopes only slightly upwards. I twist my head and look in the opposite direction. Nobody. There is only the two of us within a two-mile radius. In my idle daydreams I sometimes wonder about the perfect place to kill somebody. You could scream at the top of your lungs in this woodland and the rest of the town - let alone the rest of the world - would remain utterly oblivious. Yes, what a perfect place to commit murder. It has taken them days to discover Rob's body floating in the river. Just how long would it take for a decaying, half-eaten, worm-riddled body to be discovered here? Who actually comes here? Maybe the odd couple seeking adventure, and possibly the occasional dog walker. They'd only dare to come during daylight. Darkness plays tricks with your mind.

Apinya surpassed my wildest expectations. I fully expected Rob to join me in the churchyard. She must have kept her nerve, used brains I didn't even know she had. It was one Hell of an accomplishment; now the hard work really begins. How is she going to keep that yapping mouth shut? Is she really going to stick to the plan?

Or should I silence her before she is given the opportunity to ruin things?

"Over here," I call.

He spins in a complete circle. His narrowed eyes are bloodshot. This man is at home in the pub. His weathered, beaten face suggests he spends plenty of time outdoors, too, with the unforgiving wind blowing against his cheeks. He breaks into a smile as I appear from behind a tree. His fists remain clenched balls. He has no reason to trust me. I wonder whether he has a knife hidden in his pocket, just in case. He better not try and use it; he'll end up cut.

"Why are we in the middle of this wood, Sheena? In the middle of nowhere? Is whatever you're planning really that top secret?"

I flutter my eyelashes. Allow my tongue to circle my lips. "What do you think my plan is? Maybe I want to be alone with you? Somewhere nobody can see us..."

His laugh is throaty and congested. "To fuck me? Or to kill me?"

"Well, I'm not going to hurt you," I say.

His smile widens. Luckily, he knows I'm joking. We both know I could have my choice of men. Or women. We both know I'm not desperate. Sure, sometimes I fantasise about getting taken in the woods, up against a tree; just not by this guy.

He wipes his arm across his lips. He's not used to small talk with me; it makes him uncomfortable. "So I did what you asked me to do," he says. "What do you want of me now?"

"I'm so glad you asked."

I slide my hand inside my pocket. Pull out a brown envelope. He slows down his movements. Casually stares into space. Tries to imply he isn't bothered. He ends up looking like a teenager trying to impress the girls.

"Money?"

"No, a fucking early Christmas card. Yes. It's money."

"How much?"

"Enough. Open it if you want to see."

His shivering hand can't hide his desire to check the notes. Eying the brown envelope, the air from his mouth could blow down a straw house. I hand him the envelope, keeping my eyes fixed on his.

"I trust you," he says, folding the envelope in two, sliding it inside his back pocket. "But what's it for? You paid me for the last job."

"Another job. You've done well. You've earned my trust."

"What job?"

"The others were child's play compared to this one-"

"What is it?"

"The instructions are in the envelope. You can read them. Tell me if you're up for it."

He narrows his shoulders. Tangles his fingers together. His smile is a cross between Prince Charming and Cruella de Vil. "I'm up for it."

"I knew I could rely on you," I say.

We stand in relative darkness for a few moments. He pushes his weight from one foot to the other. I can tell from his dull, wet eyes that he's contemplating engaging in conversation. I get in there before he takes the opportunity.

"There's one last thing," I say.

He tips his head. I pull my hand inside my pocket again. He sucks in air as he takes in the metallic blade. This is the same knife I gave to Rob to kill Apinya.

"This might help you. I *don't* want it back."

My hand dangles for a few seconds. He wipes his forehead with the back of his arm. He takes the knife.

"Nice doing business with you," he says, before turning and beginning his descent of the slope.

I stay around for a few minutes, savouring the solitude and the beauty of my plans.

Katherine

The rain has stopped and yet, there is no rainbow. Not today.

With the curtains pulled apart, I can see the sky outside is blue and blemish-free. I know light seeps through the double-glazed windows, that inside the living room it is bright and airy. I *don't* know why my mind is clogged with cotton wool, why I'm freezing cold even though the heating is on (in the middle of summer), why my knees press hard against my chest, why I rock back and forth. They say that it is okay to *not* be okay; I wish somebody had sent the memo to me.

Something is wrong, but I don't know *what*.

I haven't felt like this for some time. The last time I can remember is when that grotesque man spat on me through the car window. This year I've felt much more like my younger self. I've cracked a shell I don't think even needed to be there.

There was a time, of course, when I felt like this on a regular basis. At first, Ray prodded and shook me, worried that I'd shrink to the point I'd disappear. Tears trickled down my cheeks as I helplessly watched my panicked husband try to bring back the woman he loved. Gradually, I'd reappear. Ray became accustomed to it, accepted it as part of the healing process. I guess he really did grow to believe that it was okay to not be okay.

Deep down, I think we both know I never fully reappeared.

My body jumps as the front door opens. I glance at the clock. Just gone three. Do we have an intruder? Does somebody have our key? My thoughts slowly churn. I'll have to move. I'll have to get up off the sofa. They'll see me in my dressing gown, without my makeup. This is one of the reasons I keep our bedroom clean and tidy - I'd hate a burglar to think bad of me as he rummaged through our drawers. I'd never have a cleaner because (besides the expense) I'd need to ensure the house was spotless before they arrived.

Ray appears. My big, strong bear of a husband casts a shadow over the whole room. He squints at my haggard form, all diminutive and crumpled on the sofa. His shoulders are pushed forward. It is quite striking. His back is usually straight, his shoulders back, whatever the situation. He doesn't like to show any fear.

"What's wrong?" I ask.

I sit up straighter. I don't fear whatever he is going to tell me. I knew something was wrong. I'll just be relieved to know the reason I feel so awful.

My husband has been working hard. Rob hasn't turned up for work for a few days. Ray had a big job on over the weekend, too. Rob's fretting mum called the police, reported him as missing. However, it was difficult to take it too seriously. He has a history of getting drunk and going AWOL. Ray reassured his mum he'd probably met a woman. He seemed to know something but just wasn't telling. Guys don't snitch. Regardless, he's been working on his own, coming home drained. The poor man even missed the pub on Saturday with Dave and Geraint.

My body rises as he sinks into the cushion next to me, like a bigger boy has jumped on the other side of the seesaw. He's made an effort, prepared himself for this talk. He's had a wash and sprayed his body with deodorant, masking the stale sweat. His thumb massages the back of my hand, like sandpaper on a smooth wall.

"Is it that bad?" I ask.

He sinks his head.

Clearly, it is worse.

"Ray?"

He turns to me with red-rimmed eyes. "They found a body," he says.

"What? Somebody has been murdered?"

I picture a smiling Sheena in a beautiful white dress, luscious blonde hair flailing over her slender shoulders. I imagine her pulling a knife from behind her back. Her smile turns into a throaty, sinister laugh as blood splatters and sprays across her face.

"*Murdered?* Why would you think that?"

I shrug my shoulders. Say nothing. *So why are you so upset?*

"Probably an accident," he says. "Or-"

"Suicide. They killed themselves, didn't they? That's why it's hit you so hard. Because of my parents. You're worried about how I'll react."

"Yes. Of course, it's played on my mind. You know I worry about you."

"That's not it though, is it? There's more, isn't there?"

Ray jerks his head in different directions. He thumbs his restless temple.

"We know the person, don't we? Who is it? Is it Rose?"

He turns to me. "No. Why would it be Rose?"

"She's had such problems. She's been through so much. I just thought-"

"Not Rose. They've not confirmed it yet. His mother will have to identify the body. But people are saying it's Rob-"

"Rob? That makes no sense-"

"Think about it, Kat. I haven't been able to get hold of him. He hasn't turned up for work. His mum reported him as missing. It *has* to be Rob..."

I wrap my arms around his chest. His bulky body feels so vulnerable, like a sleeping lion. No wonder he is forlorn. Rob was his mate. Despite their differences, they were getting close. I pull away. He wipes his eyes.

"What else is wrong?" I ask.

He flinches. "Isn't that enough? How do you know there is something else?"

I can't explain to him why. It defies all logic. How can I tell him the reason I know is because this news wouldn't make me feel quite this terrible, make me feel like the energy has been sucked from my body? This is tragic for so many people, my dear husband included. But not for me. I wasn't close to Rob. He was more of an acquaintance than a friend.

"Just tell me, Ray. *Please.*"

Ray wipes his upper lip. He jerks his head. "He was found floating in the river. Just like your parents were..."

Tuesday 30th July 2019

Sheena

When the doorbell rings, my face creases into a smile. Am I the first? That *is* interesting.

Two of them stand on my doorstep, the sun on their backs. The man on the left is young and handsome, with broad shoulders stretching a white pristine shirt that was probably ironed by his mum. His tangled fingers and ramrod straight back suggest uneasiness. Turning to the right, his female companion is short and squat and bursting out of grey slacks. The shine to her forehead implies it has already been a tough day. Her dark, lustrous hair shows no grey, even at the roots. The lashes appear long and natural. Despite the wear and tear and her apparent intentions to hide it, she is still an attractive woman.

"Detectives," I say, before looking down at the identification.

"Good afternoon, Ms Strachan," the female detective says. Her voice is unsurprisingly husky. "I'm sorry to trouble you. I'm Detective Inspector Hunter, and this is my colleague Detective Constable Jordan. We'd just like to have a chat with you if that's okay?"

"How very exciting," I say, holding the door open.

Leading them into the living room, I'm straight into the drinks; they're both up for coffees. DC Jordan struggles to balance a pad on his knee. His pen's thrust device is finely chewed. DI Hunter's legs are slightly parted as she leans forward in her chair.

"These are just routine enquiries, Ms Strachan," Hunter says. "I know that Pontbach is a small town, and news spreads like wildfire. I'm assuming you've heard the tragic news that Robert Campbell's body was found yesterday morning?"

I bow my head, a practiced gesture I employ at funerals when I'm not particularly fond of the dearly departed. Which is often. "I am. Such terrible news. Life can be a cruel mistress. It can throw such unfortunate hands. He had his whole life in front of him."

Squinting, Jordan glances at Hunter. When she ignores him, he scribbles frantically on his pad.

"I assure you I wasn't the one who killed him, though," I say. I make sure my laugh sounds nervous.

They both lean forward now. Perfect response. "Who said he was murdered?" Jordan asks.

Stretching back, I return the gap between us to what it was before they leaned forward. "Why ever else would you be here if there wasn't a murder to investigate? I'm sure two important detectives like yourselves would have far more pressing things to attend to..."

Jordan brushes down the invisible creases in his shirt. Hunter doesn't move a single muscle in her spongy body. "Has anybody in the town suggested that this is a murder enquiry, Ms Strachan?"

"*Please.* My mother was Ms Strachan. Call me Sheena. And no. Not to the best of my knowledge."

"Like I said, these are just routine enquiries. The most

likely explanation is that Mr Campbell died of natural causes. In the first instance, I just want to eliminate all other alternatives."

"I appreciate these are the early stages of your enquiry. And of course, it takes hours for forensics to come through. Longer when the body has drowned, I'd imagine. But you must have suspicions, just like I do-"

"What are your suspicions, Sheena?"

"Well, what reason would Rob possibly have to take his own life?" I ask.

DI Hunter rubs her forefinger across her chin. "Who knows what goes on inside somebody's mind?" she asks. Next to her, Jordan nods his head. "Mental illness is often an invisible killer. Surely the most fundamental question, though, is why would anybody else want to take Robert Campbell's life?"

I turn to the younger detective. Reluctantly, he looks up from his notepad, acknowledges my attention. "DC Jordan. Don't you think that, as a human species, we're all capable of killing anybody at any time?"

His upper lip trembles. He glances to Hunter for support. She eyes the photo's on my wall. She makes it clear he's on his own. "What do you mean? Why would you say that?"

I wave my hand, broaden my smile. "Don't worry, DC Jordan," I say. "I'm only talking theoretically. Don't you think that even the most honest, God-fearing person has the capacity to snap? To ruin a whole lifetime of moral actions with a single, horrific deed?"

Leaning forward, I clasp my hands together. I give the impression my whole life depends on his reply.

"Guess so," he says. "Unlikely, though."

I clap my hands now. "Exactly! Just what I think. Nothing is impossible, is it? But you both know, much more than me, that whilst people like to create elaborate theories, the most likely culprit in any murder is the spouse. How dull is *that*?"

Hunter coughs. "Luckily we're not in it for the excitement, Sheena."

"Very lucky."

"How well did you know Mr Campbell?" DC Jordan asks. His legs have wobbled and he's throwing punches from the ropes.

"What makes you think I knew him at all?"

I hold my gaze. He does have lovely green eyes. If only I cared.

"Well, *do* you?"

"I do. I sometimes frequent The Oak and The Swan. We've chatted a few times. I must confess, I don't know him very well. I'd probably refer to him as a friend of a friend. He's always been perfectly pleasant. Never upset me, before you ask. I was merely curious what made you think I knew him, that's all-"

"It's a small town," Jordan says. "Rightly or wrongly, I kind of assumed everybody knows everyone."

"Are you going door-to-door with these enquiries?"

"Yes, we are," Jordan says.

"And is mine the first door you've knocked on?"

"That is confidential information and I'm afraid we cannot-"

"Yes it is," Hunter says. She makes sure her face remains void of any expression.

"Is that coincidental?"

"Do you believe in coincidences, Sheena?"

I wet my lips with the tip of my tongue. "If there were no coincidences then why would the world even exist?"

Hunter smiles. I'm not sure if she means to. "Very good," she says. She looks around the room with admiring eyes. "This is a beautiful place, Sheena. Wish I could afford a place like this. What is it you said you did?"

"I didn't."

"Did you hear about the murder in Bridgend before Christmas, Sheena?"

I shrug my shoulders. "It was in the newspapers. Every loss of life is tragic, DI Hunter."

"Quite. Now you're an intelligent lady-"

"Thank you."

"So I know you understand what I'm struggling with here."

"You're wondering why it is that I've turned up in this part of Wales and suddenly you have two dead bodies."

"Exactly."

I unravel my legs. Expand my smile. "Coincidence," I say.

Hunter pushes her hands down on the sofa, ready to stand up. It is a slow, lingering movement.

"I think I have more," I say.

"More?" Jordan asks, raising one eyebrow quizzically.

I slow my breath, trying not to make it too apparent I'm keen to reel them back in. "I don't really want to say anything. It goes against everything I believe in. But I don't think I *can't*. What if I become an accomplice to a potential crime...?"

"Go on."

"Like I said. It's usually always the spouse, isn't it? Has anybody told you that Rob had a fling with Apinya Collins?"

"No," Hunter says. "You're the first. Thank you for this information."

I dab at my eyes with the back of my hand. Hunter hurriedly takes down their details.

"It's complicated," I say. "Her husband, Bernard, found them in bed together. *Their* bed. Bernard is such a darling man. But it's quite a shock, isn't it? He hit Rob, apparently."

I glance at Jordan. His forehead glistens with sweat. He has an impressive hairline. I eye his notepad. His writing is spiralling and childlike. One sentence stands out.

Husband has motive.

"Of course, it was the talk of the town. Some proper juicy gossip for a change. Naturally, I don't get involved in any of that."

"You've been most helpful, Sheena," DI Hunter says.

"There's one other thing. No. I can't see how that's relevant..."

"Let us decide that."

"Myself and Apinya are members of a group. It is a support group. We share things. But everything we discuss is in complete confidence. Like the Hippocratic Oath. We trust each other. I really can't say anything. It would be wrong-"

"It would be wrong if you don't tell us something that may hinder our enquiry..."

I sink my head into my open hands. I rub my skin so that it brings a flush to my cheeks.

"Okay. Now you've said it like that. I guess I really don't have a choice, do I? Apinya said that sometimes Bernard beats her..."

They seem in a rush to leave now. I guess they must have another door to knock on.

"Thank you, Sheena. If we have any more questions,

then we'll be in contact."

Shutting the door behind them, I allow myself a smile.

I have no doubt that they will be in touch again, whether it is to discuss *this* death, or the next one.

Bernard

Ironically, ever since that afternoon when I stopped caring what my wife thinks, her opinion of me has skyrocketed.

It feels like I'm walking around in a continuously intoxicated state. Whilst there is no euphoria, my inhibitions and self-doubts have all but disappeared. I have to admit, that does feel bloody fantastic. The nagging questions have vanished. Am I being insensitive? Who cares! Is that insensitive? Good! From what Sheena told me, my reputation is already in the gutter, so how can I possibly sink any lower? Apinya is visibly excited by my new primitive self. She loves that I take the initiative in the bedroom, that I literally just go ahead and take her, usually hard and from behind. Whilst it goes completely against my natural instinct, I can't deny that it *is* thrilling.

All of this changed a few nights ago.

She told me she was meeting Sheena. I didn't believe her, but neither did I question her; I just didn't care. She came home late; I don't know what time. I pulled the duvet off my naked body, ready to greet her, but she walked along the hallway and past our bedroom, to one of the guest rooms. Since then she has barely been in the house, and we've only exchanged a few, fleeting sentences. Whilst she hasn't been overtly unfriendly, she has been evasive; she's lowered her head and mumbled her words.

This morning I'd already had a quick workout and eaten my breakfast before it dawned on me that I was alone in the house. Tiptoeing up the stairs, I slide open the bedroom door. Apinya has such a slight frame that sometimes it's difficult to tell whether a diminutive mound is the outline of her body or merely the duvet rolled up in a ball. There is no confusion this time - the duvet is flatter than the Peak District.

When the front door knocks, my heart sinks.

My confused thoughts are thrown into disarray. Forget what she has done to me; just what sort of uncaring husband am I to not notice my wife wasn't here? Charging down the stairs, I jump the final four steps, feeling my knees creak as both feet land on the floor together.

The man and woman stood on the driveway hold up badges.

"Oh dear lord," I say. "What is it? Has something happened to Apinya?"

The female takes a step back. "Excuse me?"

"My wife! Apinya. Please tell me she's safe?"

"Why wouldn't she be safe? Sir, do you have reason to believe your wife may be in danger?"

"She isn't home. I don't know where she is. Why else would you be here?"

"When was the last time you saw your wife, Mr Collins?"

"Last night. But I did hear her this morning when I was in bed. I'd say it was about 8am."

Both detectives make no effort to hide their deep sighs. The woman makes a big issue about checking her watch.

"I'm sure she will turn up shortly, Mr Collins-"

"So that's not why you're here?"

She introduces both herself and her male companion. I glance at the identification. DI Hunter asks if they can come inside to ask some routine questions. Relieved, I follow them down the hallway.

The young man looks down, up and around - at the polished laminate floor and the Tabriz carpet, to the commissioned oil paintings and the mahogany ornaments. Slapping his hands down against his thighs, he looks ready to tell me, like they all do, that I have a wonderful home; DI Hunter's scowl silences him.

It dawns on me that, despite pretences to the contrary, this is no routine visit. I'd tried to brush it under the carpet, hadn't I, like a red bill through the letterbox? As I make the coffee, I try to quieten my breathing. I return with the cups. I'm too nervous to sit down. Instead, I stand over them.

"I appreciate I'm in a great deal of trouble, Detectives. In all honestly, I'm relieved in a way that you've caught up with me. It has been weighing me down, eating away at me."

The younger detective doesn't look sure that I'm sane. "*Sorry?*"

"I've committed a crime and now I'm ready to serve my time."

"Which crime are you referring to, Mr Collins?" DI Hunter asks. She angles her head. The question lingers. I can almost see it, floating in the air.

"With Mr Campbell," I say.

"What did you do to Mr Campbell?"

I decide to sit down now. I was beginning to feel exposed, like I was on stage. I felt compelled to talk, to fill any voids.

"I caught him with my wife. In our bedroom. In our bed. I struck him. Threw him out of the house. Quite outrageous behaviour, I know. Unforgivable. I'm really just explaining the circumstances."

DI Hunter purses her lips as she sips her drink. "I'm not sure many men would have acted any differently," she says. "We're not here about that."

"He hasn't pressed charges then?" I try not to smile.

Hunter shakes her head.

"Do you think he will?"

"It's a bit late now, Mr Collins."

I must look confused, so she explains the reason for their visit.

"*Dead?* In what way?"

"In the usual way, sir."

The younger detective stifles a laugh. They think they have a right one on their hands here.

"I just mean, what was the cause of death? He was only a young man. Oh my God, I can't believe he is dead."

"It is too early to determine the cause of death at this moment, but the most likely explanation is that he died of natural causes," the DI says.

"Natural causes?"

"That he had an accident. Or he took his own life."

I give an open-mouthed nod. This is straightforward then. Where is my wife?

"So, I gather from the incident that you made reference to, that yourself and Mr Robert Campbell were not exactly the best of friends?" DI Hunter asks.

"What do you mean?"

DC Jordan smiles. "He slept with your wife. Clearly, you weren't happy about that."

"Why are you asking? I thought you said he died of

natural causes?"

Jordan stares down at his pad. I turn to Hunter. She rests her chin in her hand. "We said that is the most likely explanation. We are just conducting a few initial enquiries. Do you not consider that to be a reasonable question, in the circumstances?"

I sit back in the chair. My trousers ride high up my leg. She's implying that I'm privileged, that I'm beyond the normal tedious questioning.

"Not at all. Most understandable. I guess I'm in shock. I didn't like Mr Campbell. But I didn't hate him enough to kill him. I'd already taken my retribution. Why would I then kill him?"

"Maybe you thought that what you did wasn't enough?"

She holds my look. Turning away, I shake my head.

"So you were in an agitated state concerning Mrs Collins when we arrived today. Why were you worried about her?"

"I don't know where she is."

"But she is an adult. She could have just popped to the shops. Seen a friend. Why would you think anything would be wrong with her?"

I bite at a fingernail. "She's been quiet recently. Distant. I don't know what is on her mind. As you can imagine, our relationship is kind of unusual at the moment-"

"I *can* imagine."

We sit in awkward silence for a few moments. I eye their cups. Why do I assume they'll leave as soon as they've drunk their coffee?

"What was Mrs Collins' relationship with Mr Campbell like after the incident?" DI Hunter asks.

"I don't know. We've never actually talked about it."

The detective nods, indicating that she understands. Her colleague still looks at me blankly.

"You've been most helpful," DI Hunter says. "I'm sorry to have taken up so much of your time. Hopefully, we won't need to trouble you again."

My body feels lighter, like I've just completed a dreaded exam. I quickly gather the cups. DI Hunter raises her buttocks from the depths of the sofa. She twists her head. Lines appear at the edges of her eyes.

Was that the front door?

We all look up in unison as my missing wife enters the room.

Her white smile is broad and welcoming. She doesn't appear distant and withdrawn anymore.

And then she removes her black sunglasses.

All three of us gasp at the purple bruise covering her right eye.

Wednesday 31 July 2019

Sheena

Her magnified face looks huge through the door. The shine of her cheeks stands out.

"Oh hello, Melanie," I say, my plastic smile bringing light to the hallway. My flamboyant hand invites her into my palace. I move to the side, probably allowing far too much room for her to enter, but I'm conscious of her wide hips, of her unfortunate, pear-shaped body. The outward feet and the waddle remind me of a duck. "I wasn't expecting to see you quite so soon."

Her nervous smile is forced, too. "Thank you for seeing me at short notice, Sheena. I'll be honest, I didn't expect to see you quite so soon, either."

She'd called earlier in the morning, when I was basking in the bath, my naked body covered with hot water, my face layered with sweat. Her breathless voice was high-pitched. Instantly, I knew that this was a difficult call for her to make. Something must have happened. Somebody must have contacted her, prompting the call. My nipples hardened as she hurriedly asked if she could see me; this *was* exciting.

"Tea with milk and one sugar, isn't it?" I ask from the kitchen, as she sinks into the sofa, fingers fiddling and messing.

"You remembered," she says. Her teeth would look

more suitable on a horse. "How thoughtful."

Of course I remembered. I was aghast that a woman of her size took sugar in her tea. Hadn't she heard of diabetes?

"I remember thinking that you're sweet enough without the sugar," I say, as I sit down on the chair next to hers, my feet dangling precariously close to her knee.

She fans her reddened cheeks with her hand. I wait for her to settle down, to take a sip of her tea, for her to get comfortable, before I lean forward to get down to business.

"So can I ask what the purpose of this specific visit is, Melanie?"

She shifts in the chair, tugs at her necklace. The poor woman is worried that I'll be upset by whatever she has to tell me. I'm sure that she has a string of qualifications to her name, that she settles down in her bed every night with a heavy book, but clearly she's short on emotional intelligence. I'd hoped she would at least give me some sort of a challenge.

"I don't want to alarm you, but we were contacted by the police-"

"The police?"

"Yes," she says, forcing a laugh. "Don't worry, you haven't done anything wrong. You're not in any trouble. It was in connection with the tragic death of a young man recently who was found floating in the river..."

"Oh yes, the delightful DI Hunter came to speak to me yesterday with her colleague. She reassured me that it was just routine enquiries. I was the first person she contacted, by all accounts, so I knew she was aware of my background. It is kind of irritating, you know? I'm trying to make a new start and yet I can't shake off my background. I guess it is just one of those things. I tried to be as helpful as I could, to aid their enquiries, and they seemed happy enough. Why did they contact you, though?"

Melanie waves her hand in the air, trying too hard to dismiss my alarm."Don't worry, Sheena. Merely procedure, as far as I could gather. The detective looked you up on the database and discovered who you are. As you can imagine, it was probably quite a shock, particularly in a sleepy town like Pontbach, where nothing really happens. I cannot tell you too much, of course, because of confidentiality rules, but she enquired whether we had any information that might assist them. Personally, I think she was looking to gain an opinion of-"

"What I'm capable of?"

She fans her face. "Yes. If you like."

"What did you say?"

"Again, I can't tell you too much, Sheena. I hope you understand? But everything I did say was positive."

"Good. I appreciate that."

"We told DI Hunter the reason you were here. I'm confident they won't take the matter any further."

I nod. Lower my eyes. Make sure she catches me glancing at her cleavage (two monumental mounds of white flesh). I glance away, pretending I've been caught out. Naughty me. "So is that the only reason you came to visit me?"

"It is a welfare visit really, Sheena. I wanted to make sure that you were okay. I can imagine that having the detectives knocking on your door yesterday and questioning you must have been quite an ordeal. We have a responsibility to check on your welfare, particularly after what you went through last year. I imagine it brought back horrendous memories."

I trace my fingers across the bridge of my forehead. She can't see my eyes, but she'll probably suspect I'm fighting back the tears. Sniffing, I look up and hold her concerned gaze. "It was unexpected, that's for sure. Initially I assumed that somebody in the town had discovered who I was and made a complaint. All the good things I've built here would be ruined if people know who I was.

"Oh dear..."

"But of course, my personal issues are trivial compared to the enormity of the incident. A young man died. He drowned. Once I realised what the detectives were attending my home for, I was really just keen to help in any way I could."

"Of course. And I know you would."

Apart from Melanie sipping her tea, all I can hear is the ticking of the clock. I wait for her to look at me before I lean back in the chair and cross my legs. Just as I thought. Behind her glasses, her eyes widen at the sight of the hem of my skirt rising. Her throat contracts as I reveal my long, shapely, tanned thighs.

I say nothing. I merely pull my skirt up a few more inches, running my fingers over my leg. My eyelashes flutter. My smile widens. My tongue grazes my teeth.

"It's okay," I say. "I look at you, too, Melanie, when I think you're not watching..."

My guest squints. Perhaps she is blinking away unwanted thoughts? She is a professional. I am her client. She wants to act appropriately. The attention - from a beautiful young woman - however, is intoxicating. How can she possibly resist? "You do? But why would you look at *me*? I'm so frumpy and plain..."

My eyes flutter over her body. They visibly undress

her, right in my living room. "I'd die for curves like yours," I say. "Me? I'm just straight up and down. You? Your body is mesmerising."

Melanie does her best to resist her urges. Slurping loudly, she finishes her cup of tea. I long to rub some ice over her burning cheeks. She runs through some formalities, scribbles down a few things on a form. She gets up to leave, heads for the front door.

Daniel will tell you that timing is everything, with nearly everything in life.

Her hand is already on the door handle when my crotch brushes up against her buttocks. She releases a long, unrestrained sigh.

"You're free to leave," I say. "If that's what you'd like to do. I'm not going to keep you against your will."

Her hand trembles on the handle, but she does not pull it down. She turns to me. Her eyes look downward. My finger caresses the underside of her chin.

"If this detective does come back, and she starts asking more questions, will you make sure she goes away? Will you do that for me, Melanie?"

Staring at my open lips, she nods her head.

"That's a good girl," I say.

I push her body up against the front door. As my fingers reach inside her skirt and pull her pants to one side, my guest sinks her head against my shoulder and releases a deep, throaty moan...

Tuesday 6th August 2019

Katherine

With my hair scraped back and my face void of makeup, I'm hardly the most glamorous exerciser. The navy-blue joggers form a loose ring around my shrinking waist, reminding me of a hula hoop. With my arms swinging by my side, I'm a baby throwing punches. My head fixes straight ahead. My eyes, though, dart here, there and everywhere, like I'm discreetly trying to swat a nuisance fly. Dangling my hands by my side for just a moment, I turn on my heels and start another lap.

This new estate is lovely. Square, green lawns lie adjacent to weed-free drives sporting two family cars. They are the ideal accompaniment to the symmetrical houses with three bedrooms and two bathrooms. And yet it is somewhat *too* lovely. Part of me wonders if the husband and wives with their two blue eyed, blonde haired children *literally* recharge their batteries when they go to bed. I could understand how a resident could go mad with paranoia, imagining they're on The *Truman Show*.

Did that curtain just twitch?

Blowing out air and digging my nails into my palms, I head out of the estate.

My heart quickens but my pace slows. Crossing the

bridge, I dare to glance down at the peaceful, rippling water. The town centre is only just awakening, seemingly with sleep-ridden eyes and a hangover. Metal shop shutters begin to rise. A few workers scurry past holding their morning coffee. An older gentleman balances a newspaper under his arm. I exchange the occasional smile, the occasional hello. I *want* to look over my shoulder. I *want* to double-check I'm not delusional, that I'm not floating in some fantasy bubble. I continue walking. I continue looking straight ahead.

The shutter is still at half-mast, but the shop is open. Ellie Goulding's version of *Your Song* plays in the background. The young, female assistant leans over the counter. She smiles when I enter, but quickly returns to her phone. Nobody else is in the shop. I look down at the polished, tiled floor. I unintentionally catch my reflection in the mirror. It doesn't mock or taunt me, like it used to. Pulling back my hair often plumps my face, but now it merely emphasises the weight I've lost. The rosy glow from the exercise isn't blotchy; it looks healthy. I allow myself a smile.

My fingers flutter across the clothes, but this time my eyes don't follow. I'm not looking to make a purchase this morning. You could say I'm window shopping, but not for anything they're selling. Casually, I make my way to the back of the shop, so my back is to the far wall and I'm facing the assistant. I pull across the plastic hangers. Pull them back.

Somebody else enters the shop.

The young girl's smile is wider this time; she holds her look for longer. She says hello. I catch her eyes wandering as the man passes. His denim jeans are loose at the heel but tight at the thigh. The short-sleeved white tee-shirt strains at the biceps. My eyes don't rise any higher.

I know who it is.

My eyes fixate on the dress in my hand, even though I'm clueless to the size, or to the colour. He pauses at the carousel at the front of the shop. I look up at the assistant. Her interest has wavered. Once again, she is mesmerised by her phone. I glance at his growing shadow. He moves closer, step by step, until I can tell that he stands next to me. His hand brushes against the garment of clothing just inches from me. I stare straight ahead.

The girl looks up now. I hold her eye as the man's thigh presses close against me. He smells like he just jumped out of the shower after a hard workout. The girl's jaw drops. So does my hand, but this is hidden from her view. She doesn't know that the other shopper - this *stranger* - grows and hardens in my open hand. She doesn't know that his own hand massages my hips underneath my tee-shirt. She *does* know that his body nestles close to me, though, and she *does* have an imagination. Her lips flicker as his hand slips inside my loose joggers...

I gently slap the hand away. My smile tells him I'm far from upset. I don't look in his face, but I briskly turn so he can hear me.

"I'll see you at the barn dance," I whisper.

All he can see is the back of my head as I head towards the exit. The background music switches to *Sweet Child O' Mine*. I turn to the young assistant and beam. I'm sure her cheeks are more flushed than when I entered.

"Have a nice day," I say.

Sheena

This has become *our* cafe. Best friends forever. I feel a tinge of guilt towards Apinya. Would she feel a sense of betrayal?

Apparently she played a blinder with the detectives. She had to. Bernard has this easy charm, a natural aura of kindness. Spend thirty minutes in a room with him and you'll be convinced he could not possibly harm a fly. Apinya walked into the room and threw everything into doubt. Of course, the female detective was straight onto the black eye. DI Hunter can switch between good cop and bad cop with the flick of her finger. I've no doubt she became Mother Teresa when my dear, meek little friend joined them. I've taught Apinya so well. She told them that Bernard did it, that he had a terrible temper (as Robert Campbell discovered). Bernard, bless him, was probably too dazed and befuddled to protest. She didn't want to press charges, though. She said she loved him too much to throw him in jail. Not only did she become the victim, but she became the martyr, too.

Now the detectives suspect both of them.

Tess is fifty yards or so up ahead, on the other side of the bridge, swinging her cream leather handbag at her side. The water ripples twenty feet or so beneath me. Of course, the bag is a fake, bought from the market. Her social media posts depict a young mother taking on the world. In reality, she signs on every fortnight and tops this up with cash in hand wherever she can get it. She is a rodent sniffing in the long grass for scraps. She lies, and she schemes. She questioned whether it was right to take the money from me. She had a young kid to feed, to be fair, and she didn't know what she was getting herself into. What isn't fake, though, is her bubbly energy and her concern for others. In a way, she is the most natural person I know. Part of my resentment stems from the nagging knowledge that I could never be like her.

The black heels, scuffed with mud, add two inches to her height (which is just as well, because she isn't the tallest). My quickening pace gains some yards, until I'm able to take in the unhealthy white flesh coating her hips, and the strain of her calves against the skinny blue jeans. I know some men lust over her soft, curvy body. She is even rounder and bouncier from the front. I'm sure she isn't short of admirers. Raising her wrist, she realises she is a few minutes early for me. She doesn't want to be loitering on her own, walking around in circles that just keep getting bigger. She doesn't realise that she'll always be a few minutes early for me. Her strides shrink. Her pace slows.

She turns right, onto the high street, just as I reach her side of the bridge. A lot of things are happening on this high street, but most people remain oblivious.

Despite her issues and her limitations, Tess lives for the moment. Without realising it, she probably puts Mindfulness into practice. I'm sure she doesn't waste time regretting her mistakes or pondering her bleak future. Whilst others lie awake over-thinking, tossing and turning, Tess barely thinks at all.

Just as well, in the circumstances.

My eyes flicker to the hanging baskets above the shop doorways, to the offers chalked on blackboards. Tess remains about twenty feet ahead, walking on the balls of her feet, straining those substantial calf muscles, edging closer to the cafe, to where she expects to meet me.

Of course, she doesn't reach the cafe.

Tess stumbles backwards, her toes upturned and her heels digging into the pavement. She lifts both hands in the air, arches her body back. Was that a shriek? Heads turn, stunned by the sudden frantic movement.

What happened?

Raising my knees, my walk turns into a jog and my jog turns into a sprint.

The heads turn to me now, glad that somebody else is taking action; I am the lifeguard in red trunks and a halo over my head running to the sea. Somebody bumped into her, didn't they? Knocked her back on her feet. Gave her a terrible fright. This happens all the time, of course; people are always distracted, on their phones or wearing headphones. In this God awful country, though, we always hold our hands up in surrender and apologise even when it isn't our fault. Good manners? We're all just zombies. We apologise at the scene and then curse behind their backs. Us Brits are just *dishonest.*

This is what makes the pedestrians blink, what makes them look again. The bulky, hooded figure keeps his head low. He does not raise his hands. He does not utter an apology. Instead, the hands remain bunched in the jacket pockets. The strides are dainty and quick. He disappears off the high street, down the lane where the drunks urinate late at night.

Tess's painted smile straightens. She puts her hand to her belly. Her dazed expression turns to bemusement.

Why is her blouse damp? Why is it tainted red? Why is the redness expanding?

"Tess!"

The shoppers turn from Tess back to me. Their mouths open at the speed of my steps, at the loudness of my shout. Tess's knees buckle and she bends at the waist. My outstretched hand grabs hold of her waist just in time to ease her fall to the pavement.

With the back of her head flat against the concrete, the whites of her eyes expand. She blinks as she looks up at me, staring down at her. She squeezes my hand.

"Sheena?" she says. "What happened?"

I'm aware of the gathering crowd circling us, blocking out the light. My knee presses against the floor. I turn around.

"Will somebody *please* call an ambulance!"

This is the one thing they all *can* do. Nobody wants to feel useless in these situations, but ultimately, we nearly all do. The group all dig into their pockets, stab the three digits into their phone.

999.

I lean forward. My lips are close enough to her ear to stick my tongue inside. I whisper my words so nobody but Tess can hear.

"You've been stabbed, Tess," I say. "Let's just hope you believe in God."

Saturday 10th August 2019

Katherine

Sheena walks up and down at the front of the room, both hands on her slim hips; she is like a pop star psyching herself to open a concert at Wembley Stadium. I don't bother looking around the room and counting heads anymore. Nobody misses a meeting. Any newcomer has to follow an induction routine. The same number of women attend this meeting as the last meeting.

She repeatedly talks about us being a family. I recall one of the last moments all of *my* family were still alive. It was late at night. I couldn't sleep. My thoughts raced. From my bedroom, I could hear my parents talking downstairs. I longed to know what they were talking about. My heart skipped a few beats as I crept downstairs. The door remained slightly ajar. I glanced through the gap. My parents were quite animated. My jaw dropped. My cheeks flushed. They were talking about Ben.

They *knew*.

"We're going to following a slightly different format this meeting, ladies," Sheena says. Her beaming smile indicates that this is a good thing. Everybody stops talking. Everybody turns and looks to the front of the room. "Kat, are you okay to come to the front? As we discussed? As we arranged?"

Synchronised heads turn now to me at the back of the room. Taking a deep breath and planting my hands flat against my thighs, I stand up. All of the women smile encouragingly. Are my ankles tied with lead? Am I walking through water? At the front of the room, Sheena stretches out her arms, pulls me close to her. She whispers in my ear.

"This is so brave, Kat."

All eyes fix on me. I may as well be a blue whale performing at Sea World. They say a good way of calming the nerves is to imagine the audience naked. With this particular crowd, that might just put me off. I clear my mind and imagine I'm talking to an empty room, that I'm talking to myself.

"Do you remember the young girl, Tess, who attended one of our meetings? It was way back before Christmas last year. She said she was sexually assaulted when she was drunk."

All of the women nod. A few of them say that she was such a sweet girl. A few others say it was terrible what happened to her.

"Well, I have reason to believe that one of those men who assaulted her was my husband."

Gasps fill the room. Looking up, a few shake their head. A few more put their hand to their mouth. None of the women question why I suspect my husband is one of the assaulters. None of the women ask what evidence I have to support this. Right now, I think they'd assume their own husbands were guilty with no questions asked.

"You poor woman," Moira says. "Living with a brute."

"They're all like that," Sheena says. "It's just that this

one got caught."

The women heartily agree.

I raise my eyes. "The thing is, last week Tess got stabbed. Right in the middle of town. In the middle of the day. It was in the newspapers."

"Oh my God! That was her? Is she okay?"

"Luckily she wasn't seriously injured," I say. "A few inches in a different direction and she'd be dead. Nobody has been convicted of this horrendous crime. I have no proof of anything, so I can't call the police. But..."

"Go on, Kat..."

"Well, I've had a heart-to-heart with Sheena about this. She's encouraged me to open up, to be brave. My natural instinct is to brush it under the carpet, to deny everything. I'm not going to do that anymore. I need to face up to the truth. I suspect that my husband, and the other man who sexually assaulted Tess, may have been behind this stabbing, too. By all accounts, they didn't mean to seriously hurt her. It was just a warning. To keep her quiet."

With my head bowed and my face flushed, I head back to my seat at the rear of the room. Twisting heads follow my movements. Sitting down, I bury my head into my open hands.

"Don't you think Kat's immense bravery - not to mention her incredible honesty - deserves a round of applause, ladies?"

The sound of clapping hands deafens my ears. Looking up, I'm greeted by smiling faces. The broadest - and the whitest - is Sheena's, at the front of the room.

"I've been mingling with Kat's husband, Ray, and his mates in the pub. I do this for the good of the group, ladies. It is vital to know what threat they pose-"

"And...?"

"They're definitely conspiring. Ray didn't commit this heinous crime on his own. I'm certain that his friends are behind it, too..."

The outraged guffaws echo around the room. I look down, at the floor. This is surreal. This is my husband they're talking about. None of it feels real.

"That is only the first of our staggering announcements this morning, ladies," Sheena says, interrupting the bedlam. "Apinya, are you okay to come to the front of the room?"

Apinya doesn't have weights tied to her ankles. She dances to the front of the room with the agility of a ballerina. I imagine a spotlight shining down on her from the ceiling. Apinya circles her right eye with her fingertips.

"Can you see this bruise?" she asks.

We all push our necks forward. The bruise has faded. Her eye does look a little purple. A few of the older dears say they can't see anything. I fear this negates the impact of what she was hoping to achieve somewhat.

"My husband did this to me. My husband hit me."

"Bernard? I can't *believe* it!"

Not many women in the room know Ray. Plenty of women know sweet, jovial Bernard. Besides, Apinya has discussed him regularly in the group.

"Yes, my darling Bernard did this to me. Just like Kat, I've never been strong enough to admit the truth before. But you ladies make me strong. He has abused me for years, both physically and mentally."

Amongst the gasps and the sighs, one of the women rises from her seat to give Apinya a hug. I narrow my reddened eyes. Bernard is an abuser?

"Do you know what I did in return? I had an affair. Maybe that wasn't right. But don't I deserve some happiness?"

"We all deserve happiness," Moira says.

I stifle a laugh. Moira *would* say that, wouldn't she? She found *her* happiness by sleeping with her brother-in law at her own wedding reception.

"But this happiness ended when Bernard found out. And you know what he did?"

Not surprisingly, nobody knows what Bernard did.

"He beat my lover, too."

Apinya lowers her hands to silence the gasps. She is like a comedian asking the audience to stop laughing so that she can proceed with her next joke. Apinya dabs at her bloodshot eye.

"That isn't the worst of it. I was forced to split with this kind, loving man. And you know what happened to him? The poor man was so distraught by the turn of events that they found him floating in the river last week..."

Every woman has heard about Rob's death. The whole town, and most of the neighbouring ones, know of his passing. I heard that DI Hunter was knocking on doors asking questions. She hounded me when my parents died, looking for something, for anything. She couldn't find anything then and she couldn't find anything now. Sheena told me that she was looking to open a murder enquiry into Rob's death, but the autopsy revealed no suspicious circumstances. Why would they? Most likely, Apinya drove him to the brink.

A sobbing Apinya returns to the shelter of her chair. The noise rattles around the room like a football stadium on match day. None of the women notice

Sheena taking Apinya's place at the front. She doesn't try to silence them. She just stands completely motionless with her arms folded across her chest until the excitement fades.

"How horrific are these stories, ladies?"

The women in the room let Sheena know in no uncertain terms that these stories are more than horrific.

"Do you agree that we need to get some revenge?"

The room roars its approval.

"On their husbands?" one of the ladies asks.

"I need my husband!"

The heads turn to Apinya. Her startled eyes show genuine fear. "I mean, I need him for *now*," she says. "I'm rebuilding my life. I have to find somewhere else to live. Get a job. I'm planning my revenge on that bastard-"

"I'm planning my own sweet revenge on my shit of a husband," I say.

"We need to play it clever. We can't draw attention to ourselves. Kat and Apinya will be the first suspects they'll look at if they take revenge on their husbands," Sheena says. "We have another man in our sights to begin with. Kat has been working hard to bring him to justice. The question is, will you support us?"

"Of course we will!"

"Whatever happens?" Sheena asks.

"Absolutely!"

Sheena eyes each woman in turn. She wants to make sure she has no doubters, no potential weak links. Her furrowed brow straightens.

"Good," she says. "I'm confident we have total, unconditional trust here. We're a family. A unit."

Sheena rubs her hands together. She leans forward at

the waist. "Right, we are going to execute our plan this Saturday 17th August, at the barn dance..."

Monday 12th August 2019

Ray

It was Saturday afternoon when things started clicking together, when I actually started using my brain and working things out.

Kat returned from her Saturday morning meeting in a bleak mood. Clearly, she had so many things on her mind. Sometimes she is overly reflective of her life. I'm convinced that now and then she ponders what her world would have been like had I not become part of it. She sat cross-legged on the sofa, mesmerised by the television screen. Black, terrifying clouds had visited her world. It was best to give her some time. She barely acknowledged my existence when I told her I was popping out. I just needed some space. To get away.

Outside, I blinked the drizzle from my eyes. I didn't head out in any particular direction. My sole purpose was to clear my mind. I just went wherever my sturdy size eleven's took me. Clearly, I must have walked in automatic pilot mode, because when I looked up, the leisure centre stood in front of me, adjacent to the playing fields. There isn't much to it - mainly just a small, claustrophobic gym and a 20-metre swimming pool. Stick up some metal goals and the badminton courts transform into a 6-a-side football pitch. Mr Brittas would *not* be impressed. I found myself walking across the rugby pitch, following my feet again. The wet, overgrown grass dampened my trainers, seeped through to my socks. What lured me to the leisure centre? Maybe it was the cheap chicken soup served in plastic cups out of the machine? No. I didn't think so.

I smiled at the young, greasy kid perched on a stool behind a plastic screen on reception. He didn't smile back.

"I was just passing," I said, "and I wondered what the building work was all about? Have us lucky locals got anything new to enjoy at our leisure centre?"

The boy arched his head. He eyed me like I'd maybe escaped from an institution.

"Building work?"

"Yeah. You know. What the workmen were here for before Christmas."

He folded his shoulders. "There hasn't been any work done here since I started."

"How long you worked here?"

"Two years."

I turned around and pushed open the glass door. I didn't need to turn around to know the kid's eyes were burning into the back of my head.

On the way back, I questioned whether I was losing the plot. That guy from the pub, the dirty bastard that touched up the young drunk girl, *definitely* said he was working on a job at the leisure centre. Why would he lie about that? My mind started working overtime. I started questioning *everything*. Coincidences? Of *course* they happen. But how outrageous do they need to be before you smell a rat? Kat told me that the guy in the white van appeared almost as soon as she left the house. Was he waiting for her to leave the house? And when I picked up the newspaper the other week and read about the poor girl who was stabbed in the town centre - in *daylight* - a picture of the sweet, young, drunk girl stared back at me.

Somebody had planned all of this.

Or was I paranoid? Maybe I was losing it?

Back home, I paced up and down in our bedroom. Downstairs, Kat remained oblivious to my presence. This wasn't just a bad day for Kat. She had changed - morphed into virtually a different person - over months and months. Catching my reflection in the full-length mirror (the one Kat absolutely *hates*) my overhanging brow and flaring nostrils reminded me of an angry bull eying a red flag. Kat's phone stared at me from her glass bedside table. More and more she's left it hanging around recently, almost daring me to look at it. Was that coincidence, too? I've always left it untouched. The lure, though, was like an ice-cold pint of lager to an alcoholic. Picking up the phone, I was stupefied that there was no password. Did she trust me unconditionally? Or was it a trap? I threw the phone down onto the bed. If she trusted me that much, then what sort of a man did that make me to snoop through her phone? I just couldn't resist, though. I retrieved the phone from the bed.

The incident with the white van man hounded me. She shared details of the incident with me when I returned home from work. She said that she located the white van, parked on his drive, and she called the man. My mind tries to think back to the approximate date and time of the incident. It was the middle of the day, for sure. It was a few months before Christmas. Probably in October. Kat doesn't call that many people. She isn't a social butterfly, or at least she wasn't back then. With the phone back in my hand, I swiped through the call history.

That was it. Digging a pen out of the drawer, I made a note of the telephone number.

I've lived with my plan hidden away inside my skull for days before I've been able to do anything about it. I set my alarm an hour early this morning, but even then, I wait, staring at the clock, counting down the minutes. Pulling on my jeans and tee-shirt, Kat begins to stir from beneath the duvet. She looks at me, eyes almost stuck together.

"Have a nice day, sweetheart," she says.

Stroking hair from her face, I plant a kiss on her forehead.

I push a mint into my mouth as I pull away. I want to get to him before he leaves the house. From the sequence of events, it didn't take a genius to work out which village Kat went to. I pass the sign within twenty-five minutes. With the sun just beginning to rise and residents pulling apart their curtains, I crawl along the streets in my own van. Up and down. Back and forth. And then I stop.

Glancing at the piece of scrap paper, I check and double-check the number on the van. I probably think the same words my darling Kat did.

Bingo.

Parked up on the other side of the road, with my backside pushed high along the seat, I stare at the house, and I wait. Whilst I wait, my anger wells inside my chest until I fear it may explode. This guy set me up. He groped and abused that sweet girl. But that is the least of my venom. You know what really makes my blood boil? This filthy bastard spat over my darling wife. How dare he?

The front door pushes open. A man appears.

Tony.

His liver-spotted hand is already outreached, ready to open his van door, by the time I get to him. He glances up, probably expecting to see the postman. No such luck. He takes a step back when he sees me on his drive, with my shoulders wide and my chest pumped out.

"Ray," he says. "This is a nice surprise. Wh-what you doing here?"

"Shut the fuck up and get in my van."

I don't need to glance back to know he is following me, a playground bully sent to the headmaster's office.

Throughout the drive, I stare straight ahead. My companion, on the other hand, has ants in his pants. He shuffles in his seat. He stretches out his legs. Pulls them back again. Tangles his fingers together. Untangles them.

"Ray? What's this all about? Where are we going?"

I don't move a muscle in my face. I don't say a word.

I park up in what, to the untrained eye, probably looks like an industrial estate. Pushing open my door and planting my foot down on the uneven ground, I sense Tony glancing from side to side as I circle the van. I pull open his door. He shrinks within the depths of his seat. I recall his bravado when he took me on at pool. The way he flexed his muscles and downed his drink. I smirk. Not so tough now, are you?

"Out."

Pulling at his collar, I give him a helping hand. With his back pushed up against the brick wall and my face just inches from his, I notice that he is a few inches taller than me. Like *that* matters.

"Did you spit over my wife, Tony?"

"I don't know what you mean, Ray."

My left fist ploughs into his ribcage. His feet leave the ground as he releases a high-pitched yelp. Spit dribbles hang from his mouth. I push his chin back up with the flat of my hand.

"Shall we try that again, Tony?"

His darting eyes look around. His face breaks into a pleading grimace. "I'm sorry, Tony. It was nothing personal. I meant no harm to you or to her. I didn't want to do it."

"If it wasn't personal, then what was it?"

Silence.

He becomes another few inches taller than me as my hand grips his crotch.

"I was paid to do it."

"That's a good boy," I say, releasing the hold. "Now we're talking."

His frown turns into a smile. Did he think we were becoming mates?

"Did the same person pay you to abuse that girl? And did they pay you to stab her? I read all about it in the newspapers."

He paused for a moment, before nodding his head. "*Why?*"

"I have no idea. I assume it was some sort of crazy vendetta."

"Give me a name."

He visibly shrinks. "I can't, Ray-"

"A name..."

"You may as well kill me now."

I raise one eyebrow. He fears whoever put him up to this more than he fears me. The poor bastard. This *must* be bad. I don't want to kill him, though. I have killed one man in my life, and I swear to God it was an accident. He was only a young kid, with his whole life ahead of him. We were scrapping at the football. I landed a punch to the side of his face. The boy fell forward. His skull cracked against the edge of the pavement. My whole world froze when I spotted blood flowing from his ears. I was never convicted, because the police didn't know which of us did it. Not a day passes without it haunting me, though. Whatever this vile man has done, I don't want to kill him.

"Take off your clothes," I said.

"*What?* What are you going to do with me?"

"Take off your clothes or I *will* kill you."

I struggle not to laugh as he kicks off his shoes and hops on one foot, trying to remove his trousers. He reminds me of a toddler getting undressed on his own for the first time. Eventually he stands in front of me naked, his two hands cupping his balls. Slowing down my movements, I pick up his discarded clothes and put them in the van. I'll throw them in the tip later.

Turning around I eye both my fists, like they have protruding claws, like I'm Wolverine.

"Run!" I say.

I give him a boot up the backside as he turns and flees, his bare feet hot against the tarmac. The poor sod doesn't realise there is a primary school just up the road. One of the teachers is an old football ally of mine. He knows he is coming.

Tomorrow morning I'll be reading about a naked man exposing himself to a group of school children. Returning to my van, I allow myself a smirk.

They don't like sex offenders in prison, do they?

Wednesday 14th August 2019

Rose

My head peers over the wall. My eyes admire the meticulous, freshly mowed lawn. In autumn, the soggy grass is smudged brown from the flattened conkers. A few tiles are missing from the slate roof. No wonder there is a horrendous draught in the winter - from here, the smeared, dirty windows appear wafer-thin.

I'm flooded with nostalgia when I spot a group of women leaving the building. We used to be close. We used to be friends. They head off in the opposite direction. They don't notice me. This is planned. I don't want to draw attention to myself. Finally, I shout out to a lone woman.

Her lined face looks up. Creases form from her eyes. I am the last person she expected to see, even though, just a year ago, I was the first person she'd see, sat at the front of the room. She stops walking. Her hands drop to her ample hips. Her thin lips curl at the corners. She doesn't see me as a foe. She sees me as a friend.

"Moira," I say. "I was wondering whether we could have a quick chat?"

Saturday 17th August 2019

Bernard

Clearly, Sheena wasn't lying when she said Apinya told the group I hit her.

Naively, I actually felt good walking to the rugby pitches hand-in-hand with my wife. I'd put on my knee-length shorts and smothered my face in sun tan lotion. Even though it was a boiling hot August afternoon, a welcome breeze swept through the air. Usually the fete is a great opportunity to catch up with people I don't get to see often. Spirits are usually high. Nobody takes themselves too seriously. I don't find any need to feel self-conscious. For the first time in as long as I can remember, I was genuinely looking forward to a social gathering.

This enthusiasm quickly vanished.

I was a marked man. My name was mud.

Admittedly, some women didn't blank me; they greeted me with a scowl. I felt daggers in the back of my head from all directions. I may as well have walked around with no pants on. The welcome breeze disappeared. The stifling heat made me itch. I looked around for a friendly face - maybe Ray or Dave or Geraint. Either they weren't here, or they saw me first.

I made my excuses and left within the hour. Apinya didn't ask any questions. She didn't try to persuade me to stay. Pecking my lips, she merely promised she wouldn't be too long.

When Apinya returned home about three hours later, with a melting ice cream in one hand and pink candy floss in the other, she announced that she didn't fancy the barn dance this year. Thank goodness. I simply couldn't tolerate anymore negativity today. Apinya said that she'd arranged to go to Sheena's flat with Kat for a girl's night in. She made it sound like they were teenage girls going to a sleepover. At first I didn't believe her, but then I questioned my doubt. After all, her lover was dead. He was found floating on top of the river. Who else would she be meeting?

Of course, I don't trust her. The autopsy did not find any suspicious circumstances; that female detective wasn't so convinced, was she? And if I didn't kill him, then who did? What sort of person was capable of committing that act? Maybe the sort of person to tell everybody her husband was a wife-beater?

Sitting on the sofa, surrounded by my gadgets and antiques and commissioned paintings, I can't remember the last time I felt so painstakingly low. Has somebody reached inside my chest and pulled out my heart? I rub my forehead with my middle fingers, before sinking my head into my open hands. Whilst I'm relieved that nobody else is around, the solitude is intensely lonely.

My mind fills with horrendous questions. What do I need to do to rebuild my life? What do I need to do to rebuild my reputation?

Not finding any answers, I'm almost relieved when the doorbell rings.

Katherine

I wasn't even supposed to be here this evening.

Ray raised both his eyebrows but remained silent when I told him I wasn't going to the dance, that I was heading to Sheena's house instead. He knew I hadn't been myself lately, anyway. Rob didn't mean anything to me (I barely knew him), but a floating body at the river - that was bound to bring back haunting memories. Ray is a loving, caring husband. I knew he wasn't going to argue with me. He merely pulled together a pained smile and told me to go and have a good time.

Forget me, though. Something hasn't been right with Ray, either. Whilst I stared absentmindedly at the TV on Saturday afternoon, he was a bunny on coke. He thinks I barely noticed him leaving the house. He used to do this when he was a football hooligan. And does he think I don't know he checked my phone? Sheena says men think it is their prerogative. He wouldn't have found anything on there, of course, but that's not the point. It's just so unlike him. What exactly is going on with my husband?

Stood in the entrance to the barn in my gorgeous red dress, I had wanted to remain inconspicuous, but the women from the group caught my eye. Some of them nodded their head. Others smiled. I knew I looked good. I hadn't felt this confident since I was a teenager. This was my moment. My eyes stopped working the room and fixed on my target.

I didn't need to seek his attention. Even though his arms were wrapped around his wife, his eyes fixed on me. I can't deny I felt a pang of excitement. Admittedly, part of the thrill was that he was taken, that he was a forbidden fruit. His wife remained completely oblivious to what was going on, to the fact her husband lustily eyed another woman. Me. Despite our scheming, despite our ill-intentions, my smile wasn't forced. I couldn't hold it back. I didn't need to gesture with my hands, or with my mouth. Our fleeting relationship isn't built on words. He hasn't uttered a single word to me. No. I merely pulled my head back, just a few inches, then I turned on my heels. I know all of the women from the group trailed Grant's movements as he left his wife to her plastic cup of warm wine and dutifully followed me out of the barn.

The control I had over him exhilarated me. His eyes couldn't stop wandering all over my body. Jesus. My skin tingled. I felt a hot flush to my chest, creeping downwards. I didn't *need* to poke my tongue inside his mouth. It wasn't *him* (as such) that excited me. It was the pure, unequivocal power, the thrill of knowing that this young, handsome man lusted after me, that he would do anything to taste me, to savour me.

The three of us agreed the plan after last Saturday's meeting. We waited for the other women (the Pawns, as Sheena sometimes calls them) to vacate before we huddled together in the room and conspired. Sheena widened her eyes as I took the initiative. Apinya nodded her head. She'd go along with anything so long as Sheena approved the idea.

I was merely the lure. I was the temptation Grant just couldn't resist. Me! And so I enticed him to the smaller barn, on the outskirts of the farm. I pushed him inside. Sheena and Apinya waited inside for him. I stayed outside. Initially he wouldn't even notice I wasn't there. He wouldn't complain, though. How could he? He was alone with two sensationally beautiful women.

I convinced Sheena and Apinya that I couldn't face tying him up, that I couldn't muster the strength to set the hay on fire. That way, in my warped mind, I was merely an accomplice to the crime. I wasn't the killer. I expected them to protest, to malign me. It was quite the opposite. Apinya's eyes expanded into saucers. She *wanted* to kill him. Sheena's reaction, of course, was not so blatant. She merely lowered her eyes. This was the best she was going to get from me. She had always doubted me.

She still thought I was the weakest link.

They reappeared from the barn and into the light with beaming smiles, high on the euphoria of what we were doing. We had come this far. There was no turning back. I couldn't show my doubts. I couldn't show my fears. I wrapped my arms around the two women and joined in with the delirious giggles. The smoke inside the barn was just beginning to build, to spread. The fire was just beginning to get out of control. The screams were beginning to become wild and uncontrolled.

"Let's split," I said. "Let's not bring any attention to ourselves. We don't want to be seen together, do we? We should meet there."

Worried creases appeared around Apinya's eyes. They softened when Sheena broke into a smile.

"Good plan," she said.

I was leading the way.

Apinya

The first time I killed was only a handful of weeks ago. Even though I had planned to kill Rob, when it came down to it, he gave me no choice. If I didn't kill him then he would have killed me. It was merely self-defence, right?

Initially I was traumatised by the enormity of what happened. I was a killer! Sat in the churchyard with Sheena afterwards, I longed to pinch myself. Was this a dream? Was this an hallucination? This can't be *me* we're talking about. Even Sheena was horrified when I told her I'd killed Rob. Apparently she only wanted me to scare him away. She didn't *say* that though, did she? Of all the people in all of the world who I thought would understand, it was in Sheena. When she didn't, I knew I was in trouble. But then her attitude changed, didn't it? The more I told her, the more impressed she was. Our roles switched. She looked at me in awe! Amidst the terror and the looming fog, I sensed bravado.

If you get life for one murder, then you may as well commit two. This is all irrelevant, though, because I'm going to get away with it. I'm now a serial killer. How many people in this world, let alone this town, can say that?

It was Kat's idea to split. The old buzzard really has impressed me. How did she manage to think so logically? I'd always assumed she'd lose her nerve at the last minute. It was only a matter of time. I was ready for her when she did. She isn't like myself and Sheena. We're *made* for this type of excitement. Sheena has said as much, but I've always been wary that Kat wasn't really committed to our cause. Sure, she's begun to say the right things and smile in the right places, but her mind always seems elsewhere. Bizarrely, considering my husband is much richer than hers, I've always had this nagging feeling that she looks down on me. How would that make sense? That would be like a girl from *TOWIE* looking down on a girl from *Made In Chelsea*. It's ridiculous!

Stood outside the barn, with the fire building nicely inside, the three of us giggled like schoolgirls. We had pulled it off. Together. As a team. My previous doubts towards Kat disappeared. She'd proven me wrong. The three of us were sisters now, like we'd taken a vow and shared blood. It was then that she suggested we take different routes, so the three of us weren't seen together. Fear seeped through my body. I didn't want to be alone. But Sheena's face lit up. She said it was a good idea. It must be, because Sheena is always right. We all embraced, and then fled in different directions.

I decided to take a longer route, along the road. I fancied a walk, to clear my mind. Now though, my calves are beginning to strain. Bernard is the walker. He likes to go for his hikes in the mountains. He likes his own company. I do feel bad about how our marriage materialised. He has been good to me. He doesn't deserve for the town to view him as a wife beater.

It isn't my fault, though. It was Sheena's idea. What was I supposed to do? We had a greater cause. There had to be a few victims along the way.

I decide to kick off my heels and walk barefoot, like I

did on one of our nights out. Oh God, it feels like my feet can actually breathe! Pulling my hand to my mouth, I silence a hiccup. Sheena said I should avoid the wine tonight, to keep my mind alert, but I couldn't resist a few cups. Even I suffer with occasional nerves. I walk as close to the grass verge as I can. With the light fading fast and the road so narrow and twisting, a car won't see me until it is too late. I don't fancy getting run over, particularly after everything we've just achieved. Sheena is right. Apart from the odd exceptions, men really are the Devil. Take that guy back there. Did you hear the way he squealed like a pig? But that was appropriate, because he *is* a pig! He had a wife and two young children, didn't he? Just what was he thinking of? Okay, I know I cheated on my husband, but we don't have children. My circumstances just aren't the same. We were doing the world a good deed by removing his life. That way he won't be able to hurt anybody else with his vile urges.

I don't want to look over my shoulder. I thought I heard breathing. I thought I heard footsteps. It must be the darkness; Sheena said it plays tricks on your mind. Why am I walking on my own? I *knew* it wasn't a good idea to split. My mind *is* playing tricks on me. Don't be a silly little girl, Apinya!

The breathing grows louder. The footsteps move closer. I can no longer blame paranoia. The muscles in my shoulders stiffen. My breathing tightens. I turn around, ready to stab whoever it is in the eye with one of my high heels. Do they realise who they're messing with? Do they realise that they have a killer in their midst?

"Oh it is *you*," I say, putting my hand to my chest. I

start laughing. I really *was* being ridiculous. "What are you doing here?"

The breathing continues to get louder. The footsteps continue to move closer.

"I am here to kill you."

Katherine

I conscientiously and methodically count one hundred steps before I turn on my heels and head back in the direction of the barn.

Maybe it is the adrenaline pumping through my body? My fingers tingle. I can barely feel my feet. Of course, everything we are doing is utterly outrageous. Disgraceful. Shameful.

And yet, I hadn't felt this alive since I was a teenager.

I quicken my pace. I need to get there before it is too late. I acted quickly before, and I'll act quickly now. Of course, Sheena and Apinya had no idea that I didn't just stand dutifully on the spot, like a good girl, whilst they were busy in the barn. No. I've wasted too much of my life standing still, watching the world pass me by. As soon as I pushed the wooden door shut, I pressed my hands down against the adjoining wall and pulled myself up onto the barn roof. Lying flat on my front, like a sniper eying his target, I glanced through the gap in the roof. Pulling out my phone, I filmed my two darling friends tying a young man with rope at the wrists and ankles before setting the building on fire.

Pretty damning evidence, I'd say.

Maybe I *am* too late? My cough is throaty. My eyes water and sting. Pulling my arms to my face, I walk through the smog. I use the flat of my foot to push away the heavy stone we placed in front of the wooden door. Pulling the door open, I dive inside, not really caring if I live or die. The cries for help are muffled. At least he is alive. I grab hold of his ankles and drag his body out of the barn.

Outside, his body lies floppy against the muddy ground. His eyes are dotted red. All colour has seeped from his face. His hands press flat against his chest as he splutters and coughs.

He'll live.

Untying the rope, I plant a tender kiss on his darkened forehead. I twist his face so it looks straight up at me.

"Promise me you won't tell anyone I was involved in any of this."

He struggles to produce any words. I press my fingers into his cheeks.

"I promise," he says.

"Good. Now you go back to your wife and be a good boy. Okay?"

He nods.

I spring to my feet and run to the metal gate.

I've got some catching up to do.

Sheena

Rose used to be the only person to have a key. God. It seems so long since she led from the front. Whatever happened to her? Now Kat has a key. Apinya has a key. I have a key.

Passing the chest-high wall, I glance up at the pitch-black sky. Bright, shiny stars cluster around the sleepy half-moon. I push the door. No movement. It doesn't open. I must be the first here. That's a surprise. Sweet, deluded Apinya was so hyped from the thrill of taking another life that I'm surprised she didn't skip here. Maybe she took a detour? Honestly, sometimes I wonder what on earth goes through that girl's mind. Kat isn't here, either. She *is* more of a worry. Maybe she had second thoughts? She has surpassed expectations so much tonight. Maybe she just cracked? Maybe - *finally*- her guilty conscience got the better of her? I crinkle my nose. Frankly, it doesn't really matter if she breaks. She must realise I've considered all alternatives, that whatever route she takes, none of them will lead to me? What could she possibly do? Blabber to that knucklehead husband of hers? Go to the police? I've got so much dirt on her, she may as well lock *herself* up.

I turn the key and slide open the door. A stray bird flutters somewhere upstairs. Could that possibly be the sound of a mouse scurrying along the floorboards? Kat says that this place gives her the creeps. Who can blame her? The darkness and the dusty odour remind me of returning to an empty student flat after the summer holidays. Looking down, I half-expect to see a pile of red letters scattered on the floor. Pushing my arms out to my side, like I'm a trapeze artist, my fingertips graze the bumpy, rough, flaking walls. I don't turn on the corridor light, as agreed; we don't want to bring any attention to the building. To all intents and purposes, the school lies empty tonight. Opening the door to the hall, where we hold our meetings, I switch on this light. Our room lies to the back of the building. Nobody can possibly see us from here.

I take a chair at the front of the room and stretch out my legs. The room feels much smaller and more depleted without the excited chatter, without the rows and rows of occupied chairs. We've worked wonders over the last year to bring the group back to life. My eyes rise to the ceiling, to the yellow stains and the cracks that spread like varicose veins from wall to wall. My feet tap on the dusty, hard floor. These are exceptional circumstances but - *still* - I don't like waiting. This is the second time in a handful of weeks that I've had to wait for Apinya. Folding my arms across my chest, I resist the urge to check my watch. Daniel would say that checking my watch shows a lack of patience, that it depicts nerves. He has an infinite amount of time to pass these days. I don't bother to look at my phone. We *never* communicate by phone. Not anymore. Those are the rules. Daniel says that the small details are the ones that make all the detail.

The sound at the front door makes me sit up straighter. Hesitant, muffled movements make their way down the corridor. The door pushes open.

"Kat," I say. "I thought you'd be Apinya."

"She's still not here?"

"No."

"Not to worry," she says. "You know what she's like. She's probably taken the long route, just to make sure nobody saw her. That girl has to do things her way, doesn't she?"

"Yes. I'm sure you're right."

I stand up and take Kat in my arms. Her thick, dark hair tickles my nose. Her perfume is wonderfully alluring. Her body curves in and out in all the right places in her wonderful red dress, like a man sculpted her. I hate to admit it, but she was the perfect lure, like a worm to a fish. Who would have imagined it six months or so ago? Sometimes even I'm amazed by the impact I have on people.

Kat pulls out a chair on the front row and sits down opposite me about four feet away. I expected her to frantically pace up and down the room, to incessantly ask non-stop questions. I know she suffers with dark, horrific moods that attempt to suck any remains of joy from her body. I assumed she would be panicky and anxious. In contrast, she sits perfectly still, with her hands flat against her thighs. Maybe she is beyond anxious? This can happen when somebody suffers from a panic attack. Is she numb with fear?

"So why are we here, Sheena?"

"We're just waiting for Apinya."

"I know we're waiting for Apinya. But once she's here - what then?"

I inhale air to extinguish my sigh. I don't want any unnecessary arguments. We went through all of this after the meeting last Saturday. Why does she feel the need to ask again?

"We're hiding. Letting the dust settle. Waiting for the fire to get out of control, for the police and the fire brigade to attend the scene. We're keeping away from the pandemonium. We don't want to be anywhere near the scene when it all kicks off. And believe me, it *will.*"

Kat nods. But then she looks out of the corner of her eye. Up at the ceiling I observed moments before she arrived. "But why didn't we go to your flat? That's where we're supposed to be. That's where I told Ray I was going. That's where Apinya told Bernard she was going."

I shake my head. Maybe she *is* losing it? Is she not thinking straight? "That's the first place they'd go," I say.

"Why?"

I can't help but scrunch up my face now. She is an annoying child that keeps asking questions. "*Why?*"

Kat crosses one leg over the other. She rubs her hands together. "Yes. I mean, why would the police even think of going to your flat? Why would they think you have anything to do with the fire? What link could they possibly make to you?"

These questions are getting harder. I look to the door. Where *is* Apinya? I hold up my hands. "I've got some history, okay? Why do you think I appeared in this goddamn town out of nowhere? I was escaping my past life. That charming DI Hunter knocked on my door first when they found Rob's floating body. Do you think *that* was coincidence?"

Kat shakes her head. "I don't believe in coincidences."

I hold her eye now. I'm getting irritated by this conversation. I need to silence her, before I lose my temper. She doesn't look away. "The police won't come here. Hunter won't think of finding us in this dump. That's why we're here."

"I've had some experience with DI Hunter before," Kat says.

"Oh yes?"

"When my parents died. She was a nuisance. She always had suspicions. She was like a dog with a bone."

"She seems like the type," I say.

Kat breaks into a smile. "I was just thinking on the way over here," she says. "My mind was racing, to be honest with you. It's not surprising really, is it? Anyway, I came up with a different theory of why you chose to bring us here."

I *do* sigh now. "What theory is that then?"

She grazes the tongue stud against her teeth. Sucks in air. "I think you and Apinya wanted to bring me here so that you could kill me, Sheena."

I pull my head back. My laughter echoes around the room. The silence, when I stop laughing, startles me. I scan Kat's face for a trace of emotion. She remains a wax doll. "Why would you think that?" I ask. "That's crazy."

She shrugs her shoulders. "You *are* crazy, Sheena," she says.

I go to argue against this, but then realise I don't have much of a defence. I *am* a crazy bitch. That's why I'm so special.

"There's only two things wrong with that plan," Kat says.

"What's that, then?"

Kat looks around the room, then to the door. "Apinya isn't here, is she?"

"No. She's not," I say. "I'll give you that. What's the

second reason?"

Kat slides her chair forward a few inches. Her face is within arm's reach of mine. Her smile appears wide and delirious.

"Well," Kat says. "I am here to kill *you*."

Katherine

This building has always stirred negative emotions. They're much more potent at night, though, when the place is virtually empty. I swear the walls have eyes and ears. Of course, I've never, *ever* been able to separate the building from my dead, older brother, Ben, which is a shame. Usually I picture him in his grey shorts and socks walking to school, dreading the day that lies ahead. Now I imagine him sat at home during the summer holidays, counting down the days until he has to return to this horrific place.

Sheena shuffles in the seat opposite me. She likes to be at the front of the room, of course. It is a power thing. Originally she made myself and Apinya the leaders. We were merely a distraction. She didn't want to draw too much attention to herself. We were there to give her a foot up. She is shrewd, I'll give her that. Right now her eyes don't move away from me for a millisecond and her right hand caresses the blade hidden away in her pocket; she reminds me of a school ground bully who has been put in her place. Doubts have replaced her bravado.

"You really have *no* idea who I am, do you?" I ask.

She laughs. Her shoulders widen. She thinks she has the upper hand again. "Oh, Kat," she says. "You worried me for a moment there. But now I know you have *nothing.*"

"Why do you think that?"

She leans forward in her chair now. Closer to me. "Because I know so much more about you than you could ever imagine, Katherine."

I give her an encouraging smile. "Tell me everything you know, Sheena. I'm all ears."

She is a master at hiding her true emotions, of course. I don't even think she knows what her true emotions *are* anymore. She morphs into whatever people want her to be, to whatever they want to hear. It is a tremendous skill. She does it to the group, to the men (including my husband) in the pub. She does it to me. Now, though, her flushed face suggests uncertainty.

"I moved to this town because of *you*, you silly bitch," she says. "You are the catalyst for all of my plans."

I glance at my polished nails, looking for any cracks or imperfections. I look up at Sheena. Release a bored sigh. "But who *am* I?"

Sheena gives a condescending raise of the eyebrows. "Ooh, somebody's getting philosophical tonight, aren't they?"

I don't say anything. I just leave her to fill the void.

"You're Benjamin Conway's sister-"

"And who's Benjamin Conway?"

"He was murdered by the serial killer Daniel Perry on 5th June 1988. He was his third victim. Rose's daughter, Marie, was his fifth victim."

I raise my own condescending eyebrows. "*Very* impressive, Sheena. You've done your homework, haven't you? I'll give you an A star. Good girl."

"What has gotten *into* you?" she asks. She doesn't like me mirroring her. It tells her I'm aware of her behaviour, of the little games she plays. I can see the spit coating her teeth, the subtle cracks in her lips.

Everything feels magnified. My senses have heightened to a completely new level. "Maybe you should be asking who I am?" Sheena says.

I push my knees together. Straighten my back. "Oh. That's a good question. Who *are* you, Sheena Strachan?"

Her smile widens. "I'm Daniel Perry's girlfriend. Yes - the man who killed your brother. He sent me here, Kat. Daniel sent me here to kill Rose. He sent me here to kill you. He enjoys torturing the lives of those he has already destroyed..."

I look down at my body. "You haven't done a very good job of that yet, have you?"

Sheena smirks. "Where *is* Rose? How do you know I haven't killed her yet?"

"Fair play," I say. "I don't."

"So I need to give you some credit, Kat. Maybe you were right."

"What's that?"

"Maybe I am here to kill you?" Sheena says.

"Maybe you are. You *do* realise I knew who you were the very first time I saw you?"

I sense Sheena's bluster fade. She played her trump card and I wasn't floored.

"More importantly," I say, "he doesn't love you, you know?"

Sheena twists her fingers together now. I catch the whites of her knuckles. "Who doesn't love me, Kat?"

"Daniel."

She blows hot air from her mouth. "And why do you think he doesn't love me?"

My eyes glance around the room. I roll my tongue over my lips. I know this annoys her. "Because I'm the only person Daniel's ever loved, that's why..."

Sheena

I glance to the door again. It has become a compulsion. I've never wanted to see anybody as much as Apinya right now. I long for the door to swing open, for her to walk in uttering breathless apologies. Apinya worships me more than any woman in the group. I truly am her leader. She'll be on my side. There is another reason I keep looking at the door, though. I keep checking who is closer to the exit -me or this stranger I suddenly find I'm sharing the room with.

"You're psychotic," I say, spitting out the words.

Kat shrugs her shoulders. "Maybe I am. Maybe I'm not. Did he tell you that you were the Queen in this little game of his? He sent you to *me,* Sheena."

I hold her eye. "So what happened, Kat? Did he reply to one of your fan letters from prison? Not only are you psychotic, but you're deluded, too. You're a sick, pathetic bitch..."

She looks down at the floor. "Sticks and stone, Sheena, sticks and stones. I wish I was deluded. I wish I never met him. I truly do."

I decide to go along with it. I want to hear what she has to say, even if it is just a sick fantasy. "When did you meet him? Did you have an affair? Does Ray know about it?"

She shakes her head. "He was my first love. When I was a teenager. He was my *only* love."

Her gleeful smile vanishes. She looks forlorn. She

doesn't love Ray?

"Sheena. You know I'm sometimes overcome with dark moods?"

I nod. I may be heartless, but even *I* think they sound painful. I don't envy her.

"Do you know why I get these moods?"

I shrug. "Depression, I guess. The death of your brother? The death of your parents? You've always played the victim, Kat. It could be any number of reasons."

She looks up at me. The light in her eyes indicates she sees some humanity in me, even if it's just a glimmer. I don't want her to see humanity, though; Daniel says it's a sign of weakness. "You're right in a way, but not in the way you think. I *do* get depressed. Awfully. It suffocates and strangles me. But I don't think it is my natural state. I sometimes feel like that because I fight against this life of mine. This dull, predictable life is *his* creation. He made me live it."

"So why on earth would he do that, Katherine?"

"To avoid bringing attention to myself. So that I remained invisible. Just like he did for all those years. Until the urge became too much, until he got caught last year..."

I clench my fist. I might just finish her now, just to stop her talking.

"I know you think you're the real deal, Sheena. But I don't believe you've actually killed anybody, have you?"

I dig my nails into my palm. I consider arguing against this, but I'm beyond caring now. Didn't I kill a defenceless man with Apinya a couple of hours ago? Admittedly, I didn't want to. My plan was always to get my followers to commit the killings. Daniel said you can learn from Charlie Manson. Kat forced me into a corner. My eyes burn into her skull. She doesn't seem to notice.

"You know what brings me down? What makes me feel so low I can barely move some days? Boredom. The lack of excitement I so crave, just like Daniel does. Can I tell you something about Daniel that you don't know? That nobody knows?"

"You've shared your fanatical story that you were once with him-"

"Not that."

She looks around the room. Over my shoulder. At the door. "You said that your boyfriend killed my brother-"

"Yes. Benjamin Conway."

"He didn't kill Ben."

My waved hand dismisses this outrageous comment. "Of course he did. He left his trademark sign-"

"Oh, *that* was him. He *was* there. But you know who stabbed him? The person who pulled back the knife and plunged it into my brother's chest?"

I shake my head. My upper lip trembles.

"That was me."

I stifle my gasp with my hand. What is she saying? Who *is* this woman? I pull my chair back. Whoever she is, I'm ready with my fists, with my teeth, with the knife in my pocket. She had better be one *crazy* woman if she wants to be crazier than me.

"My brother, Ben, was in love with Daniel," she says. "So many people were. Not just women. Daniel didn't mind. Far from it. He encouraged it. Just like you, he craved the power he had over people. But it drove *me* mad with jealousy. Plus, it just wasn't right. It was impure. Ben worried my parents wouldn't approve of him lusting after other men. He was wrong. Our parents were good, decent people. I overheard them talking about it. They knew all along that he was gay. They loved him whatever his sexuality. *I* didn't approve. I wanted my brother dead. Daniel knew this. He knew everything. He read my mind, just like he read yours. He told me that he'd already killed that weird couple. You think they were his first? Think again. I'd never heard anything quite so exhilarating. It made me feel alive. It fucking thrilled me. And-"

"*And*? What did he do?"

"He dared me to kill my brother. He said it would create an unbreakable bond. We would both be killers. So I did. In front of him. I pushed that knife into his chest so hard that the blood splattered all over my face. I proved to him I could kill. That I wasn't a coward..."

"You were a coward because you did what he told you to!" I shout. "You killed your brother, Kat. How is that *possibly* a good thing?"

I realise now that I believe everything she tells me. She may be psychotic. She may be crazy. But she isn't deluded. Not totally.

"That's only the beginning," Kat says.

She bows her head. She smothers her face with her hands. Could I jump on her now? Overpower her? I stay still. I'm addicted. She knows I won't do anything. I want to hear what she has to say.

"I lived this awful, dreary life with Ray for so long. Day after day after day acting like this perfect housewife. Do you know how *exhausting* that is? I did it because Daniel told me to, not because Ray did. And then I cracked..."

"*Cracked?* How?"

I think I know the answer. I just don't want to face up to it.

"I wanted to defy him. I wanted to make him aware I was still out here. I was still a danger. I wanted to show him I was still capable of taking life-"

"You killed your parents, didn't you?"

She looks up at me. The whites of her eyes are blotted red. "You know why I was the perfect lure tonight, Sheena? Why you were so *impressed* with my performance? I've done it before. The compulsion to do something utterly awful ate away at me for so long. The three of us picnicked. I threw off my clothes and jumped in the river for a swim. I wanted to be outrageous, to make my parents gasp. It was only when I was in the river that the compulsion overcame to me. What could possibly be more impressive to Daniel than killing my own parents? It *was* a compulsion. It was totally uncontrollable. My head disappeared beneath the water. I could barely make out their panicked outlines on the river bank. I didn't think I could do it. They were taking too long. I'd have to come up for air. And then they both dived in-"

"Oh my God, Kat..."

"They couldn't find me in that dirty brown water, of course. They didn't realise I kept pulling my head above the water for air. And then when they did find me - or when I found *them* - I grabbed their weakened bodies and held them under the water until - one by one - they stopped breathing..."

I take a deep breath. I look to the door. Apinya isn't coming, is she? What's to say this crazy bitch hasn't killed her, too? I don't have any options left.

I slide the knife from my pocket. She looks up just as I launch at her. Her outstretched leg hits me straight in the belly. The blade spins in the air and lands on the floor behind me. My hands grab Kat's red dress. I pull her down onto the floor. She lands on top of me. Reaching up, I snatch a handful of hair. Kat brushes aside my hand. She straddles me. My writhing body can't push her off. She is stronger than me. Her fists crack the sides of my head. I shut my eyes tight and brace my whole body as she lands punch after punch on my softened face...

"Get up! Both of you. Get up now!"

My dazed eyes look up. The room spins. I expect to see blue uniform. I expect to see badges.

I take a second look.

Rose stands over us. I look past her shoulder. Ray and Bernard glare down at us.

Rose

It was Monday evening when Ray knocked on my door.
His forehead glistened. His fingers fidgeted. He looked
like he was in two minds whether to turn around and
walk away.

"May I come in, Rose?"

We sat in the front room. "I was sorry to hear about
your colleague," I said. "I guess you're not doing too
well, are you?"

"I'm not, if I'm honest."

I knew this wasn't a man to share his emotions. He
told me about his day. I must confess, it was much
more exciting than my Monday. He said that this man -
Tony - admitted that somebody had paid him to
commit these diabolical crimes.

"Who do you think was behind it all?" I asked.

He rubbed his ruddy cheeks. "Sheena. I just can't see
how it can be anybody else. Kat changed beyond all
recognition as soon as Sheena joined Pontbach. I know
everybody else thinks she is wonderful; I just don't trust
her-"

"I don't, either," I said.

"You know what worries me, though? That this is just
the tip of the iceberg. That these incidents were battles
in a much bigger war. I think she's playing all of us-"

"Playing who?"

Ray scratched his bald head. I could tell he was
talking from the heart, that this was unbearably

uncomfortable for him. Even he questioned his theories. He needed to share what was on his mind to gain reassurance he wasn't going mad. I know how he feels. I have done the same thing with Bernard for months and months. "Us guys in the pub. The women in the group. I think she's turning everyone against each other..."

I reached forward and smoothed his hand. "I think you're right, Ray. I've been saying as much to Bernard. He suspects I'm losing my marbles, but I swear I'm not-"

"I don't think you are-"

"I tell you what. I'll speak to the women from the group. I still have a few allies. They care about me more than Sheena realises. And you speak to the guys from the pub. Is that a plan?"

"Yes," he said. "There's just one other thing..."

"What's that, dear?"

This time Ray looked away. His pained face tried to contain his feelings. "I'm not sure I know who Kat is anymore, either..."

"I was thinking exactly the same thing, dear."

I spoke to a few women from the group. Did Sheena really think they would stay quiet with me? They weren't as gullible as she imagined. Some of them were desperately trying to keep their emotions from bubbling over. They had already questioned Sheena's approach. They struggled with guilty consciences. Dave and Geraint opened up to Ray, as I knew they would. Sheena had apparently told them to keep their eyes out for Ray and Bernard, said they couldn't be trusted. How dare she? Did Sheena really think that the guys would choose *her* over their mates?

What became chillingly clear, from every conversation, was that the women sought revenge at the barn dance on Saturday night, 17th August.

What Kat didn't realise was that the women from the group were watching *her*, and not Grant. Myself, Ray and Bernard watched (from behind the wall) the events unfold at the barn. If Kat hadn't returned to untie Grant, then we would have done so. Admittedly, Ray couldn't resist giving Grant a few slaps around the face before letting him return to his wife. Who could blame him?

Just as they split, so did we. I trailed Sheena. Ray trailed Kat. Bernard trailed Apinya.

We waited outside for Bernard to arrive. We both agreed Apinya must have taken a detour. Finally, Bernard arrived, flushed and apologetic. Whoever was last in the building must have locked the door. Of course, I had a key. I guess they didn't see me as a threat; otherwise they would have changed the locks. I'm sure Sheena's sadistic boyfriend would have told her, at some point, not to underestimate anybody. The three of us waited in the dark corridor for the optimum time to strike.

And, as we waited, we listened to events unfold.

Neither woman notice us enter the room. They are too busy fighting. Even after I shout at them to get up, they both stare at us nonplussed, with open-mouths and dropped jaws. And so I decide to hurry things along. I pull Kat off Sheena by tugging at her long hair. I silence her shriek with a slap to the cheek. Accidentally stepping on Sheena's face as I pass, I look up and catch Bernard and Ray exchanging glances.

With my hands on my hips, I look around the room. There it is.

I don't pick up the knife until I've put on my white velvet gloves, the ones I sometimes wear to play lawn bowls. Katherine and Sheena sit down opposite each other on those awful wooden chairs. Both fold their arms across their chests. Their brows hang heavily over their eyes. Katherine exchanges a brief, awkward glance with her husband, who fills the doorway.

"How long have you been there?" Kat asks.

Ray sighs. "Long enough, Kat."

I wave the knife in the air. "I'll get down to basics, ladies. We don't have much time. We've already called the police. The lovely DI Hunter and her handsome partner will be here shortly-"

Sheena smirks. "What are they coming for? Are they going to arrest us for fighting? You don't have anything on us."

I make sure my smirk is wider than Sheena's. I may be an old dear, but I'm not too old to play mind games, too. "Oh, quite the contrary, dear. Luckily Katherine over there has worked out how to use the video on her phone. She managed to get quite a good view of you and Apinya in the barn. Who would have imagined she was athletic enough to lie on the roof? I'm sure her video would have put Steven Spielberg to shame..."

Sheena's smirk disappears. Kat cranes her neck forward and grins.

"Unfortunately for Katherine, she shouldn't look quite so smug. You see, I managed to get the recorder working on this old phone of mine, too. I've got her on tape confessing to - how many?- oh *yes,* three murders..."

Kat's body slumps. She looks up at me. Holds my look. She doesn't have much to lose, does she? "Make that four, you stupid old bitch. Who do you think went back to your husband's house after you paid your visit? He said you tried to put the frighteners on him with your own knife. Well, I did more than that. I proper stitched you up, didn't I?"

"I didn't like the man anyway, dear," I say. "As you said, I was considering killing him myself."

The two men in the room smile at that.

"Here's the thing." I glance at both women. "*Your* sick boyfriend killed my darling daughter. Now that is *not* alright. The problem I have, Sheena, is that a whole roomful of women say you were planning murder tonight. Two men from the pub are willing to testify that you were conspiring, too..."

I look up at Bernard and Ray. I soften my face when my eyes fix on Ray. His whole life has been destroyed. What he believed to be the truth was merely lies. The woman he loves with every inch of his being is a fraud. What I am about to propose will undoubtedly cause him untold pain.

"Gentlemen, would you be prepared to stand up in court to testify that you witnessed Sheena stab Katherine to death?"

I hold my breath. Bernard nods. Ray's face falls.

"Yes," he says, bowing his head.

"What the fuck are you saying, Rose?" Sheena says.

I pull another knife out of my pocket. This is the blade I threatened my husband with. I wave it in my air. Without thinking, Sheena's open hand takes her own knife back.

"I'm giving you two choices, Sheena. Either you use your knife to stab Katherine to death, or I use my knife to stab *you* to death. Personally, I don't want to get your blood on my lovely top, but I'm prepared to make the sacrifice if that's the choice you decide to make-"

"Don't do anything stupid, Sheena," Katherine says. She glances at the exit. Swivelling her head, she eyes the window. As usual, the drab curtains are pulled wide apart.

"If you make a move," I say, "I'll bludgeon you to death myself."

Sheena's body trembles. She stands up. Katherine kicks out with her legs. Ray and Bernard move either side of her, close enough to strike, but far enough away to avoid any splashes of blood.

"Just do it, "Ray says. "Please, just get it over with it."

"I'm sorry Kat," Sheena whispers. "But I don't want to die."

Pulling the knife high above her head, Sheena plunges the blade deep into Katherine's chest, again and again and again...

Sheena screams at the top of her voice. The front door pushes open. DI Hunter and her colleague charge into the room. Hunter's jaw drops at the sight of Katherine's slumped, bloodied and motionless body. Sheena bends at the knee and tries to shimmy past Hunter. The detective sticks out her leg. Sheena stumbles to the floor in a crumpled heap.

"Sheena Strachan, I'm arresting you for murder. You do not have to say anything, but it may harm your defence if you..."

Bernard

My exhausted body slumps onto the sofa. Normally I would have been in bed hours ago, but I know I still won't sleep. Not after tonight. My body aches, but my mind races.

And besides, I don't sleep well when I have the bed all to myself.

We agreed that I would tail Apinya. My wife. Of course, Apinya had to take the scenic route from the farm, didn't she? She thought she was sightseeing. Her body slumped when she turned around and saw me, trailing just a handful of steps behind her. Who did she fear was following her? Did she think I might be a dangerous man? That handful of steps quickly shrunk. Apinya froze when I continued walking towards her. Within seconds, her face dropped.

I told her I was there to kill her.

And so, I am alone again. This time potentially for the rest of my life. I just don't have the energy to fall in love again.

Sheena planted the idea in my mind. At first the anger and the resentment simmered. Over weeks and weeks, however, it boiled over. Apinya humiliated me. She abused me. She deserved to die. I *wanted* her dead.

I know she took Rob's life. My wife is a murderer. I am not quite sure how she did it, but it's linked to the missing chainsaw from the garage. My wife is shrewder than people realise.

I stretched out my arms, ready to take Apinya's slender throat in my hands. I knew I could squeeze the life from her body within a few seconds.

And then, my dad's shaking, disapproving face appeared before me. Dad was a strict disciplinarian, but he was old-fashioned. He never hurt a woman. And neither have I.

"Go home. Pack your bags. Catch a flight..."

Apinya didn't ask any questions. She turned around, and disappeared into the dark night, without a backwards glance...

Daniel

With my hands nestled behind my head on the hard bed, my eyes focus on the ceiling. Apart from the toilet and the sink, there is very little else to focus on in this six feet by eight feet concrete atrocity.

I resist looking at my watch. After all, as William Langland said, patience is a virtue.

I sit up. My arms wrap around my knees. I peer through the steel bars. Soundless shoes patrol the corridors.

"Excuse me, Warden," I say. "I just wondered whether you had the opportunity to check the news, like we discussed?"

His kindly face smiles. He looks at me in awe. Some of these wardens aren't sure if I'm a magician, or the Devil. "Something crazy did happen tonight, just as you said it would. That's quite a skill you've got there. A woman has been found dead in a small, sleepy town in mid Wales. Stabbed to death. Another woman has been arrested."

I smile. It fascinates me that I still have the power to inflict death and misery whilst confined in my prison cell. "How tragic," I say. "One last thing, if you don't mind? Do you happen to know the name of the unfortunate victim?"

His eyes narrow. Why on earth would I want to know the name? He dismisses this thought. The question may sound insane, but then I am supposed to *be* insane. He glances at his phone. I am sure this goes against protocol, but I don't complain.

"Katherine Roberts."

Kat.

A tear trickles down my cheek. Kat was the *only* one I ever loved.

"Thank you, Warden," I say.

I lie back on the bed. Close my eyes. Hope that time passes quickly.

"No problem," the man says from the other side of the bars. "You have yourself a pleasant night, Spartacus."

****

If you enjoyed *I AM HERE TO KILL YOU,* then please read the prequel, *30 Days in June.*

The residents of south Wales were thrown into a state of panic on the 1st day of June 1988, when a married couple were brutally murdered in their own home. The killer, nicknamed Spartacus by the press, did not flee the scene immediately; instead, he used a cut-throat razor to carve Roman Numerals into his victims' chests.

This was the beginning of a month-long killing spree.

Seventeen-year-old Jeffrey Allen was to be the final victim, on the final day of the month. He became the only survivor, and the only real witness.

The killings end as suddenly as they began.

Jeffrey relocates to London, changing his name, and his identity, to Marcus Clancy. His past life is merely a dark secret.

On 1st June 2018, 30 years to the day since the first killing, a mysterious figure refers to Marcus by his old name.

Is Spartacus back? If so, does he have unfinished business?

And so begins 30 days of terror for Marcus Clancy, culminating in dramatic fashion on the final day of June.

About the Author

Chris Westlake was born in Cardiff and brought up in Wick, a coastal village seven miles from Bridgend. He now resides in Birmingham with his wife, Elizabeth, and two young children, AJ and Chloe.

After completing a Creative Writing course in 2010, Chris's short story, *Welsh Lessons*, was awarded 1st place in the Global Short Story Award. He followed this up with 1st place in the Stringybark Erotic Fiction Award and 2nd place in the HASSRA Literary Award.

He has written three previous novels, *Just a Bit of Banter, Like, At Least the Pink Elephants are Laughing at Us,* and *30 Days in June.*

You can find out more about Chris at his website, chriswestlakeauthor.co.uk

Printed in Great Britain
by Amazon

13953463R00202